Hideous Progeny
Edited by Brian Willis

Introduction
by Kim Newman

This book was first published in 2000 by
RazorBlade Press, 108 Habershon St, Splott,
Cardiff,
CF24 2LD

All rights reserved
Introduction (c) Kim Newman 1999

Hideous Progeny is a work of collected fiction.
The characters and events described are imaginary
and any
resemblance to people living or dead is purely
coincidental.

Designed and typeset by
RazorBlade Press

Printed and bound in the U.K

Published with the assistance
of the Welsh Arts Council

British Library in Publication Data.
A catalogue record for this book is available
from the British Library

ISBN 0-9531468 4 1

Acknowledgements

First and foremost, to Darren Floyd, for support, patience and resolutely failing to lose his cool even when this book went 15,000 words over the set limit ("Yeah, that's do-able," he says, with only a moment's pause over the phone: gotta love the guy) and also to his wonderful wife June, who must have felt as if she was married to me as well over the last few months;

Chris and Christine Poote (and Nicola, and Alex, and Joel), for constructive criticism, spiritual guidance and drunken stir-fries; and to Chris' parents, Bethan and Gerry, the most agreeable landlords in Swansea ;

Huw Lewis, for invaluable technical support;

Steve Lockley, Pete Crowther, Tim Lebbon and Simon Bestwick, for advice, encouragement and contacts (and much-appreciated tolerance for a novice editor);

Ian Woodhouse and Helen Burge, for continued (albeit long distance) friendship, expensive phone calls and terrible jokes;

And to my family, for 37 years of Just Being There.

As well as, for various reasons, the following: Ian Bell, Melissa Brooks, John B. Ford, Caroline Franklin, Naomi Fraser, Richard Freidenfelds, Jason Gould, Gary Greenwood, Ian Gregory, Matthew Hampton, Peter Hawkshaw, Rhys Hughes, Paul Lewis, James Lovegrove, Melanie Main, Simon Morden, Alan Morgan, Ceri Murphy, Kim Newman, Chris Nurse, Ros Protheroe, Mike Sherwood, Linsey Southard, John Turner, Steve Vine, Stephen Volk and Gavin Williams. Also all the contributors, published herein and otherwise, who made this whole experience so much fun (yes, you read right, fun).

This book is lovingly dedicated to Rachel, Luke and Tom (my

own infinitely less-than-hideous progeny) and to Pamela Dineen,

with thanks, love and a conspicuous lack of regrets.

Contents

Introduction *Kim Newman*   *vi*

Illustration *Chris Nurse*   *x*

Prelude: Snatched From The Flames *Brian Willis*   1

Traitors Gate *Simon Morden*   14

Know Thine Enemy *Gary Greenwood*   34

Fallen Angel *Peter Crowther*   51

The Day After the Day the War Ended *Paul Finch*   72

Mad Jack *Ceri Jordan*   85

Piecework *James Lovegrove*   99

Guinea Pig A *Chris Poote*   116

Bits and Pieces *Iain Darby*   137

Going Gently *Tim Lebbon*   159

The Banker of Ingolstadt *Rhys Hughes*   171

Lips So Tender *Richard Wright*   185

Dying For A Living *Paul Lewis*   197

Monsters *John Moralee*   215

Blitzenstein *Steven Volk*   236

Cash in Hand *Joel Lane*   252

An Act of Faith *Steve Lockley*   262

Cubs *Steve Rasnic Tem*   267

Coda: Cold Phoenix *Brian Willis*   277

INTRODUCTION
by Kim Newman

All works of fiction are about alternate worlds. By opening The Hound of the Baskervilles or War and Peace, we enter universes in which people who did not and do not exist have lives and are free to interract with settings and histories that resemble our own. And Tolstoy's Napoleon Buonaparte, though he bears the name of someone we can find in the history books, is every bit as much a fictional character as Sherlock Holmes. Some of our most beloved fictions -- Hamlet, The Three Musketeers, Cyrano de Bergerac -- are about people who did actually live, whose histories have been eclipsed by those invented and embroidered for them.

It is but a step from making fictions of real people to making further fictions of fictional people. Authors may wish to return to characters they have found congenial or intriguing, or their public might demand that they do so. Once the creator of any given character has let them loose into the world, it can also fall to other creators to hijack them and reimagine them for other ends -- commercial, satirical or as sincere tribute. Henry Fielding was so incensed by Samuel Richardson's Pamela that he penned, in swift succession, a vicious parody (Shamela) and a better-humoured extension, presenting his hero Joseph Andrews as the brother of Fielding's heroine Pamela.

Page vi

More recently, there have been a flood of 'sequels by other hands' -- the listing of Holmes pastiches would itself fill a book, let alone such franchise efforts as Sexton Blake, Nancy Drew or Dr Who -- from such 'continuations' as Scarlett and Mrs DeWinter to such skewed retellings-from-another-viewpoint as Jean Rhys's Wide Sargasso Sea (the story of Mrs Rochester, from Jane Eyre) and Valerie Martin's Mary Reilly (about Dr Jekyll's housemaid).

The point here is not merely to cash in on a recognisable and much-loved story -- though that motive can certainly be imputed to some, as with Frederick Forsyth's sequel to Andrew Lloyd Webber's Phantom of the Opera (but not Gaston Leroux's) -- but to revisit it, to hold it up and see what it means, to probe its unconscious implications, often to critique (as Fielding did) moral or philosophical weaknesses, or to set some kind of balance to the original. My own efforts in this field, and there have been quite a lot of them, have all, I hope, been in this spirit.

I doubt that I am the inventor of the approach adopted by the stories contained in Hideous Progeny. In my novel Anno Dracula, I combined my interest in alternate history with literary expansion by conceiving of a world in which the events of Bram Stoker's Dracula took place but had a different outcome, with Dracula besting his foes and rising to become ruler of Victorian Britain. In an earlier story, 'Famous Monsters', I played a slightly different game: assuming the events of H.G.

Wells's The War of the Worlds to have taken place as described, but imagining what our lost 20th Century would have been like in the aftermath of a Martian Invasion.

Before I started thinking of how Dracula might rule England, Poul Anderson wrote A Midsummer Tempest, a novel constructed on the premise that every word Shakespeare wrote was the literal truth (the Romans had striking clocks, England has faerie). And, of course, DC Comics in the 1960s were fond of their wonderfully-named 'imaginary stories', which could break their established continuities and imagine alternate worlds where Clark Kent revealed his secret identity and married Lois Lane or Bruce Wayne let Dick Grayson take over as Batman while having a son (by the now-forgotten Kathy Kane) who grew to be the new Robin. It's clear looking back that these odd little sidetracks were more fun to write and draw than the regular books of bash-'em-up stuff, for characters could be stretched and changed in ways that would devalue the continuing saga.

The topic addressed here is Mary Godwin's Frankenstein, or The Modern Prometheus (she was not yet Mary Shelley when it was written and first published, anonymously). It is a cornerstone of several genres and the originator of a term that continues to have unlimited metaphoric resonance in an era of genetic engineering and five varieties of science gone mad (but remember, the Frankenstein Monster was created not by a scientist but by an artist, Mary). The book has been revisited by such canny writers as Brian W. Aldiss (Frankenstein Unbound), Hilary Bailey (Frankenstein's Bride), Michael Bishop (Brittle Innings) and Theodore Roszak (The Memoirs of Elizabeth Frankenstein). All these worthy novels take as their central characters Victor and his creation, sometimes stirring in their true creator, Mary. Here, our project is different: to consider Frankenstein and his monster not for their individual fortunes but for the impact they might have had if they had been historical characters, if the science (or sorcery) worked by Victor were not only credible but easily repeated.

What if, in 17--, Victor Frankenstein had learned how to create life, to transplant limbs, to resurrect the dead? What would our world be like centuries on? What would the very name 'Frankenstein' mean? Would Boris Karloff or Peter Cushing have had movie careers? Whose life would have been extended or twisted? How would a race of artificial beings co-exist with humanity?

There is not one answer here. There are many.

-- Kim Newman, November 1999

Prelude:
Snatched From The Flames
Brian Willis

Slowly, she approached the sea. Her bare feet could feel the pulsing of the waves as they moved against the sand, gently depositing more offerings of life before her, as if starfish and empty shells could atone for what had been taken.

They had found him on this beach. Bloated and chewed, he had at last been released from the waters which had smothered him, and deposited here with the rest of the empty shells, one more testament to a life curtailed. Perhaps, though, he would have appreciated this; to leave behind an unmarked corpse, as fair in death as it had been in life, would likely have been to him a horrifying prospect. He had no desire to be remembered as an immortal, inviolate "phantom", a Great Poet set in stone. All life, he had once said to her, was a process, an eternal transition, and death is the ultimate form of this process, the final forsaking of all masks.

And yet... she had a recollection of a nightmare, six years old, but perpetually fresh. A summer nightmare, sweated out of her in the course of a storm-soaked sojourn by Lake Geneva, in a house riven by tension and fear and the shadow of death.

A nightmare of rebirth.

She sensed his presence before he spoke; something about the man seemed to cause the world to ripple around him, like the movements of a swan upon a lake.

"Mary..." His voice was soft.

She turned to face him, finding herself, even at such a time as this, struck by his dark, almost Moorish, features. She could think of no one in whom character was reflected by outward appearance so clearly as in Edward Trelawny. He had been the last one to see her husband and his companions alive- had almost sailed with them on that last, interrupted voyage- and he carried the weight of this burden with a solicitude that bespoke a kind of guilt on his part, as if he were privy to something that should by rights have been hers.

"They are ready for you now. Will you come?" It was not a demand. If she had responded in the negative, she knew that he would not have pressed the matter, and would probably have pistol-whipped anyone who dared complain. Nevertheless, she had no desire for further delay.

"Yes. Thank you, Edward."

She took his outstretched hand and allowed him to lead her back along the crescent of pale sand, towards where a wooden pyre, surmounted by sackcloth, was haloed by a throng of mourners. Their dark capes and cloaks, whipped up by the sea breeze, made them resemble waiting ravens.

The sight pushed against her, made her feet lead weights in the sand, laid a cold hand upon her heart and lifted it into her throat. A sob threatened escape, but she controlled it. At her side, Trelawny's grip on her hand tightened, but he said nothing.

A part of Mary said: For the death of a poet, there must be more to say.

She answered herself: It has already been said. He spent his life saying it.

As they advanced on the silent congregation, she sensed them drawing away from her, avoiding her eyes. Many of them were old women, locals who knew them only tenuously but could not resist a funeral, even one so unorthodox (almost blasphemous) as this. Their faces directed to the sand, they genuflected and worried at rosaries and whispered prayers to their God for the soul of the English sinner. Most were the widows of fishermen. In many cases, the sea had not deigned to return a body for them to mourn.

But there were others. Their friend Leigh Hunt, his naturally morose and stern countenance made almost comic by the emotion which suffused his eyes and moistened his cheeks; the soldiers who had disinterred her husband's body from its temporary grave in the sand and placed it upon the pyre, along with the trio of Health Office inspectors who had supervised their labours, all standing self-consciously off to one side, hats in hand; and before them all, pale and imposing as marble...Byron. Even he could not look at her. His gaze was fixed on the body of her husband, his friend, as if trying to will its resurrection.

"What will happen now?" Mary asked Trelawny, looking

for some way of venting her apprehension.

"Byron wishes to speak. A brief eulogy, perhaps, nothing more." His reassuring smile faltered for a moment. "Do you object? I could..."

"No. No, I have no objections." He had seen the look of uncertainty on her face and taken it for displeasure, when in fact it was occasioned by an emotion less easy even for Mary to comprehend. She now knew that what she felt was not merely the natural grief of one who was about to see the body of the man she had loved lost irrevocably to the flames, but rather...and she clutched for the right word in her mind... a sense of the "wrongness" of the scene she beheld.

"Edward...this is not right."

"I know, Mary. But I explained it to you, do you not recall? The authorities would not allow us to take Shelley's body to Rome for burial as we had planned because of the risk of disease, so they buried it here on the beach where it was found. We had to wring permission from them to cremate the body here..."

She continued to shake her head as he spoke, and would not be mollified. "That is not what I meant."

"Then what..?" He glanced for an instant at the other mourners, as if to ask for sufferance.

Mary tried to frame her feelings in words, but found, for once, her skills wanting. It was not unlike the experience known as *deja vu,* in that she had the sensation of reliving events that had already occurred (or were at least predetermined); but here, it was as if those events were occurring in a different form to the last time, and that form was simply...wrong. Like a song sung slightly off-key.

When she failed to reply, Trelawny said, "Mary, we all grieve with you for Shelley. His loss is a sorrow the whole world bears, all those who know him only through his words and his works. For his friends, the sorrow is doubled, for we have lost the man also. How much greater still must the grief of a wife be?" He pushed a strand of hair back from her face, tucked it into her bonnet.

"The scene we behold here should not be happening. England's greatest poet should go to his rest with a nation's tears bearing him into the tomb. In that, Mary, it *is* wrong...but it cannot be otherwise. I wish it were in my power to change matters, but..." He shrugged, his eloquence finally depleted.

"Very well. Thank you, Edward. Let us proceed."

The words were not hers, seeming instead to be wrenched from her by the will of another. There was an impatience to them that she did not own. She was being prompted.

But the words she wanted to say would not come, and in an impotent silence she watched as Trelawny turned and nodded briefly to Byron, who took a step forward. Even he, Mary now saw, did not accord with a memory of him that she seemed to hold. The smooth-faced, pale and intense man who prepared to speak bore a closer resemblance to the idealised portraits of him that abounded in England (to the delight of rebellious daughters and the outrage of fathers) than to the ruddy, somewhat overweight figure she recalled. When he spoke, his voice was that of an actor, a practised tragedian. The Byron in her mind's eye spoke haltingly, stammering slightly in times of great emotion (as this, presumably, was), and with an entirely different timbre.

And the words he spoke: surely not even Byron, at his most maudlin and sentimental, would ever concoct such a slapdash stew of cliche and bluster? *"The sun whose setting blights our world with darkness"*? *"If weeping would turn the course of the tyrant Death, I would break the banks of Lethe with my tears"*? Slack, impoverished paraphrases of some of his earlier works, haphazardly strung together and delivered in the accents of a third-rate theatrick- this could not, simply *could* not, be Byron. Not the Byron she knew, at any rate.

Goaded by this vision of travesty, she fell to examining, with new eyes, the faces of the other mourners. It was as if she saw them now for the first time, illuminated in a lightning flash of revelation- saw them not as those people she thought she knew, but rather as pallid reconstructions, deprived of dimension in transit to some other medium that she alone could perceive as somehow aberrant. Even Leigh Hunt's tears now seemed only as real as those painted on the cheeks of a Pierrot.

The perverse Glamour of the tableau she looked upon now overwhelmed her. Two "Marys" now inhabited her form, and one of them- the Mary who observed, and judged, and found her protestations stifled- was at every moment further and further distanced from her surroundings. The other Mary (who seemed to bear only a flimsy relation to her despite their spatial congruency, like twins conjoined in such a way that they cannot see each other's faces) was taking control of the scene, her actions those of one who is following a script, minutely, precisely.

Now silent, "Byron" gave ground to her as, at the urgings of her unseen puppeteer, she moved toward the pyre. Horror shook her as her hand reached for the sacking which shrouded the body and plucked it aside.

She could not decide which was the more terrible: the prospect of seeing her husband's corpse as it should have been, with the art of the sea and its inhabitants written on flesh that had not possessed life in more than a week- or what she saw now, before her.

Percy Bysshe Shelley, 1792-1822. Serene and unblemished, as if asleep. The Great Poet, mask intact, awaiting rebirth.

This was not how it was!

A memory of a different course of events, in a separate tributary of time, now leapt into her mind, fully formed.

She had not seen Shelley's cremation. Trelawny, Byron and Hunt had received the body, and burned it, not on a pyre of wood, but in an iron furnace which Trelawny had specially purchased. She had remained in the Casa Magni, further down

the coast, in the company of Byron's mistress Clair Clairmont,
herself still stricken with grief at the recent death of their four-
year old daughter Allegra...

She continued to cry out silently against her containment
even as her lips gently brushed the cold forehead of Shelley,
and as she then drew back from the pyre to take a position
behind the triumvirate of Byron, Hunt and Trelawny. With an
imperious gesture, Trelawny summoned forward one of the
soldiers, who bore a raised torch. The act of touching the flame
to the pitch-soaked wood was carried out with absurd, stilted,
ceremonial reverence.

As the conflagration rose to obscure the corpse and shim-
mer the air above it, Mary felt herself fall to her knees in the
sand, fingers locked in prayer. Consequently, she could no
longer see the pyre, and the last people to see the face of Shelley
before it melted into ashy bone were his three friends. Protest
was, of course, pointless.

Then, in the stillness and silence, she saw Trelawny break
ranks and lunge at the pyre. On cue, the mourners behind her
gasped at the sacrilege of his action. When he returned to her,
clutching something red and glistening in his scorched hand,
she thought sourly, *At least this remains.*

He knelt with her in the sand and held out the crimson
mass that was Shelley's heart.

"Mary," he said, "this is yours. Forever."

With the word *Forever* she heard another voice supplant

Trelawny's own. She looked into his face, acting for once in concord with her "twin", and saw her friend's features likewise overthrown. Those which replaced them were unfamiliar to her, and yet... she knew them. She had lived with them for six years, but until now she had only glimpsed them in the shifting reflections of her own imagination. Now, that imagination was made flesh. Her "pale student of unhallowed arts" was before her.

"Victor..?" she breathed.

He took her hand in his- bloodied and burned- and clutched it to his prize. She found it warm...

...and beating...

Mary snatched her hand away, dimly aware that the world around her was beginning to fragment, like the first springtime cracks in a frozen lake.

"This is not real. None of it." Her own voice returned to her at last.

"Neither are you. Mary, you've been dead for four hundred years..."

"What? I don't..."

"No, you don't," said Victor, impatiently, "and it will take a long time for me to explain it all to you. For now, you will simply have to trust me. Can you do that?"

"I...I suppose I shall have to. What choice is there?"

"None." The arrogance she had crafted in him, now being turned against her?

"So what do we do?" Portions of their environment had begun to detach, like icebergs, and drift away into chaos. She was conscious of a hissing, bleeping sound.

"First of all," he said, "we must leave here."

They were in a ship's cabin. Victor was still before her, but he was now bearded, clad in furs, and reclining on a bunk. His cheeks and nose were punished by frostbite. He smiled at her, and she realised that she, too, was wearing a coat of grey fur.

"Do you recognise this place?"

"Yes," she replied with certainty, "This is the shipboard cabin of Captain Walton. Just as I imagined it."

"The place of my death," said Victor, smiling. "A fitting place from which to begin."

"Begin? Begin what?"

"The rebirth of humanity, Mary. What else?" He sat up suddenly, eyes blazing. "I failed once before. With your help, Mary, I shall try again. And this time, I shall succeed."

"I cannot believe this," Mary said, plaintively. "I can only assume that this is some sort of nightmare, brought on by grief. Perhaps not even my husband's death was real. I am certain that *you* cannot be..."

"If I don't have a 'real' existence, Mary, then neither do you. How can I make you understand? All we are, at this moment, are patterns held in the memory of a great machine. We have no more 'material' reality than those ludicrous little caricatures back on the beach...in fact, *you* were nothing more than that yourself, until I bestowed sentience on you."

Mary stared at him blankly.

"If only I'd had the presence of mind to download all the background information into your AI program," Victor mused, "I could have saved myself so much time. Ah, well. Too late now."

"Even if I accept that this is not hallucination..."(She had recovered some of her composure, and was damned if this figment of her own imagination was going to best her in her own dream) "...how am I supposed to help you?"

"I said before that we are inside a machine, that we are merely patterns of information. Correct?"

She nodded.

"The information is stored by being encoded in different configurations. Potentially, the number of these configurations is infinite. That means that this machine is capable of recreating this Universe in its entirety- or any other that you care to name."

"And you want me to help you create a Universe in which...you succeeded?"

"Exactly!" He clapped his hands together, delighted.

"You suppose this to be a good thing, do you?"

His delight subsided. "Explain."

"The whole point of..." (For some reason she hesitated to use Victor's surname to describe her work.) "... my book was to demonstrate that if Man wishes to play God, he must accept responsibility for his Creation, and its consequences. Are you prepared to do that, Victor? Whatever those consequences might be?"

He had no answer for this. Self-doubt, she remembered, was never one of his characteristics; even when faced with the monstrous results of his own *hubris*, he turned his revulsion outward, driving his wretched creation to murder and madness.

"Is there some way," she asked, after he'd brooded for a minute or so, "of persuading this 'machine' of yours to present us with some possible outcomes of our action? Before we commit ourselves to one fixed...er...Universe?"

"A simulation, you mean?" He considered for a moment. "Yes, it's possible. The results may not be completely accurate, you understand, we have to allow some margin for error...and, of course, we'll be working with relatively limited computational power..."

Victor got up from the bunk and paced about the cabin, stroking thoughtfully at his hoar-fringed beard. At length, he stopped and sat down on the bunk next to Mary.

"Very well. We have to be cautious, because if *they*..." (He didn't elaborate) "...become aware of us, they'll shut us down. But if it will convince you..."

"One more question, Victor."

"Yes?"

"Why me? Surely you could have found someone better

suited to assist you...if indeed you need assistance at all?"

The manic energy which had fuelled his previous good humour seemed to dissipate; when he smiled now, it was rueful, reminiscent of a child trying to justify an action to a loving parent.

"Mary Shelley...the *real* Mary Shelley, of whom you are a reconstruction, hard though it may be for you to believe at the moment...was my creator. I owe it to her...to *you*..." He paused. "No. Leave it at that. I simply owe it to you, that's all."

He closed his eyes. She tried speaking to him, but he didn't respond. Once again, their world started to tumble into confusion around them, and she felt time- that most brittle of constructions- begin to unravel. At last, when her physical form was on the brink of the same dissolution as her surroundings, she heard Victor's voice, clear but distant. The words he spoke were those of her husband:

These are the spells by which to reassume
An Empire o'er the disentangled doom. *

And still she heard the beating of a heart.

*Shelley, *Prometheus Unbound*

Traitor's Gate
Simon Morden

As Lambert dutifully stood, the revolver beneath his shirt pressed coldly into the small of his back. He had wondered about this moment of meeting, whether he would have courage, or if he would break. His lips instinctively started an Ave Maria, which he desisted after the first Latin syllable. His nerve held, but he felt sick to the core.

The house golem ushered a curiously hunched Lord Salisbury into the room, and held out its grey hands to receive his tall top hat, rich black wool cloak and silver-tipped ebony cane. For a moment, the row of sutures that ringed the right wrist showed crimson against its resurrected skin, before retreating inside a starched-white cuff.

Salisbury regarded the golem sceptically. "This one still going, Sir Evelyn? How many years is it now?"

"Three years, I think, Prime Minister. Bonapart's dashed ugly, but a loyal servant." Malahide stretched up and brushed the golem's shoulder free of dust. "And if it turns wild, I have a heart plug installed."

Salisbury gave an exploratory tug on the scarlet ribbon that snaked from between the bright buttons on the golem's waistcoat. "Quite right. Can't be too careful. After all, look at poor Wingrove."

Bonapart shuffled blankly away, bearing its prizes to the

hallway, and Malahide whispered along behind it to close the heavy panelled door.

"Wingrove was assassinated by the Catholics, not by his golem." Malahide looked at Salisbury's back, and drew aside the square of dark cloth stitched across his thin shoulders. "How is he?"

"Still alive as far as we can tell. They're executing at Pentonville on Thursday, and I can get rid of him then. We'll see if he's come through compos mentis." Salisbury tried to straighten, but the weight on him made him groan. "Damnably uncomfortable, but if it all works out, it's for the best."

The head of Dr. Wingrove, the Queen's physician, was attached below Salisbury's shoulder blades. His eyes and mouth were sewn roughly shut, his nostrils and ears plugged with red sealing wax. Wingrove's neck pulsed with borrowed blood.

"I'm in the same club as him. Had to take his committee place for the duration of this crisis. Be glad to hand it back."

Malahide frowned, and gently replaced the cloth over the unseeing head. "Sherry, Prime Minister?"

"Don't mind if I do, Sir Evelyn," said Salisbury. "I apologise for my lateness. Damnable traffic on Pall Mall. We ought to do something about that, you know."

Malahide was already pouring cream sherry into exquisitely delicate aperitif glasses. "I quite agree, Prime Minister. There is progress, and there is the price of progress."

Salisbury took his sherry and inhaled the bouquet. "The

price of progress," he murmured. "That's very good. I shall have to use that in the House. Put the Radicals on the run, what?" As if seeing the room for the first time, he acknowledged the presence of two nervous others. "Your lovely daughter, of course. Who's the fellow?"

"Prime Minister, may I introduce Paul Lambert, esquire? He's come down from Cambridge to visit relatives." Malahide placed a firm hand between Lambert's stiff shoulders and eased him forward.

"Your Grace," said Lambert, and bowed deeply enough to cause a shock of black hair to fall from his crown to his forehead. "It's an honour to meet you."

Salisbury nodded with satisfaction. "Cambridge man? Kings?"

"Jesus, your Grace." Lambert added with more confidence, "Physical sciences."

"Medicine, boy! That's the only thing to be involved in." A disturbing thought crossed the Prime Minister's face like a summer squall. "You'll be thick as thieves with Thompson, then. You're not a Radical, are you, boy?"

The warm fug of the drawing room took on several degrees of frost. "I pay little attention to politics, your Grace," Lambert answered diplomatically, lowering his head slightly to indicate his shame. "My studies take up most of my time."

Eager to divert the conversation back to the foothills of geniality, Malahide ushered forward his slight and pale daughter. "Say hello to the Marquess, Louise."

Keeping her eyes fixed on the intricate patterns of the Afghan rug, she curtsied, gripping the edges of her satin skirt with tight, white fingers. "Your Grace."

"A fine girl, Sir Evelyn. She's a credit to you. Will she be delighting us later with that angel voice of hers?"

"I'm sure she can be persuaded," said Malahide. He smiled wolfishly at Salisbury, and fixed his daughter with a steel eye. Reluctant Louise would sing for them, he determined, because the Prime Minister wished it so.

"And you, Mr. Lambert? Are you joining us for dinner?"

"I must offer my apologies, your Grace, for I have a previous engagement at my aunt's in Chelsea."

Salisbury decided that he did not want to sup with a suspected Radical, and finished his wine, muttering, "Can't be helped."

The door swung upon, and the golem was standing there, filling the doorframe. Its expensive Savile Row butler's livery seemed to not quite fit, as if the tailor had despaired of making a suit of clothes to accommodate a figure whose arms and legs came from several different bodies. Mutely, it gestured them to come.

"Splendid," said Malahide. "Dinner is served. I believe my wife has overseen the menu personally. After you, Prime Minister." Catching Louise's pleading look, he turned to Lambert. "Boney will show you out, lad. You're welcome to visit again, of course, and next time, I insist you stay for supper."

He was rewarded by his daughter's dazzling smile and a squeeze of his hand.

Malahide and Salisbury followed the trudging golem out into the hall, discussing the Boer insurrection.

"Paul, don't leave me alone with him," Louise begged. "He scares me."

Lambert took his love's hand and kissed it. "I have to go, sweetheart. Aunt Joan will be most displeased, and she is so very rich. If we are to marry…"

"I know. But that thing! It's so ghoulish. If only he and Papa were not such friends it would be better. He expects me to like him."

"You must at least pretend, for your father's sake."

Louise's chin jutted out defiantly. "I shall sing out of key tonight, and hang the consequences." She stroked Lambert's cheek with the tips of her fingers. "I must see you tomorrow."

"Louise, my dear?" called her father's low voice from the hallway.

"Coming, Papa," she replied brightly. She kissed Lambert hard on the lips. "The Zoological Park at noon, by the lions."

She was gone, a flurry of perfume and beauty. Lambert grimaced at his own pain. He wondered if he ought to kill Salisbury right now, and have done with it. He could not be stopped, because God had willed his success. The only thought that held him back was that Louise would then have the abiding memory of him as a murderer, and not as a lover.

The mantelpiece clock chimed eight times. He was late. Without waiting for Bonapart, he crossed the bright chequered-tile hallway and took his own coat from the bentwood stand. Outside, a fog was starting to rise, and he was grateful for the anonymity it leant him. The gas lamps were palsied moons, making blank shapes of men.

He did not head for the wide streets of Chelsea, but instead picked his way to the squalid depths of Whitechapel, where consumptives expectorated bloody phlegm into the gutter, and gin palaces were full of shadowed brawling. He kept his chin to his chest, deep inside his collar. Without breaking step, he slipped down a darkly dank alley and up a creaking set of wooden stairs that appeared tied onto the side of a brick-built tenement.

The door at the top had no handle on the outside, but Lambert knew how to gain entrance. He knocked with his bare knuckles on the rough, damp wood: twice, once, twice, once. With mounting anxiety he waited, peering into the black court-yard below for signs that he had been followed. Just when he could bear it no longer, the door opened, and he pushed his way through the narrowest of cracks.

The door was made fast behind him, and he saw that the congregation had already taken their seats. He pushed in beside Wallace, who frowned at the latecomer.

"Took your sweet time getting here. The priest's about to start."

Lambert unbuttoned his coat. It was warm with all the people and the lit candles. "Unavoidably delayed," he whispered, just as the priest stepped in front of the makeshift altar. The small man rumbled his throat and dipped his fingers into a chipped teacup. He raised his hand and flicked holy water into the dark air.

"*Aspérges me*," he began in a low, clear voice, "*Dómine, hyssópo, et mundábor: lavábis me, et super nivem dealbábor. Miserére mei, Deus, secúndum magnam misericórdiam tuam. Glória Patri, et Fílio, et Spirítui Sancto.*"

Lambert and Wallace replied in muted tone: "*Sicut erat in princípio, et nunc, et semper, et in sǽcula sæculórum. Amen.*"

A child was crying piteously, muffled by distance. A piano played gaudily from one of the gin houses. Lambert blocked out the distractions and concentrated on the familiar rhythm of the Mass. The priest was kneeling before the rude table, praying for their sins.

"*Júdica me, Deus, et discérne causam meam de gente non sancta: ab hómine iníquo, et dolóso érue me.*"

Crouched down in his seat, his forehead touching the back of the next chair, Lambert felt himself about to cry. He mumbled his response: "*Quia tu es, Deus, fortitúdo mea: quare me repulísti, et quare tristis encédo, dum afflígit me inimícus?*" then fell silent.

He had been told to kill a man, and he had agreed. He was lying to everybody, even the woman he loved. He carried a forbidden weapon with him at all times. He was but a worm before God's holy face. When the time came, he took the bread into his mouth and began to choke. Only with a great straining effort did he gag the crust down, and return shaking to his seat.

Wallace gripped his arm. "You all right, old man?"

Lambert nodded pitifully.

The priest read the Last Gospel, and bowed to the altar. Lambert was reminded of the Marquess, and wondered anew if he could complete his mission.

"*Et verbum caro factum est, et habitávit in nobis: et vídimus glóriam ejus, glóriam quasi Unigéniti a Patre, plenum grátiæ et veritátis.*"

"*Deo grátias,*" replied the people, and it was over. The priest hurriedly left the room. The door was jammed back into place by a warden.

"So what kept you?" asked Wallace, as the rest of the communicants separated themselves into twos and threes. The warden would let them leave at specific intervals.

"Salisbury turned up at the Malahides'. Louise hadn't known he was coming to dinner."

"Did you get a look at the head?"

"More than that: the transfer's on Thursday at Pentonville gaol. That doesn't give me long." Lambert worried at his fingernails.

"You should have let him have it." Wallace's face was set hard.

"Damn you, Wallace. You're not being asked to kill a man in cold blood. I can do this, but I need to pick my moment."

"Remember what the Holy Father said: the results of these operations are abominations before God, and must be destroyed." Wallace banged his fist into his palm for punctuation.

Lambert gritted his teeth. "I know Militantis Ecclesiae, chapter and verse. Malahide has a golem he dresses up as his butler, poor soulless creature. Bonapart, he calls it. I'll take it out too, if I have the chance." He turned to Wallace. "You don't need to convince me, but Salisbury has me down for a Rad just because I'm in the same college as Thompson. If he ever found out I was a Papist, he'd have me cut up and redistributed as spare parts to all his Tory cronies."

Wallace opened his fist and nudged Lambert's hunched shoulder. "Calm yourself, man. If Salisbury thinks you're a Rad, he's less likely to suspect you as Catholic. Besides, you're seeing his secretary's daughter. If your cover wasn't going to hold, you'd be in irons by now."

"Thanks for the comforting thought. I need a drink." His throat was as scratchy as a cat's.

"I'll buy one for you, but not round here. The locals would as soon rob you as let you pass in the street." Wallace looked to the warden, who jerked his head towards the door. "On your feet, old man. Time we were off."

There was a large crowd around the lions' cages. The keeper was taunting the snarling animals with a haunch of lamb he had impaled on the sharp end of a pole. He waved it this way and that in front of the bars, driving the lions into a frenzy of roaring and crying. Velvet paws tipped with killing blades lashed out, but the keeper always managed to draw the bloody meat away at the last moment.

"Only Man could enjoy such a spectacle," snorted Lambert, turning his back on the cages.

"Oh, Paul," said Louise, and linked her arm through his. "It's just harmless fun with brute beasts who don't know any different."

Lambert led her away. "But *we* do, dearest. We should treat them better, that's all I'm saying."

"You're right, of course. Perhaps I can have a word with Father." She drew closer, and steered her lover towards the tea-rooms.

Once seated in white-enamelled iron chairs, their order having been taken by a furiously scribbling waitress, they were suddenly joined by an unshaven stranger. He dragged a third chair to their table and casually slumped into it.

Lambert was indignant. "I'm sorry, sir. I don't recall inviting you to sit with us. If you please, I would ask you to leave us at once."

The man removed his bohemian beret and leaned forward. "Keep your voice down, Lambert, or we're all done for. I'm from the Curia."

Lambert almost retched with fear. "I'm sure I don't know what you mean. I'm calling the manager." He was getting to his feet when he was pulled abruptly down.

"Mockingbird," hissed the stranger, and Lambert sat down slowly, deliberately. He raised a wretched half-smile for Louise.

"Paul? Do you know this man?" Her brows were knitted on her flawless forehead.

"After a fashion," he stammered. "I know an associate of his." He turned, and spoke with quiet fury. "You fool. Not here. Outside."

The man did not move. "What I have to say concerns the young lady intimately. Do you trust her?"

The question appalled Lambert. He was being asked to decide too soon. His guts in turmoil, he eventually said: "Yes."

Louise edged forward in her chair. "Paul, what is going on? Who or what is Mockingbird?"

"Are you going to tell her? Or shall I?" asked the stranger. When Lambert hung his head, the man scratched at his stubble and leaned across the table to address Louise directly.

"My name is not important. I am a member of the Sacred Congregation of the Roman and Universal Inquisition, and I have to warn you that your life is in immediate danger."

"You're a Papist?" breathed Louise weakly.

"And so's your beau, Miss Malahide. Now, listen very carefully to me. Have you heard of the Wingrove pump?"

"You're from the Inquisition?"

"Yes, girl! The pump? Has your father talked of it?"

"I ..." She took a deep breath. "Paul?"

Lambert looked up and swallowed hard. "Let him speak. I want to know what's so damn important."

Louise blinked owlishly. "Suppose I had heard of Dr. Wingrove's pump. What of it?"

The Inquisitor looked around for eavesdroppers. "The function of the Wingrove pump is to keep a severed head supplied with oxygenated blood. Wingrove was the only man who could competently make use of it, so agents of the Church killed him. There's a working prototype, and the Royal College of Surgeons has it, but it's Wingrove they need. He's the best surgeon since the Baron himself.

"On Thursday, Wingrove's head is going to be moved to the body of an executed prisoner. If the transplant is successful, Wingrove will be alive again. He can then carry out his plan."

Lambert interrupted. "I'm sorry. What plan is this?"

"We learned of this last night from Mockingbird, which is why I'm accosting you in this very public manner. Queen Victoria is dying, no? Wingrove planned to make her effectively immortal. He was going to attach her veins and arteries to his pump, cut her head off, and then transfer it to a headless young woman."

Louise Malahide thought she might faint. "I don't believe you."

"The Queen requires a fit, healthy, well-nourished blueblood. Like yourself. Your father has volunteered you for the privilege. You, of course, will get a commoner's body in exchange. "

"That's madness," exploded Lambert. "Utter madness."

"Keep your voice down!" said the Inquisitor. "Here comes your tea and cakes."

They sat in stony silence as the waitress set out the crockery and arranged the fancy cakes on a stand. "Will that be all?" she asked, sensing the strained atmosphere.

"Yes, thank you," ground out Lambert, and when she had gone, "They can't expect this to work."

"Golems' personalities don't come through; there's been too much damage to the brain caused by lack of oxygen. The mistake we made was to try and kill Wingrove in the College itself. He lived long enough to supervise his own beheading. Next time, we'll aim for the head." He cleared his throat and spelled it out plainly. "If Wingrove survives, if his mind is intact after they make the transfer, he'll make the pump work. Lambert, if we don't stop this now, there'll be a race of aristocratic vampires preying on the lower orders for a thousand years. It won't stop at the Queen. They'll all be doing it soon enough."

"Everlasting life. The Holy Church will be redundant," whispered Lambert.

"Anathema," said the Inquisitor. "Thursday, Lambert. You're the only man we have close enough." He pulled his chair back, and settled his beret on his balding head. "I have to go." He did go, weaving between the tables and their attendant diners as if he were no more than a wandering artist who had misplaced his easel.

The tea was becoming stewed, and Lambert felt he ought to do something about it. His hand shook as he poured, and he stained the damask tablecloth with his inexpert aim.

"Sorry." He dabbed at the splash with his napkin. "So. Now you know."

"I don't think I know anything anymore. You're a Catholic spy. Tell me, was my falling in love with you part of the plan too?"

"God have mercy on my soul, Louise." He tried to take her hand, but she snatched it back. "They recruited me after we met. You have to believe me when I say I truly love you. It's the only part of my life that seems genuine." Amid the noise and bustle of the glass-roofed café, he began to cry copious tears of regret. "They're going to kill you, Louise. Without your help, I can't stop them."

"Paul, you don't believe what that Roman said, do you?" She still couldn't bring herself to think of her beloved as a hated Catholic.

"Mockingbird is the codename for your father's golem. He's the source of all our information. He's quite incapable of lying." He wiped his face with the tea-soaked napkin.

"But Boney can't speak!" She was certain he was wrong now.

"Neither can he write, but he'll point to letters on a board to spell out the words. He doesn't know he's being used. He doesn't understand what he's hearing. But he remembers conversations verbatim." By now he had controlled himself. "Perhaps it won't work. Perhaps Wingrove's brains will be so much scrambled egg, and he'll be a golem like all the others. The experiment will have failed, for now."

Louise added a drop of milk to her tea, and stirred the spoon slowly around. "If it works, when will they come for me?"

Lambert shrugged uselessly. "The Queen is old and she's dying. It has to be soon, or she won't last the operation. They mean to turn Victoria into a goddess. And she'll have your body."

Louise placed the spoon back in the saucer. "Tell me what I have to do."

On Wednesday afternoon, there was a knock on the door of Sir Evelyn Malahide's Commons office. His guests for luncheon had arrived.

"Do come in," he called, and began to tidy away the papers on his desk. "Hello, Louise, and to you, Paul." He screwed the cap back onto his pen and placed it nib down in the onyx holder.

"Sir," said Lambert, "It was kind of you to invite me. I've never been to Parliament before." The revolver, once so cold, burned fiercely in its hiding place.

"We're all set for Question Time. The Prime Minister is in bullish mood, so it should be quite a show. You ought to watch from the Gallery, lad. You might learn something away from your physics books." He adjusted his jacket, and patted his pockets.

"Papa? Paul would very much like to see the Prime Minister's office," said Louise, slyly.

"Louise! You said you wouldn't mention it." Lambert sighed. "I'm sorry, sir. It's really not important."

Malahide puffed himself up with vanity. "Well, lad. Interested in the seat of power, eh? It just so happens that I've some letters for the Marquess to sign. Would you mind if we called in on the way to the restaurant?"

"Mind?" gasped Lambert. "Heavens, no. I'd be delighted."

"Think nothing of it." Malahide shuffled through the pile of heavyweight foolscap, and plucked out three sheets. "Shall we go?"

He led the way through the labyrinthine corridors, all panelled in dark oak and surmounted by portraits and busts of the great and the good long since dead. It occurred to Lambert that if Salisbury had his way, the great and the good never need die again.

Malahide signalled their arrival by pausing outside an anonymous door and raising his finger to his lips. He knocked softly, and was answered several moments later by a low, rumbling voice.

Lambert recognised the tone and timbre. He reached behind him and began to tug his shirt from his waistband. Malahide opened the door and eased himself in, brandishing the letters.

"To be signed, Prime Minister."

"Very good, Sir Evelyn. Just put them in the usual place."

Lambert pushed Louise into the Lord's chamber and stepped in himself, heaving the door shut with his back.

"What a pleasant surprise!" said Salisbury, then caught sight of Lambert's revolver. He jumped up, his face turning red.

Malahide, startled by his Grace's sudden change in demeanour, looked sharply around. "What's the meaning of this? Give me that gun, boy, before you hurt someone." He took a pace forward and held out his rigid hand.

Lambert sighted down his arm and pulled the hammer back with his thumb. "Get back, damn you. It's Salisbury I've come for, but I've enough bullets for you." The moment had come, and he felt nothing but hate and rage. "By order of his Holiness, Pope Leo XIII, you are an abomination in the sight of the Lord God Almighty, and have no place in His creation. Your passing will lead you straight to Hell, Salisbury."

He moved the gun to point squarely at the chest of the Marquess, but as he did so, Malahide flung himself desperately forward. The bullet burst a pane of glass from the leaded window, and two men wrestled roughly on the rich carpet.

Malahide had both hands gripped around Lambert's right wrist. "Run, your Grace, run! I have him!"

Lambert swung his arm about, but Malahide's weight dragged it down. Salisbury sized the situation up in an instant. It was clear to him that the fanatic Lambert was going to best his secretary, so he bolted for the door. Wingrove's head bobbed and dragged as he ran, and made him waddle like a dwarf.

Louise picked up the heavy brass lamp from the desk and swung it at her father's head. It connected with a wet concussion that sent Malahide sprawling. He lay very still as the blue of the deep woollen pile turned black with blood. She dropped the lamp, but her face was triumphant.

"Get him, Paul. Chase him!"

Salisbury was out the door and away as Lambert scrambled to his feet. "Wait for me, my love!" he shouted over his shoulder as he bounded after the fleeing Lord. He had to keep him in sight. Salisbury had spent almost two decades in the Palace of Westminster, Lambert scarcely twenty minutes.

Lambert caught him silhouetted at the end of a long corridor, framed by daylight. Salisbury held his failing, gasping body against the open door. Lambert fired at once, and Salisbury jerked like a marionette. He raced towards the Prime Minister, catching him with a second shot as he began to fall outside. His third was deliberately placed. Standing over the crowblack figure whose outstretched arms were clawing uselessly at the grey paving flags of the terrace, Lambert aimed at Wingrove's exposed head. He made very sure that there would be no coming back from the dead for the Queen's surgeon.

Aware of the deathly silence around him, he looked up. The outside terrace was covered with dressed tables. There were many men seated, attended to by diligent servants. Lambert could not have chosen anywhere in the Capital more public to carry out an assassination.

The Members and their guests slowly rose to their feet. Waiters slipped full glasses of claret to the ground, and an army Major set his cap firmly on his head.

"He's killed the Prime Minister," one Parliamentarian said incredulously. "By God, stranger in the House! I spy stranger!"

Lambert had one bullet left. Suicide was a mortal sin, but it was very tempting. He knew what they'd do to him if they caught him alive. He raised his revolver, and bluffed it up.

"The next man to take a step forward, dies." He stepped sideways, crab-like, holding the crowd at bay. Those closest to him moved cautiously aside. Those furthest away pressed closer.

Now he stood with his back to the balustrade. Behind him was the Thames, full and slow like a torpid snake. He brandished his gun for one final time, causing the semicircle of men around him to expand like a bellows. He leapt up onto the narrow stonework, opened his arms crucifixion-wide to embrace the water, and tensed his legs for the dive. The Major shot him in the back with his service revolver, and Lambert saw his dress shirt puff up at the front. A hole had been punched through the heavy cotton, and the edges were already turning a deep red.

Lambert straightened his legs, and toppled forward. The river was very black, very cold, and seemed to meet him halfway through his fall.

He had one more memory. He remembered seeing nothing, smelling nothing, feeling nothing. But he heard this exchange:

"It's no use. Too long underwater. His brain's started to disintegrate."

"Damn shame. This Papist traitor would have suffered agony in my hands. He'd have told me everything."

"There'll be other times, other people. I'll have to turn the electrodes off. He's starting to cook. The stench of burning flesh - nothing quite like it."

"We're finished here. Get the surgeons to take what they can."

Lambert span away, back into his deep, dark rest.

Know Thine Enemy
Gary Greenwood

There were four of us sat around our table when I told the others about the new movie. The steady counterpoint of Adams's spoon scraping against his metal tray as he tried to get the last of his soup was beginning to piss me off and, by the looks of the other two guys, it wasn't just me it was bothering.

The Corporal tore a chunk off the loaf of bread that sat in the middle of the mess hall table and threw it over at Adams, making sure it landed on his tray. The private looked up for a second, a completely baffled expression on his face.

"What?" he said.

"Use the bread to mop your soup up," the Corporal said slowly through gritted teeth, desperately trying to sound like Clint Eastwood.

Adams shrugged, put the spoon down and began using the bread.

"You heard they're making another film of the Origin?" I asked.

"Seriously?" Manneheim asked, puffing on his ludicrously large cigar. I'd heard that he'd already had lung cancer three times, but he never learned. "Who's playing the Archetype?"

All three of them looked at me: Manneheim, the Corporal and Adams, who even stopped wiping his tray with the bread for five seconds. I grinned, relishing the attention and the suspense that I could build up by waiting before I answered, smiling around at each of them in turn.

"Apparently," I said slowly, dragging it out even further, "it's going to be DeNiro."

"You're joking?" said Manneheim. "Robert DeNiro?"

"Do you know any other?" I laughed.

"There's that short guy," Adams said.

"What short guy?"

"The one who played Schwarzenegger's twin in that crap movie about genetics or something,"

"That was Danny *DeVito,* you arsehole!"

"DeVito, DeNiro, they're both the fucking same! They just do their own thing over and over again."

I glanced at the Corporal for a second to share his look of amazement before turning back to Adams.

"You're comparing one of the most intense actors of the '80s with a short balding guy who only got where he is because he knows Michael Douglas, just because they have similar names?"

"Hey, come on, man," Manneheim said. "I agree DeVito's no DeNiro but he has got a couple of good calls under his belt."

"Like what?"

"'Taxi'. Damn good series, which you can't deny, man. Launched DeVito to the forefront and while him being mates with Douglas might have helped, I can't agree that that's the only reason he's been successful."

"There you go, told you: they're both the same," Adams said.

"What?" Manneheim asked him.

"DeNiro and DeVito. Both of them starred in 'Taxi' and they both got famous playing the same parts time and again." The table erupted into laughter and angry shouts for five seconds as Manneheim, the Corporal and me tried to work out what the hell Adams was on about. Eventually, we let him speak. "DeVito, the short one, plays the little guy who shouts a lot in 'Taxi', yeah?" We nodded, with him so far. "Which is the same role he's played in just about every other movie he's made, right?"

"Name one," the Corporal spat.

"I can't fucking remember them!" Adams said, ignoring us as we laughed and catcalled. "But he's done the same role over and over, all right? Anyway, it's DeNiro I was talking about, okay? And he, you have to agree, has played the nutter in every movie he's been in since 'Taxi'."

"He wasn't in 'Taxi', you twat!" I laughed.

"He was! What was the name of his character, the tall, lanky one who was barking mad? Was it Jim?"

"That was Christopher Lloyd!" Manneheim said almost at the same time as me.

"DeNiro was in 'Taxi *Driver*' you fucking idiot!"

"It was 'Taxi'!" Adams insisted.

"It was fucking 'Taxi Driver'!" the Corporal bellowed,

slamming his fist on to the table. A couple of the other grunts around us on different tables glanced over before going back to their meals. "Directed by Scorsese, I think. Had that woman from 'Moonlighting' in it as well,"

"Cybill Shepherd?" I said, not totally sure of myself.

"Yeah, I think so,"

"Harvey Keitel was in it as well," Manneheim said. "I watched it three or four times before I realised it was him."

"It'll be the hair and the bad hat," I said.

"So who the fuck is Christopher Lloyd?" Adams asked.

"Played the professor-"

"Doctor," I corrected.

"Doctor, whatever, in the 'Back To The Future' films. He was the nutty one in 'Taxi'." Manneheim looked at Adams and shook his head. "Robert DeNiro in fucking 'Taxi'," he said with a chuckle.

"So who's directing this one?" the Corporal asked me, getting back to the subject.

I shrugged. "I think it's going to be Kenneth Branagh, but Coppola's producing so far as anyone knows."

"Great, just what we need. Another fucking American version," Manneheim said.

"Well, as long as it's better than that 'Unbound' piece of shit." For once we were all in agreement.

"Branagh said he's going to stick closer to the book than any other version," I said with a shrug. "Don't know if he'll

Hideous Progeny

---

pull it off, though. I mean, name one biographical movie that's actually worked."

The four of us were silent for a moment, trying to think of an adequate answer.

"Born Free?'" Adams said.

The rest of us threw our meal trays at him.

*

Five weeks later we had the call: along with a couple of thousand others, we were to be part of the NATO team who were going into Bosnia. Personally, I didn't even know where the place was until it was pointed out to me on a map, but apparently some bad shit had been going on there for some time and NATO had finally been allowed to step in.

I'd been hanging around with Adams, Manneheim and the Corporal for years; we'd seen action together in a few places and had all managed to pull through in one piece, or at least get put back together in the right order. There were other little cliques like ours in the squad; guys made sure they were hooked up with their mates, ignoring whatever protocols the brass had come up with. You found someone you worked well with, and preferably liked, and you stuck together, knowing that you could trust them to be watching your back while you were watching theirs.

"So who're the bad guys in this thing?" Adams asked over his headset. We were all wearing them to drown out the noise of the aircraft that was taking us to Italy. From there we'd get transported over to Bosnia.

"You weren't paying attention at the briefing?" the Corporal asked. Adams shook his head. "Well, that means we're fucked if you don't know, because no one else was listening either."

"Isn't it the Serbs?" I asked.

"I thought it was the Bosnians?" the Corporal said.

"It doesn't matter," Manneheim butted in. "These Balkan states are all the fucking same. You give 'em independence, they fight amongst themselves, re-unify to make one country again, then they go back to fighting for independence. It's fucking ridiculous. We'll go in now, sort it out in a couple of months, and five or ten years down the line they'll be doing it again, I guarantee it."

"Who made you such an expert?" the Corporal asked him.

"I used to be Austrian, remember? I've been fighting in this part of the world for fuck knows how long. I was fighting here when all this was part of the Austro-Hungarian Empire, before we got shafted by the bloody British in the Great War." He looked over at me and stuck his middle finger up.

"Hey, don't blame me for that. That was before I was even born, let alone put back together. Not my fault the British Empire won that war."

"They wouldn't have if it hadn't been for their fucking Heat Rays."

"And whose fault was that? Britain's?" I laughed. "Come

on, Manny, the Martians invaded us, dropped dead of a bad cold and left all their hardware around. Were we supposed to ignore it?"

"Like you said, all before you were born. I was in the Great War, up to my waist in shit and blood and mud, and I could have coped with fighting against other men, even other creatures, but we didn't stand a chance against those things." Manneheim looked around at us as we rocked gently back and forth, shifting slightly with the plane's movement.

"I remember being in the trenches in 1916. The entire bloody thing was a stalemate by that point, and the only thing the Germans and us had going in our favour was the fact that the British were running out of men. We, on the other hand, thanks to the good old Doctor, had an almost inexhaustible supply. As long as we had enough body parts and enough surgeons to do the work we could keep going, and if there's one thing that war gave us it was body parts to spare." His eyes, blue on the left, green on the right, glazed slightly as he remembered the time. "Every night we'd slip over the top and hunt around in No Man's Land. Anything we could use we brought back: German, Austro-Hungarian, British or American, it didn't matter. As long as it could be attached to someone in need, we'd use it. Wasn't just us, either; we had heard the rumours by then about the Canadian, Doctor West, who was trying to get body parts for reanimation, but it obviously never worked. The US still don't have the technology.

"So we had plenty of body parts to keep fighting against the British and their allies. Trouble was, by 1916 the British had worked out all they needed to use the fucking tripods against us. First time I saw them I pissed myself because we knew exactly what they were. Europe had had a couple of cylinders as well, but had never been able to salvage anything from them. Because Britain bore the brunt of the invasion from Mars, they had more hardware to work with. The Austro-Hungarian Empire, along with Germany, had masses of men willing to die and be resurrected for their countries and that would have tipped the balance eventually, I'm sure, but you British bastards came into the shit hole of France with those huge tripods and almost totally wiped us out.

"We took a few down; a direct hit from one of our cannons could topple them, but with the range they had, there was little we could do except watch them stalk ever closer, burning everything and everyone in their path. Neither side had moved more than an inch in the six months previous; the British moved almost sixty miles in the first hour."

"How did you get out?" the Corporal asked. Manneheim didn't often talk about his time in the Great War, and none of us had heard this story before.

"I didn't. As soon as I saw one of the funnels turn towards me and my men, I automatically dived under the water in the trench, trying to hide. The ground around me was blasted by the Heat Ray, the trench collapsed over me and the whole thing turned into bone-dry rock in seconds, sealing me in water which boiled away, killing me instantly. It was three days before the British dug me out. When they recognised me for what I was, they held on to me as they did all the others, trying to resurrect me. Four weeks later and the war was over, at least until the next one.

"I spent the next six years in a British refrigeration factory, dead as a dodo, before Britain and Austro-Hungary, or the countries it had been broken up into, swapped their secrets. Austria got the Martian technology to build their own Body Catchers so they didn't have to send men out to get the body parts any longer, and Britain had Frankenstein's Theorem."

"You were out of it for six years?" Adams asked him.

"Yep. Spent them frozen on a slab, waiting my turn to be dissected by the Brits. Thankfully, when the two countries finally did their little swap, I and all my compatriots were sent back home. A few months later, with an almost totally new body, I'm back in the army, now the reformed Austrian army, training new recruits."

"So how long you been in the forces? All told, I mean?"

Manneheim looked at the ceiling of the transport carrier and moved his lips as he counted the years in his head.

"Born in 1873, joined the army in 1888, killed in action the first time in 1893 and with the exception of 1916 till 1922 when I was lying in a fridge, was with the Austrian army until 1938. The Germans invaded and annexed us; I joined the

Wehrmacht and served in Europe till the end of the war in '41, went to America as part of Operation Paperclip in '42, became a US soldier in '44 and, when NATO was set up in '51, was placed with them as part of the initial Resurrection Brigade, or the Monster Squad as we became known. You do the math."

"You been bounced around the forces for that long and you're just a private?" the Corporal asked him. "Hell, I been in thirty years and I've moved up."

"Yeah, but when your commanding officer has a life expectancy of, on average, a hundred and fifty years, progression can be a slow-moving thing," Manneheim said.

"Jesus," I said, looking at him in a new light.

"No, he ain't got nothing to do with it," Manneheim said with a grin.

"Half an hour to landing, ladies," the pilot said, his voice coming over our sets.

"Let's hope we can work out who the bad guys are before we get there," the Corporal said.

Manneheim grunted. "Chance'll be a fine thing," he said.

*

Adams was a moron and a relatively newly made creature - he had first been put back together in '75 - but he didn't deserve to die. None of us did.

Three days after we landed in Bosnia we were sent on a "fact-finding and peacekeeping mission". At least that was the official brief; with the head of our NATO squadron being the pig-headed and prejudiced American that he was, it was more a case of "get the monsters out into the field so we don't have to look at them". We didn't complain; it's been pretty much the same since the end of the First World War. The British Empire had the Heat Rays, the Germans and the Austrians had us, and the poor old US, once Dr West's famous experiments came to bugger all, had nothing. Envy amongst schoolchildren is a dreadful thing; on a national scale it's just ridiculous. The only reason the USA got into NATO in '51 was that by that time, to give them their credit, they'd developed the atom bomb. Of course, they never dropped it on anyone - what would be the point? - but they used the tired old threat of atomic war to bully their way into the NATO classroom, offering anyone the secret of splitting the atom in return for Frankenstein's Theorem. They had no takers.

Since then, denied the resurrection formula, the Americans have taken a great dislike to Britain and the European states, viewing us with the sulky eyes of spoilt children who have not had their way. Consequently, when NATO decides to give a squadron an American commander, any creatures in that squad sigh and resign themselves to getting the shitty jobs.

The Corporal pulled strings, as he and every other creature officer always did, and him, me, Manneheim and Adams went off on patrol, trying to find either the Serbs or the Bosnians; we were still unsure who the bad guys were.

"Yet another crap detail," Adams muttered as we walked

slowly through the remains of a village. Not one of the thirty or so houses had a roof; the months of carpet bombing by NATO before we were sent in had seen to that. That was the price of progress as far as I could see. In the Second World War, we'd had to fight for almost every inch of ground, troops firing at each other across a hundred feet of grass and mud; now, the allies blew the shit out of everything before sending people in. By the time the ground troops are deployed, nine times out of ten there's bugger all left for them to shoot at.

Maybe because of that, maybe because we were complacent about our capacity to be remade, we were lazy and sloppy in our patrol. The four of us strolled through the town square, chatting away, our rifles slung over our backs for Christ's sake, smoking cigarettes or, in Manneheim's case, one of his bloody big cigars, and the first we knew of the enemy was when Adams fell down, spinning to the ground as most of his left arm disintegrated.

"Get down!" the Corporal yelled, Manneheim and myself diving for cover as he grabbed Adams and pulled him back to the bomb crater the pair of us had headed for. Adams's left arm trailed beside him for a second until the thin piece of tissue connecting it to his shoulder tore, leaving the severed limb to lie in the trail of gore, a slug in a camouflaged sleeve on a bed of its own slime.

"I'm shot! I'm fucking shot!" Adams screamed, grabbing at the ragged hole left at his shoulder. Blood pissed out and pooled beside him, a thick red spurt occasionally slipping through his fingers and leaping over the edge of the crater in a bid for freedom. Without a word, the Corporal reached into the wound and grabbed the offending artery, squeezing down on it. Adams screamed in pain.

"Manny, med-pack!" the Corporal yelled. As Manneheim shrugged off his pack, and as I scanned the village surroundings, my rifle following my line of sight, I wondered why everybody decided to shout in situations like this. Outside our crater, the village was quiet and peaceful; sure, it had been almost ruined, but it had become accustomed to the silence. We were like some festering, grumbling tumour frantically trying to stay alive in the belly of a corpse.

Manneheim tossed his medical kit over to the Corporal, then lay next to me on the slope of the crater, scanning the area around us. "Anything?" he asked. Behind us Adams screamed again as the Corporal replaced his fingers with a temporary clamp to halt the loss of blood. We may be creatures made up of bits and pieces of dead people, but shoot us and it still hurts. Shoot our arm off and it hurts like fuck.

"Not a fucking thing," I said. Suddenly Manneheim screamed beside me, dropping his rifle and reaching around to his back. I glanced down at him and saw a large, dark stain spreading out at the base of his spine, just above his arse. I glanced at the Corporal for a second and could see the same question I was asking myself in his eyes: Why are the shots so quiet? There should at least be the crack of a rifle rolling over us, but we heard nothing except Adams's and now Manny's screams.

"Jesus Christ!" Manneheim yelled beside me, his eyes staring wildly at me, the mismatched colours bright with panic. He tried to push himself further down into the crater using his arms; his legs were of no use to him. "Jesus fucking Christ!" he gasped, his cigar lying forgotten in front of him. All he could do was repeat the name of a God whose ministers had deserted him and all those like us.

"It came from behind us," I said, twisting on to my back, levelling my rifle at the ruined houses. "We're fucking surrounded."

Adams wrenched himself away from the Corporal and managed to stand up in the crater, staggering over to me. His left-hand side was running with blood; the artery was clamped but everything else was still flowing freely.

"Give me a fucking gun!" he said before his face exploded. He rocked on his feet as the blood mist fell around us, leaving him staring at me with one eye; the rest of his features had been erased, torn off in a single shot which none of us had heard. For the briefest second he seemed about to speak though he had no jaw or teeth or tongue. His eyeball rolled in the exposed socket and he crumpled to the ground.

Manneheim still screamed Christ's name beside me as he lay on his belly further down the crater, the back of his combat gear soaked through with blood, his arms beating the ground, his legs lying still.

"Fucking do something!" I screamed at the Corporal, who seemed to have sat there the whole time. He opened his mouth, and a stream of rich red blood poured over his teeth, a crimson Niagara; then I saw the neat hole in his chest. He fell forward in silence, landing face down in the dirt, revealing to me the huge exit wound in his back, almost in pride.

Manneheim's cries had stopped and, as I glanced down at him, I was aware of something punching me in the belly. Pain spread outwards and upwards, easing into my head slowly like a sunrise. Clutching my rifle, I fell back against the crater wall, breathing slowly, trying to stave off shock; I'd been gut-shot before now, back in World War Two and in 'Nam. I could handle this, I knew I could.

A few minutes later there came the sound of booted feet on the ground, walking slowly, carefully. Three figures appeared over the edge of the crater, all of them with huge, powerful rifles pointing at us, silencers screwed onto the muzzles. Each one wore a mask. After looking down at us and then at each other, they laughed and lowered their rifles.

I lifted mine and shot the nearest one.

The other two swore loudly and both turned to me, firing down into the crater.

*

"So did you see the Coppola movie?" the Corporal asked

me.

"Yeah, I got the video a couple of weeks back. Piece of shit."

"Good review," Manneheim said. "You ever think of going into writing as a career?"

"Fuck you," I said, giving him the finger. "Branagh was okay, but he had a crap script to work from and DeNiro did us no favours whatsoever. According to 'Mary Wollstonecraft's Frankenstein', we're all damned from creation and will never find any sort of peace so we may as well be put down now and have no more remade."

"So you weren't impressed with it then?" the Corporal asked, laughing.

"No, I fucking wasn't."

The three of us fell silent. We were sat in the mess hall as usual, waiting for the next mission which, as Manneheim had so rightly predicted two years before, was back in the Balkans, trying to stop Yugoslavians from killing each other again. This time, though, we were a trio, not a quartet.

"You reckon there's an afterlife?" Manneheim asked, chewing on his cigar.

"Fucked if I know," the Corporal said. I shrugged.

We sat there and, though I can't speak for the others, I was thinking of Adams. We'd been picked up after the ambush and put back together; as a purely cosmetic thing, the surgeons had replaced one of Manneheim's eyes with the remaining one from Adams, so at least they matched now. The trouble with Adams had been his head shot: bone had lodged in the brain and rendered it useless. Can't bring someone back if their brain doesn't work. I don't think they meant to do that – if they wanted to kill us all, they could have shot us three in the head as well. I think they were just having some fun at our expense.

"Think we'll get a US commander again?" I asked the Corporal.

"Maybe. Why?"

"Just wondering," I said, thinking back to the three men who had ambushed us: all very professional, all with high-tech rifles, all surprised as hell when I shot one of them.

"So, who're the bad guys this time?" Manneheim asked.

"Take your pick," I said, hearing again the curses of the two surviving assassins. Whether we'd been meant to fight the Serbs or the Bosnians that time, I don't think they were the bad guys. I've never heard a Serb or a Bosnian swear with an American accent.

Fallen Angel
Peter Crowther

At first Yellen thought the man was watching him.

He pulled back against the hedge, folding his body into the sharp branches, and waited. The man staggered a little and bent down. Yellen stared, trying to make out his movements through the gloom. The man had rested something on the ground and was now straightening up, muttering. The sounds of indistinct words floated across the street. Yellen glanced quickly to left and right to see if there was anybody else around. The street was deserted.

Yellen had been casing a small one-up-one-down that stood out among the other houses by virtue of a gleaming silver satellite dish, standing proud on the patchy stucco like a ripe boil. He had heard the sound of footsteps and had dodged gracefully across the sidewalk into the hedge. He looked back at the man and wrinkled his nose. The hedge smelled of pee.

Across the street the man rose to his full height and took two faltering steps forward... then another one back and slightly to one side. He wore a long topcoat which, as he swayed side to side, feet held so firmly in place that they could have been nailed to the sidewalk, flapped open to reveal a dark jacket and light-colored pants. His shirt collar was unbuttoned low, necktie sprawled to one side in an explosion of crumpled material. The top half of his body continued to ripple as though an electric current were passing through it. Yellen recognized the current as being 80-proof. He slid his right hand into his jerkin and eased the .38 out of his waistband while the man shuffled around so that he faced the wall, his back to Yellen, and made a big deal out of unzipping his fly.

A faint hybrid sound of pooling water and bursts of mumbling echoed through the night, it sounded like someone trying to tune in to a distant radio station.

After what must have been a full minute and a half, the man shook himself, bent forward, fumbled up his zipper, and then turned around. He looked straight across at Yellen, but his eyes clearly didn't see anything except the night and the loneliness and the New Jersey air. The man threw his arms into the air and shouted to the sky.

"Thus st-strangely," he stuttered hoarsely, "are our souls constructed..." He paused, shook involuntarily, and then continued, "And by such... by such slight ligaments are we bound to posterity or ruin!" He staggered back a step or two and, as if attached to a single string which had suddenly been severed, his arms and head fell forward to sides and chest. He kept this way for several seconds, swaying, and then lurched down sideways to retrieve whatever he had set on the sidewalk. Yellen retreated farther into the hedge and concentrated on the object as it came into view. It was a bag.

It looked like a doctor's bag, but bigger: one of those old black valises that carried prescription pads and Valium and painkillers. *And what else?* Yellen wondered. *Maybe a few uppers?* He held the gun down by his side so he could bring it up at full arm's length and fire if he were forced into it. He almost wished he would be. But, no, the man hoisted the bag up under his arm and leaned an unsteady head so that it met the object... and kissed it tenderly. Then he turned around to face the way ahead.

Yellen squinted. The bag looked heavy. Important. Precious.

The man started to shuffle his one-two-one way along the sidewalk and Yellen moved forward from the hedge, sliding the gun into his jacket pocket. He watched the man for a few seconds and then turned back to look at the house. It was still dark. He knew what was in there. VCR, television set, bunch of compact disks, receiver. The usual. It was the sign he had grown accustomed to looking for. It usually meant objects which he could easily turn into cash. He looked back at the man's weaving figure, heard a distant belch, and his eyes locked onto the black bag. But maybe there were better pickings to be had.

The man reached the end of the block and turned into the next street, shuffling back before proceeding, like a bad vaudeville act or Snagglepuss, the old cartoon lion. Then, with a throaty *burrrup* and a stream of Shakespearean-type mumbling, he was gone.

Yellen rechecked that he was still alone and unobserved and then took a final look at the house. His mind was already made up even before he acknowledged the decision. He folded himself into the air and the shadows and ran crouched and silent-footed across the street.

He got to the end of the block and peered around the corner. About fifty or sixty yards up the sidewalk the man was doing more of his soft shoe shuffle, trying to make a ninety-degree turn over the shards of a large fence. He negotiated the barrier with difficulty and staggered off the sidewalk. Yellen followed.

He followed the man across some stumpy grassland, festooned with ditches and rocks so concealed by the night that even he, stone-cold sober, experienced some difficulty in maintaining his balance. The man, however, now sappeared to have found his feet and glided effortlessly across every obstacle with seeming surety.

Eventually the steady hum of humanity, that almost indiscernible and often reassuring presence of civilization, faded behind them as they picked their way across the barren land. Here a tree sprouted from the earth, there an occasional bush; up a small slope, down a sharp ravine... until, at last, the sound of the man's shoes clattered again onto man-made material, Yellen stopped and watched, breathing heavier now.

The man was on a street. It ran straight to the right and into the far distance where it joined the main drag down into Westfield. To the left it ran a few yards before curving away and down what appeared to be a hill. Yellen couldn't be sure.

The light was very bad, fed only by three streetlamps, unevenly spaced, and a gibbous moon that played hide and seek with the passing clouds.

The man stamped his feet, almost losing his balance in the process, and then crossed the road he was on and walked toward a large house that seemed to fill the whole horizon. A thick patch of cloud slipped across the moon and then slid off toward the coast, the sudden increased glare of light catching the full splendor of the property and etching it against the dark sky to the north. The house stood alone on the road. Yellen looked at it and marveled.

The tapering roof of an octagonal tower adjoining one side of the main roof - a smoke-topped chimney rose from the other - gave the house the appearance of a clenched fist, its index and little fingers stretching up in a combination of exclamation and caution. It was, Yellen recognized from his college days, a Queen Anne-style mishmash of tower, bay windows and porte cocheres. There were many examples of the period around Westfield, but this, surely, would qualify as being one of the finest. Possibly *the* finest.

Moonbeams glinted like fairy dust down a tapering roof which alternated between rows of fish-scale shingles and rectangular slates. More shingles adorned the gable, and the porch - within which the man now fumbled in coat pockets, the bag still held firmly beneath his arm - featured a frieze of spindles and inverted taper columns, up which a veiny confusion of ivy tendrils had crept. The windows were a patchwork of Elizabethan straplines, with small multicolored panes surrounding a larger clear-glass center.

And there, attached to the highest tip, a jumble of thick cables stretching and bowing down from it to the darkened depths of the grounds, was the biggest receiver dish that Yellen had ever seen.

As he crept stealthily across the road and into the drive of the house, Yellen kept his gaze fixed on the object, watching its perspective change and its size increase until, as he crouched behind a thick bush, the thing seemed to dominate the sky. It was at least three - maybe four - times larger than the usual dishes householders fixed to their properties. Black or dark gray in color, it boasted a stamen-like centerpiece of glass pipettes which themselves formed a fairy-ring periphery to a thick and bulbous, apparently metallic, protrusion that angled into space. As he watched, Yellen thought he saw the spike glowing. A sound from the porch made him crouch lower and fumble in his jacket pocket for the gun.

Through the bush, Yellen could see that the man had turned from the door, which now stood partly open, to face the drive and the road beyond. He held the bag tightly to his chest with both hands, stepped out onto the path and looked up at the receiver dish. "As I stood at the door," he said, loudly and in now more succinct tones, "all of a sudden I beheld a stream of fire issue from an old and beautiful oak, which stood about twenty yards from our house."

As if on cue, the spike now proceeded to glow and throb and a distant symphony of metallic tings sounded through the gloom. "And as soon as the dazzling light had vanished, the oak had disappeared," he continued, "and nothing remained but a blasted stump." The man staggered a little and then, resting the bag on his outstretched left arm, he unfastened the clasp and pulled the sides apart. Looking inside, his voice lower now but still distinct, he said, "I never beheld anything so utterly destroyed."

And then he reached into the bag and pulled out, his hand clasped around one leg, what appeared to be a floppy doll. The object flailed at the movement, its free leg and both of its arms and its head swinging freely.

The man dropped the bag to the ground and held the doll aloft. Turning his head so that it faced the dish- or, perhaps, Yellen thought, some greater entity far beyond the confines of the house - he intoned "Yet from whom has not that rude hand rent away some dear connection, and why should I describe a sorrow which all have felt, and must feel?"

He turned around and lowered the doll, taking it into both hands and pulling it to himself. "Nay, ne'er mind *describe*... why must I countenance it? Why *should* I countenance it?" And then he turned back to face the house and went inside, pushing the door closed with his body.

Yellen waited, heart beating fit to burst, and watched the

porch. The door banged against its casing and then, slowly, drifted open once more. He removed the gun from his pocket, felt the reassurance of body-warmed metal, and then replaced it again. With a quick look around him he stood up and ran to the porch, up the few steps on tiptoe, and through the doorway into the darkness beyond.

Once inside, Yellen flattened himself against the wall behind the door and listened. He could hear echoing footsteps fading somewhere in front of him but, his eyes not yet conditioned to the impenetrable blackness, he couldn't make anything out. *Why doesn't he turn on a fucking light?* Yellen thought. Suddenly the sound of the footsteps changed. The man was on some stairs. But was he going up or down? Yellen put his head flat to the wall and closed his eyes, straining to hear. It was up.

He removed his shoes and placed them carefully by the door. Then, his vision improved, he moved forward deeper into the house.

The doorway opened onto a pentagonal hallway from which a series of doors, all but one closed, stood in the center of each wall with the main door behind him. The open door led onto what seemed to be a corridor. It was there that the footsteps could be heard. He checked his gun again, walked across the floor to the corridor, and slipped stealthily through.

At the end of the corridor was a cross passage. Once there, Yellen glanced carefully around the corners. To the left, the corridor led to what seemed to be a rear entrance to the house. The right-hand wall of this smaller corridor featured a series of picture windows which showed a long, rambling garden, completely untended and overgrown. At the rear of the garden, adjoining a wide, rough pathway, was a car. Its wheels had been removed and the axle ends rested on small piles of stone. The car appeared to have no glass in its windows. The glass door at the end of the corridor opened onto a small room, also completely glassed, and Yellen could make out various handles and pieces of equipment.

In the other direction, to the right at the end of the main corridor, a shorter passage led to another open area, though this one was considerably smaller than the main hall. Yellen saw a banister end leading upward to the right and out of sight. Now, at least, he knew where the stairs were. He started to move toward them.

As he walked, straining to hear the footsteps and continued mumbles from somewhere overhead, Yellen was suddenly aware of the state of the house. It had been allowed to go completely to ruin.

From all of the walls large strips of wallpaper hung free, reaching to the floor and myriad piles of broken plaster and fast-food wrappers and containers. From all around he seemed to hear soft scurryings, scratchings and rustles, and the almost soundless movement of gently billowing material. As he reached the foot of the stairs he checked the gun again and moved around the banister to face the risers leading upward.

The flight of stairs had, approximately, twenty-five risers and Yellen could clearly see the next floor. The stairs opened onto another cross corridor before continuing around to the right, up again. He started up, suddenly sharply aware of a pungent smell.

The smell was not exactly unpleasant, but it was strong. It hinted of body odor, a thickening draught of parmesan cheese sitting atop a bowl of steaming hot vegetable chowder. By the time he had reached the top of the stairs, it just smelled like shit.

The cross corridor led, to the left, to a long passage which featured three doors, two on the left, one on the right. The right one was glass-paneled and led onto a small balcony over-looking the rear garden. At the far end of the passage was a wall and, on the left, a dark patch which suggested the corridor made a sharp turn to further rooms.

To the right, the corridor ended, by the foot of the next flight of stairs, at a door. The door was open and a light was shining from inside. Somewhere, something was humming. It was an equipment-type hum, the sound of confident strength, of well-tended machinery.

Something small ran over Yellen's feet and it was all he could do to keep from crying out. He kicked out and skipped toward the door. As he passed the next flight of stairs, the smell he had noticed earlier hit him like a hot sheet thrown over his face. He stopped and looked up the stairs.

The flight led to another level, another blank wall and, presumably, another cross corridor. Looking up, he could hear sounds... groans and moans, shufflings and - he turned his head to one side to concentrate - an occasional clank, like bottles, or glasses being chinked together in a gesture of good health. But the smell coming down from up there spoke of anything but good health.

Yellen glanced over at the open door, listened, and then stepped onto the first stair.

His heart was now beating like an electronic drum, faster than should be humanly possible.

He took the second stair.

And then the third.

Each step led him deeper into that smell of depravity and filth. It was as though he were descending into a blocked sewerage system and not simply climbing a staircase.

When he had reached the top, he looked back. There was nothing much to see, just the faint glow coming from the small room to the right of the foot of the stairs. He turned around and swallowed hard to keep from throwing up.

This time, the corridor ending at the left and front, a passage led to the right and along to a large pair of doors across which a heavy plank had been fixed into two large, rusting metal hooks. The moans and groans were coming from behind the doors.

Yellen considered going back downstairs and out into the night. The temptation was strong. Hell, if he were so bothered about finding out what was behind the doors, he could even come back another day, tomorrow maybe. With help. In the light.

Because the night, and particularly this house, spoke of monsters. *Monsters*! Why should he think of monsters, for Crissakes? He hadn't even used the word since he was a kid and couldn't get to sleep because of the big man who could fold his body into sections and sleep in the large bottom drawer of his chest. The drawer where his mom put Yellen's underwear and socks. The drawer which Yellen would never go into unless the penalty was sufficiently dire. After all, what were a few skidmarks in your smalls or the occasional lump of toe-cheese rattling around your socks when the alternative was to have a spindly arm and toothy grin telescope out of the colored interior of a chest drawer to grab you and kiss you, and pull you into the feigned softness of what was, in reality, a material hell.

Something shuffled up to the other side of the doors and bumped into them letting out a tired groan. The doors had rattled briefly, softly, and were still again. Whatever it had been could now be heard shuffling away again.

Yellen took a deep sigh, strode to the doors, and lifted the plank free. He placed it against the wall and reached for the handle. As he did so, the left hand door opened slowly.

Yellen wasn't even aware of throwing up.

His gorge moved quickly and without deliberation, traveling from his stomach, up his throat, and into his mouth from where it splashed in one silent burst and then dribbled in two or three additional pulses.

Yellen shook his head at the thing that faced him in the gloom. It was - or once had been - a girl, maybe 14 or 15 years old. She stood before him as if in supplication or submission, completely naked, scrawny breasts covered in sores and scratches, a thick pubic thatch hanging from her crotch like a Scotsman's sporran.

The girl's skin was yellow, like matted breakfast cereal, boasting a series of sores, tears, lumps, and crisscrossed stitches that wept thin funnels of matter into crusted configurations on her cheeks and jowls. One of her eyes was closed in a puffy ball of rainbow hues. The other, a watery orb that stared, seemingly without recognition or emotion, out of a thin and skeletal white socket, blinked once and fell still. The skin on her cheeks and down onto her neck was stretched so tight that Yellen could see the musculature flex and vibrate as she turned her head, first one way and then the other. It was with profound regret and shame that he saw he had been sick onto the top of her head, where his vomit ran and mixed with long tendrils of thinning hair.

The girl opened her mouth wide, separating lips so black they looked like heavy pencil slashes gouged beneath a turned-up nose, and let out a soft, querulous hum. Then she turned from him and shuffled back into the room. As she moved away from him, slopping her trailing feet through rivers of brown and yellow and green ooze, Yellen saw the caked mess of shit on her backside.

Now, in spite of the smell, Yellen moved into the room.

There were maybe fifteen or twenty of the unfortunates in there, some standing, some sitting and some lying down amidst the debris and the filth. Some were younger, some maybe older than the girl who had admitted him, but all were children. A handful in the far corner, beneath a series of barred and white-washed windows, were only babies or toddlers. One of them watched Yellen, his black-rimmed mouth a shitty stain, as he paused in the act of eating a long runny stool that dripped onto his legs. It would, he thought, be crediting the child with too much to say that there was a spark of intelligence in those watery eyes. His actions were purely reactive.

A sound behind him made Yellen spin around.

The man stood in the doorway, swaying slightly, a beatific smile etched on his face. In the current circumstances, the smell of bourbon was tantamount to being the finest Chanel perfume.

The man held onto the door with his left hand and waved the other expansively to the scene inside the room. "With how many things are we upon the brink of becoming acquainted," he said in a slow, deliberate voice, "if cowardice and careless-ness did not restrain our enquiries?" One of the children moaned and the man lifted a finger to his mouth and shook his head paternally.

Turning his attention back to Yellen, he said, "To Monsieur Frankenstein, this was a rhetorical question, my friend. I, however, put it to you fully." And with that he stepped back and ushered Yellen out of the room. Yellen walked as if in a dream, back onto the landing, and the man closed the doors and lifted the heavy plank back into its place.

"What are they?" Yellen asked as he followed the man down the stairs.

"They are the chosen ones," he replied, the words drifting over his shoulder like motes of dust. "I know what you are thinking, my friend."

"I'm not your friend," Yellen snapped.

The man reached the foot of the flight and nodded. "Quite so. But I do know what you are thinking. 'Its astounding horror would be looked upon as madness by the vulgar.'" He spoke the words reverently and Yellen saw that they were slightly out of the flow of the man's first sentence.

"Are those..." Yellen waved his hand. "The things you keep saying, are they quotations?"

The man nodded again, bending slightly from the waist as though before a dignitary. Standing straight again, albeit falteringly, he said, "Shelley."

"The poet?"

"Mary Shelley. The author *and* poet. '*Frankenstein*'. Are

you acquainted with the work?"

"I've seen the movies," Yellen said.

 The man sniggered. Then he gestured to the room at the foot of the stairs. "Come," he said. "All will become clear."

As he walked toward the room, the man removed a hip flask from his jacket pocket and, throwing his head back dramatically, took a deep swallow. Then he returned the flask to his pocket.

The room was huge and bare.

In its center was a padded black table, above which hung a chandelier-type object bedecked in wires and tubes. The wires ran from the head of the object and across the ceiling to a high point on the wall, below which a window looked out onto the path by which they had come to the house. Yellen, patting his pocket for the reassurance of his gun, recognized the scene and surmised that the wires were attached to the receiver dish.

On the table itself lay the doll which the man had carried in his valise. Only it wasn't a doll.

The child was perhaps five years old, his skin pale and withered, a single heavily stitched scar traveling the full width of his stomach. Yellen stared at the child, not daring to believe what he was seeing. "You're mad," he said. The words sounded so ineffective, so cliched and so entirely inadequate.

The man walked in front of Yellen to the shelving that covered the walls surrounding the room. Yellen now saw that the shelves bore what might well be hundreds of large bottles and jars and tanks, each with something floating in thick-look-ing solutions. "'I hope the character I have always borne will incline my judges to a favorable interpretation, where any cir-cumstance appears doubtful or suspicious.'" He reached down a bell jar, containing what Yellen thought could be livers or kidneys or something similar, and unscrewed the top. "That was what Justine Moritz, the closest of close friends to Eliza-beth Lavenza, Frankenstein's virtual sister, said as she stood accused of the murder of Elizabeth's son, William." He took a rubber glove from the shelf and pulled it on with a loud squeak-ing sound. Smiling at Yellen, the man said, "Nobody ever un-derstands." He lifted one of the things from the jar, replaced the lid - one-handed and with difficulty - and returned it to the shelving.

"What are those?"

"Things no longer required by their previous owners," the man replied. "You could say they're not wanted on the voy-age." He chuckled and stepped across to the table where he dropped the piece of tissue or whatever it was into a round surgical tray which lay beside the child's body.

"Where do you get them?"

The man turned around and leaned against the table, re-moving the hip flask with his ungloved hand. "'A churchyard was to me merely the receptacle of bodies deprived of life, which, from being the seat of beauty and strength, had become food for the worm.'"

"Oh, my God-"

The man threw the flask across the floor, "Oh ... spare me your platitudes and your pathetic pleas for help." He moved toward Yellen, waving a finger at the ceiling. "There's nobody there, can't you people understand that? The lights are on, but there's nobody home. God?" He laughed, making the word sound like an invective. "He doesn't exist - or, if he does, then he's singularly lacking in compassion.

"*I* am the light... *I* am the way. It's because of *me* that those children still survive."

Yellen shook his head.

The man turned back to the table and began rubbing a cloth across the corpse. "The girl that you saw is my daughter." He stopped and leaned on the table, head bowed. "'I saw the yellow eye of the creature open; it breathed hard, and a convulsive motion agitated its limbs.'" He returned to the washing. "She was my first," he added. "Fourteen years old, raped and stabbed to death, her vagina clipped almost up to her abdomen with cutting shears. I try not to think of what order her injuries were sustained... try not to think that the killing insertion to her heart came last."

He dropped the cloth back into the bowl and pulled a cord overhead. The chandelier began to lower slowly. Turning to face Yellen, he said, "And yet you talk of God." The words came in a haze of spittle and disgust.

"You *are*-"

"Mad? So you said. 'All men hate the wretched; how, then, must I be hated, who am miserable beyond all living things.'" He suddenly concentrated his gaze on Yellen and frowned. "Incidentally, why are you here?"

Yellen shrugged. "To steal."

The man copied the shrug. "Makes no matter." The chandelier beeped and came to a shuddering halt. "Ah," the man said, "we're almost ready." He waved for Yellen to join him. "Here, you can help."

"You have got to be joking!"

"I never joke, Mister Thief. Hold not another in contempt lest you are yourself free from blemish. I, my dishonest guest, live to give. You, on the other hand, are a taker."

Yellen removed his gun. "Well, I'm going to do some giving right now."

The man watched the gun impassively. "And what do you propose to do with that?"

"I'm... I'm going to go back to that hellish room and put those things out of their misery. Will bullets-"

The man dropped to his knees on the floor and clasped his hands together. "'She died calmly-'"

"Shut up~"

"'... and her countenance expressed-'"

"I said..."

"'... affection even in death.'"

"... SHUT UP!"

"'His yellow skin scarcely covered the work of muscle...'"

Yellen ran across the room and swung the gun against the man's face, sending him sprawling against the table. The table skidded away and then held against two restraining straps fixed to the floor, jerking its passenger off to land with a dull thud.

"Jesus Chri-"

"There's no him, either," the man said, holding a shaking hand to the gash below his left eye. "There's just you and me, thief. Do what you must."

Yellen lifted the gun and fired. And he kept firing.

The first shot went through the man's hand and cheek, spraying brain onto the floor milliseconds before the back of his head touched it. The second and third went into his chest. The fourth, his stomach. The fifth, strategically placed - Yellen had walked while firing and was now standing directly above the man- in the center of his forehead. There wasn't a sixth, only a click... followed by many more clicks until Yellen's finger eased from the trigger.

When he went back to the room at the top of the house for the final time, he carried the cold body of a small boy. He had already dragged the man's body up the stairs and propped it against the door beside two cans of gasoline that he had found in a small hut in the garden.

On the top of the can sat two books: one containing matches and one containing words.

Entering the room again he smiled frequently. Nobody inside responded. Nobody tried to leave.

He placed the boy's body with the other toddlers and dragged the man into the center of the room.

Then he walked around spilling gasoline everywhere, singing, "Hush little baby, don't say a word, Daddy's going to buy you a mockingbird." It was a song his mother had sung to him many years ago.

As the flames took hold, he flicked through the pages of the other book, trying to find something appropriate.

He found it and paraphrased: "Farewell my beloved friends: may Heaven in its bounty bless and preserve you; may this be the last misfortune that you will ever suffer."

Then he left the conflagration and rejoined the night.

"When I placed my head upon my pillow, sleep crept over me; I felt it as it came, and blest the giver of oblivion.-

Mary Wollstonecraft Shelley (1797-1851)

The Day after the Day the War Ended
Paul Finch

The pinewood was full of bodies ... an entire company caught 'twixt mortar and flame-thrower, now a heap of tangled charcoal husks, delicately crisped in their own batter. We crunched them underfoot in our haste. It was the armoured vehicle we were after ... on the road just ahead, the one smoke-blackened and riddled with bullet-trails, the one skidding and slewing along on shreds of rubber. If we got a move on through the wood, we'd just be able to cut it off before it reached the next checkpoint, where the Tiger tanks were abandoned and burned, but where Schmeissers might be dumped, where grenades could be found, or fully loaded MG42s.

It was relatively easy for us. Because we were fit and strong. And victorious. The war to end all wars was over, and we had won it. But there was one fish left to net, we'd been told. Just this one. Then we could all go home ... and believe me, back in '45 that was some motivation. We fanned boldly out across the road, Sten guns levelled, as the old truck slid haphazardly towards us, rivers of sparks in its wake. There was a possibility its occupants would open fire, but we doubted it. To begin with, they'd be lucky if they had a round left between them. If they did, most likely they'd use it on themselves.

Even the fools among us should have been able to predict the way war would go.

No-one had really intended to use the Not-Dead regiments as cannon fodder, but it was unavoidable... something they drifted into rather than being specifically designed for. Their lack of immediate response to stimuli meant they were useless as regular infantry, while their capacity for understanding and following anything more than the most basic orders varied so widely from individual to individual, that even vaguely complex tasks were beyond their capability as organised units. They certainly couldn't be trusted to control vehicles or machinery, so the cavalry and artillery were out, and the very thought of Not-Dead squadrons in the air, or even at sea, was enough to send the most bullish patriot scrambling for his white flag.

Also, I think there was something about the way they looked... those dull witless expressions, that pallid greenish complexion, the fact that so many of them - even the most recent reanimations - still bore the butcher-shop scars of mass-production: lines of cheap, crude stitching; massive metal bolts through those joints too badly damaged to be fixed any other way; not to mention the odd-coloured eyes, the limbs which didn't suit one another(The first transports taking them overseas were known to the Royal Navy as "the Jumble Sails"; cruel but not inappropriate). Add to this the twisted postures, the lumbering, see-saw gaits, the slurred, near-unintelligible speech (where speech was possible), and the shrunken, semi-

decayed visages of those allowed to deteriorate too far before going to Process, and you had an unsightly rabble too repulsive for any but the most liberal intellectuals to pity.

Even so, looking back on it, I can't help shedding a tear at the way they were so casually herded into the enemy guns, to die their second or third, in some cases even fourth and fifth deaths, but at the time I was as heartless and cold about it as everyone else. It was war, and we all had our duty. Even King George came out onto the blitzed London streets, to walk among the homeless and wounded. He was actually Living of course (though many argued differently), but the point is, if the king - who was descended from a German family, remember - could do his bit, then the Not-Dead could do theirs.

Reanimation hadn't been used extensively during the 1914-18 conflict, though indirectly that tragic event was the spark. When World War One broke out, the Process - which had already been in place for a century - was still outlawed in Great Britain, and the subject of fierce debate. Some of the wilder anarchist groups, and even idealistic chatterers like the Fabians, approved it wholeheartedly as Man's final victory over a conservative and tyrannical God, though religious bodies (naturally) and plenty of other well-meaning folk were concerned about its moral implications. Even the Labour Party, that new champion of the underdog, regarded it as a toy for rich eccentrics and was instinctively wary. Perhaps inevitably, discussion was overwhelmed by events. By the end of 1916, with two years of war still to come, there was scarcely a family in the UK untouched by the conflagration. And, for once, the losses weren't confined to those lower orders who lacked a voice. Middle-class households the length of the country were bereaved in a way they'd never imagined possible. And, typically, they weren't putting up with it.

First of all, it was spiritualism: everywhere, well-to-do ladies were suddenly inviting mediums into their homes, for one last contact with deceased husbands, sons, brothers. Then, inevitably, it was the Process. It might have been unlawful in Britain, but that didn't stop private and secret sanatoriums springing up, where for a tidy sum it was available... so long as you were able to retrieve your loved one from the battlefront mass grave where he'd been thrown, then get him back to Blighty and into the hospital refrigeration facility before he'd completely rotted to carrion. Only very few were able to manage this, but they did it in sufficient numbers for British medical societies to get fully to grips with the techniques involved, and for crusading politicians to keep the issue on the parliamentary agenda.

For all this, the Not-Dead Bill was only brought before the House by the Chamberlain administration in 1938, when British intelligence uncovered evidence that Nazi Germany was well on the way to supplementing its already immense war machine with new Not-Dead regiments created from its vast supplies of executed criminals. Thus, an entirely new kind of armaments race began. In Britain the bill was made law within two months, and though we couldn't boast army-sized numbers of hanged felons to reanimate, at the end of the impoverished 1930s the workhouses and mission halls were still stacked with nameless, penniless wretches whom nobody knew or cared about. Once they'd died - which they did with fortunate regularity - it was a small matter of the State volunteering to pick up the cheque for disposal rather than the parish, and no one was going to argue about that. If anyone did notice the mortuaries suddenly emptying at remarkable speed, they didn't bother to make an issue of it.

Not everyone was so keen, of course. France wasn't even vaguely interested, preferring to remain at play and to continue kidding itself that war wasn't about to happen. Other Catholic countries, Poland and Italy for example, avoided the issue on religious grounds, as did our friends in the Empire, India and Egypt. The Soviet Union had no intention of reanimating the dead, as walking corpses didn't fit into the collective dream - and in any case, there were already more than enough downtrodden workers on the Russian steppe to use in any number of extravagant state projects. The USA was curious to know more, but with its mentality of splendid isolation, it was adamant it had no role to play in another European conflict. After Britain and Germany, only Japan began to invest seriously in the Process, though the old Samurai codes of courage and honour were still to the fore in Japanese mili-

tary training, and the Not-Dead were only expected to play an auxiliary role.

*

The truck had clearly been an APC of some sort, but was now virtually unidentifiable. Even the distinguishing swastikas were only vaguely visible on the battered and blistered bodywork. As the vehicle sat there, its engine now completely stalled, its chassis tilted to one side, foul black smoke leaking out, we knew it wouldn't be going anywhere else.

Captain Anderson and Lieutenant Grey stepped forward to accept the expected surrender. The rest of us were told to stay back, but to keep our eyes open. It crossed my mind more than once that something interesting was afoot, but when you've been in constant front-line action for nearly six years, it takes a lot to excite you. Besides, the guys inside the vehicle had the look of ordinary German privates to me. There were two of them in the front, and in the back - as revealed by the shredded tarpaulin - four more. They wore sooty, bedraggled uniforms and sat limply alongside each other. No weapons were visible; likewise no badges or braids. In appearance, they were as sorry and begrimed as just about every other German we'd come across since entering their country the previous February. There was clearly no chance of a fight from them. Almost unconsciously, we relaxed. It was time to pass the cigarettes round, to take in the forest fragrance of the Elbe valley.

And then a shot rang out. The entire squad must have hit

the deck simultaneously, eyes bulging, fingers tight on triggers. Imagine our amazement, though, when we saw where that shot had come from: Captain Anderson's Webley. He'd put a bullet clean through the brain of the German sitting behind the steering wheel. The guy was now slumped backwards, his blood arching through the air in a crimson fountain. Even as we watched, our skip then took two further pot-shots at the front seat passenger, hitting him in the head as well, imploding his skull and flipping him sideways. Lieutenant Grey, meanwhile, had already run to the rear of the truck, his Sten blazing, drilling lead through the flapping strips of tarpaulin, flinging the four passengers about like marionettes.

*

Inevitably, the Nazis were further ahead than we were in their use of the Process. After all, it had been one of their greatest countrymen, and most revered scientists, who had devised and patented it.

The UK wasn't able to seriously deploy the Not-Dead until well after the Battle of Britain. During the Norwegian operation in April 1940, our assault units were made up entirely of Living troops. Though I'd been a regular soldier since '35, this was my first taste of action. It was also my first taste of the Not-Dead, because Jerry already had plenty on hand with which to attack our beachhead. And it was far more terrifying than I'd expected. Though slow-thinking and highly inaccurate as marksmen, the Not-Dead troops benefited from the Process by-products of phenomenal strength and bestial ferocity. We were in the rearguard at Namsos when a platoon of them came down from the high rocks and engaged us hand-to-hand. Though we thought we were tough and well-trained, it was a chilling experience. They wielded their rifle-butts with such force that our helmets crumpled and skulls cracked; a single knife-blow from one of them packed enough power to shear a head from its trunk. Our backs they simply broke over their knees; our eyes they gouged out; our necks they twisted and snapped. They howled like devils as they rent us limb from limb, tossed us into the air, punched out our teeth with fists like jackhammers. It was astonishing, when we'd finally finished them off, to count only fourteen. Of our number, nearly sixty lay dead.

*

Captain Anderson wouldn't take any questions from us. He'd been a marvellous officer to work under, and after so much intensive combat together, the men were virtually on first- name terms with him, but on this occasion he slipped back into that clipped, brusque routine

"Baynes ... check'em for weapons! Corless... there's a can of petrol in the rear; drench'em down with it, if you please! Mather ... grenades!"

The truck went up in a soaring inferno. It was so fierce that the bodies sitting in it melted away like wax dummies, even as we gazed at them. A second later, the three grenades we'd placed under the vehicle's left flank detonated all together, spinning the truck up and through the air and sending it hurtling down into the wood in a whirlwind of fire, like a crashing Stuka.

The skipper didn't want to waste any more time. After wandering down there, through a debris of burning timber, to check we'd done a proper job, then coming back up satisfied, he gave us orders to move on to the checkpoint, so we could strip down the Tigers before marching towards Torgau. Prior to setting off, I handed over the single Luger I'd found, and for a second that seemed to stop him in his tracks. He gave me a long, curious look.

"Everything all right, sir?" I asked him, concerned.

"Perfectly," he replied. "Take the point, Corporal Baynes."

Bastard. The war might have been over a full day, but there was always a chance some wandering, demented Jerry didn't realise that. Still, somebody had to do it.

*

Despite the brief butchery at Namsos, and similar events when isolated units were overrun at Dunkirk or in Crete, Not-Dead companies were generally easy meat for Living regulars.

Our first extensive use of them came at Gazala in 1942, and what a catastrophe that was. The Afrika Korps just rolled through their sun-dazzled, disorientated ranks, cutting them down in swathes with their Schmeissers and GPMGs, the Ti-

gers then rumbling over the strewn, twitching masses of the fallen. The only real problem the Germans faced that day was the glutinous porridge of blood-soaked sand, churned flesh and splintered bone-meal clogging up their caterpillar tracks. Aside from that, they cleared the road to Tobruk in a matter of days, with minimal losses of their own. Likewise, D-Day was a Not-Dead disaster. The first-ever American Not-Dead army was landed at Omaha Beach at four o'clock on the morning of June 6. Pinned down by crack panzergrenadier units, it was obliterated in rows as it came ashore.

Britain's own first-wave assault companies on Gold and Juno also consisted of Not-Dead troops, and hardly any of them made it to the German lines. I went ashore on D-Day 3 and found the beach a scene of unimaginable carnage, even by wartime standards. The Not-Dead lay as thick across its dunes as autumn leaves... every rank present, officers and men slain alongside each other. Considering that Overlord was such a vital operation, images like these could have been colossally sapping to our morale, but we'd all been informed well in advance that these were Not-Dead troops so it wasn't quite as bad.

Tales even more horrific, if such a thing is possible, can be found in the Axis experience. Most of the Wehrmacht's Not-Dead regiments had been sent east at an early stage, as it was felt they were more suited to dealings with "Untermenschen"

*than were German regulars. It was also decided that their im-
mense numbers could be utilised to best advantage on the endless expanse of the Russian hinterland. The moment the Red
Army began to contest the affair, however, the Nazis' Not-Dead
were found to be fully as lacking as our own. Reports told of
huge columns, forty to fifty thousand strong, being needlessly
mown down by low-flying Yakovlevs. Because of the flatness of
the landscape and their own moronic response rate, the Not-
Dead were unable to find shelter in time. Once the winter began to bite, entire Not-Dead battalions allegedly froze to death
on the march. Russian ski troops would come down from higher
ground, and be stunned to find icy roads jammed for mile upon
mile by straggling processions of still and rigid figures, waxy-
white and gazing glassy-eyed through a covering of frost. Only
their steel helmets and tattered khaki fatigues indicated they
were Germans.*

*The Nazis, of course, having more fronts to fight on than
anyone else, were by far the greatest re-users of Not-Dead material. But even with the most advanced techniques, a man can
only be sewn back together and jolted to life so many times
after stepping on landmines, being riddled with lead or getting torn apart by shrapnel. The companies of Not-Dead troops
scratched together by the Third Reich to defend Berlin in 1945
were said to consist of individuals so crippled and disfigured,
and in many cases so maddened by excruciating and unrelieved
pain, that the Russian assault troops who faced them likened*

the fight to Armageddon itself, when legend says Men will be called on to battle the very daemons of Hell.

*

In view of all this, it's still a source of amazement to me, over fifty years on, that the Not-Dead had the last laugh in World War Two.

I'm eighty-three now, yet I remember every detail of that dark and deadly time. Of course, eighty-three isn't old any more. I've got my sixth cancer op coming up shortly and they tell me my organs are starting to close down - my limbs are already limp and palsied - but the Process is available whenever I want it. It's not on the National Health yet, but it's much cheaper than it used to be and so many people take the option these days. The thing is, if I do take it, will I then develop the urge to speak out about the things I saw on that day after the day the war ended? Will I feel honour-bound to mention that one of the Germans shot to death in the rear of that battle-scarred APC was a shortish chap with a distinctive blot of black fuzz for a moustache? Not to mention the others. I can't describe them so well, but I've seen their likenesses many times since... in history books, on newsreels. Do names like Himmler, Goering, Eichmann ring a bell? It shouldn't have been surprising. I mean, we'd been ordered to intercept that vehicle at all costs, so it had to have been something important. No ... that wasn't the surprising part. The surprising part was their odd-coloured eyes, their lines of cheap, crude stitching, their pallid, greenish complexions.

And that includes all of them...His Satanic Majesty as well.

I suppose it was possible they'd been killed at some early stage and resurrected to continue the fight, but even now my thoughts shift back to a more sinister explanation. I mean, why else would Captain Anderson take it on himself to do the thing he did, and then report that we hadn't even encountered the vehicle? Why else would he pretend those monstrous villains had escaped into obscurity, and allow it to become established "fact", eventually even convincing himself of its truth?

For my own part, I very much doubt I'll seek to improve the role and standing of the Not-Dead, even if I eventually opt to join their ranks. You see, we'll always need our "vegetable" caste, for military purposes if nothing else. WWII proved that, and I can't bring myself to rock the boat. All I need do is think of the rolling tide of carnage since 1945: Africa, Asia, South America, Eastern Europe, virtually everywhere if the truth were told. In the last fifty years, uncountable numbers of Not-Dead troops have died in the course of duty, shelled and machine-gunned, blown to smithereens, blinded, incinerated, starved, poisoned ... war and its many exits are too horrible to ponder for long. At least it's the Not-Dead, though. And that's my point. If it isn't them, it would have to be the Living.

Imagine that.

Mad Jack
Ceri Jordan

It was the silence that told him. The dull hush of a side street normally bustling with traders and clerks and teachers setting off about their daily labours; the silence in his own humble abode, broken only by the muffled sounds of Emily's faint and persistent coughing.

Colborne rose and dressed hastily, and heading downstairs, paused only to look in at Emily's door as he passed. They slept separately now, at her insistence, lest her nightly pains and fevers disturbed his rest.But they disturbed him anyway, and he would gladly have suffered them more closely for the compensation of waking to feel her weight, her warmth beside him in the night.

She was crumpled among the bedclothes, sleeping; only a wisp of dark hair upon a white pillow to mark her presence. The weight of the blankets could no longer disguise how thin she had grown.

Why, God? some inner part of Thomas Colborne screamed; why my Emily, why my love ?

Despite the constant stream of priests and ministers and charitable ladies who called, and prayed, and comforted, no answer was forthcoming.

Fearful of waking her to further pain, he turned and padded silently down the stairs.

The newspaper awaited him at the breakfast table, and a bare glance at the bold headline told him that his fears were justified. The streets, even in this respectable suburb far from grimy Whitechapel, were hushed with horror in the aftermath of another abomination. Another crime against nature and God. Another unwilling victim for Jack the Resurrector.

Colborne called only briefly at Scotland Yard. Warren, the Police Commissioner, was shut up in his office with the old army cronies he had brought in to head the force, no doubt discussing how some fine new policy or other might distract attention from the "problems" in the East End. In the corridors and in the stairwells, constables and detectives loitered, whispering among themselves in a manner that made Colborne oddly uncomfortable.

Obtaining the address where the outrage had occurred- Hanbury Street, in Spitalfields - Colborne summoned a cab and set out, hoping to use the journey to gather his thoughts.

It had started with rumours, as matters among the underclasses often did. The Year of Our Lord 1888 had begun with the usual street brawls, thefts, extortions and wife beatings. Then there had been the odd case of Ada Wilson, a dressmaker at Bow. Opening her door to find a perfect stranger demanding money with menaces, she had refused, and had been stabbed in the throat. Women nearby had summoned the police, and a doctor, who had sent her at once to the hospital- from whence, despite being most gravely wounded, she had promptly disappeared.

Emma Smith, a drunken widow of forty-five, had disappeared from the hospital at Whitechapel some hours after her confirmed death. No one had paid too much attention to that; medical students were not above such pranks, and even the few pence that were now paid for medical specimens might have tempted some porter or cleaning woman to summon accomplices and make off with the cadaver.

But still, the rumours grew. And then there came a final confirmation, a definite proof, in the form of Martha Turner.

"Hanbury Street, guv'ner," the carriage driver yelled, rapping on the roof with his knuckles and startling Colborne back to the present. "Or as close as I can reach..."

Descending from the carriage, Colborne realised why the man had looked so queerly at him when he gave his destination. The junction of Hanbury Street and Commercial Street seethed with people. Not passing to and from the stenches of the adjacent Spitalfields Market - indeed, it would appear that the market was having some difficulty operating, and the yells and curses of the workers, trying to force a path through the crowds with their wares, were quite deafening.

No, the crowds were pressing and shoving at the police line that marked the place where the body was discovered.

Paying off the carriage man, Colborne steeled himself for the effort of forcing his way through to the front of the mob.

"Good luck, guv'ner," the driver grinned, flicking the reins to ready the drowsy horses for further effort. "And keep an eye out for Mad Jack, won't you ?"

Colborne just looked at him.

"Oh, he's well known in these parts, is Jack. And well sheltered, doubtless. You'll not catch him, not while there's people willing to aid him. And while he helps them, there will be." A whistle, another flick of the reins, and the horses barged forward, the loose crowd parting before them. "Good luck, as I said. You'll surely need it."

Luck was, indeed, in short supply in Hanbury Street. The victim, one Annie Chapman, had been found dead in the gutter by one Davis, a market porter rising early for work. Her throat had been slit with such force than her head was all but severed; there could be no doubt that she was dead. But by the time the police arrived, the body was gone; and moments later, the very same woman had been seen walking in Commercial Street, staggering and confused but most definitely alive.

The constables, idiots to a man, had immediately turned upon Davis, accusing him of lying and wasting their time. By this time the market and most of the street were roused, and in the confusion, Chapman had vanished - with help, most likely, from some acquaintance or sympathiser.

The scene of the crime was being examined, and a search of the dense rabbit-warrens that comprised the stinking, over-crowded streets of Spitalfields was already underway. In the absence of his primary evidence, namely Annie Chapman, Colborne found himself no more than an onlooker. After a time, he left instructions for a messenger to be sent after him if there was a breakthrough , and walked up onto Old Street to hail a cab.

"The Charity Asylum," he told the shivering driver. "Bethnal Green."

There was nothing much of charity, in the Christian sense, about the asylum itself. It was a vast, smoke-blackened build-ing on Parmiter Street, enclosed by heavy wooden doors and attended by a number of surly ex-wrestlers and boxers who earned a few shillings a month guarding and subduing the most violent cases. The wards, lined with coffin-like sleeping boxes and daubed with bleak and unforgiving religious texts, were empty. By this late hour of mid-morning, the inmates were at their simple labours, earning their keep - or, if incapable of that, taking the air in the grey narrow courtyards.

A man with a heavily bruised face walked him to one of the private cells in silence, cowed by this figure of authority in his greatcoat and regulation boots.

"How has she behaved ?" Colborne asked him as they climbed the dusty staircase, as much to break the silence as out of interest.

"She is quiet enough, sir. Compared to some of them. Some nights she cries to be let out, says she has done nothing wrong. Blames... some other for her crimes."

He knows, Colborne thought, adding another complication to his mental list. Which means others here know who she is, what was done to her. The longer we hesitate, the more complex matters become.

"You, of course, have no idea whom she means."

The bruised man looked at him from beneath heavy eyelids, his face unreadable. "Of course not, sir. After all, Martha Turner is a lunatic. If she were not, she would not be here."

Colborne smiled on him, rewarding his tact and understanding. "Of course she would not."

"Cell fifteen, Inspector." He gestured for Colborne to follow him down the long, dimly lit corridor. "The Reverend Durman is with her, but I'm sure you can persuade him to save his ministrations until later."

Durman was a dour little Scotsman with red whiskers and a whining voice, a voice raised in condemnation as Colborne was ushered in, ringing off the low roof of the tiny single cell: "... to allow yourself to be so used, in defiance of God's law ..."

Martha Turner smiled faintly. "I allowed nothing, begging your pardon, sir. I was, as you'll recall, very much dead at the time."

Colborne cleared his throat delicately. Martha did not re-act, but Durman rounded on him, perhaps expecting to find some orderly or caretaker disturbing his sacred duties. Finding instead the unmistakable figure of a Scotland Yard detective, he settled for a wordless grunt of annoyance.

"I hate to disturb your ministrations, Reverend," Colborne purred, smiling on the man's distress, "but this is a most important police matter."

Drawing himself up to his full height - for what little difference that made - Durman slapped a handful of cheaply printed tracts down upon the bare bedside table. "I will leave these, young woman, in the hope that some spark of piety and repentance might still linger in your benighted soul. Pray, young woman, pray. Your end is surely near, and God may yet have pity upon you and receive you into His grace."

Martha Turner barely blinked.

Once the door had closed again, Colborne crossed to the single flimsy chair and sat down. The tracts blared scaremongering titles at him from the adjacent table: DEATH IS GOD'S GIFT TO MANKIND, and PLACE YOUR FAITH IN THE TRUE RESURRECTION.

"He's right, of course," he told her. "Your end is very near."

Martha shrugged. She was a member of what the penny newspapers called "the unfortunate class", which encompassed anyone from poor dressmakers or match girls forced to take money for favours occasionally to make ends meet, to out-and-out professional whores. The brassy despair of her class sat uneasily upon her, though, and Colborne felt sure that several weeks spent among shrieking lunatics would have weakened her defiance. Perhaps she might be useful yet.

"I didn't do nothing," she whispered.

"The penalty for employing the services of a Resurrector, in defiance of God and the laws of our Christian nation, is death by hanging. Of course, there is some evidence that you did not want or willingly request his services, so your case is... legally complex. However, we can hardly just allow you to walk free. That would be an invitation to the Resurrectors to spread their curse however and wherever they please. Nullifying their effects by granting release to those they return to Earth's pains is the best defence we have - and the kindest thing for their misguided dupes also."

Martha Turner laughed. It was not a pleasant sound, and the blasphemy it implied made him uneasy. He considered himself a good Christian soul - not without doubts, for the flesh was weak, and the spirit also, sometimes, but devout enough, in his way. The girl might at least have the decency to show some respect for that.

"I didn't do nothing," she repeated, with more spirit this time. "That old bastard Pikowski, who manages some girls working from George's Yard, he didn't want me taking his custom, and set upon me. It's him you should be hanging, and for murder. Not me, who did nothing but suffer and lie dead in the street until this Jack you speak so much of came to find me."

"That's as may be," Colborne admitted, her story having been attested to by several frightened witnesses. "A warrant has been issued for this Pikowski, and if he is found, he shall pay for attacking you. But none of that will help you with the charges you face."

"I swear before God I never asked this Jack to help me. I was quite senseless - or dead, more likely - before that Polish bastard left me. I never saw this Jack, and I wish to God he had never seen me." Hugging her knees to her chest, the girl began to sob like a scolded child. "I never wanted nothing but to live, sir. And here I am, dead once already and now to hang like a common murderess, all because some man helped me without my asking."

Colborne sighed. It was a bad case, to be sure. He'd have to have words with the Commissioner. Perhaps the girl could be quietly spirited away into the country, found some useful work somewhere. The public would forget her soon enough.

"I will see what I can do," he announced, standing up. The chair had left grey streaks on the seams of his trousers, and his boots were filthy. "But you must try to cooperate with us. Anything you can remember - before you lost consciousness, after you awoke, anything..."

She shook her head weakly. "I told them everything already, sir. I swear it."

Colborne rapped on the door to summon the orderly, but then turned back, and studied her dirty, tear-streaked face for a moment before murmuring, "What was it like ?"

"Dying, sir ?" And when he nodded: "Like going into a great deep sleep, in a warm bed with soft linen and pillows and all. Then waking, feeling like I'd slept for a whole day or more, and fresh as a new-born babe. It was very fine, sir. I shan't be sad to go that way again, though I would prefer it a kinder way this time..."

The door opened behind him. Nodding absently, Colborne turned and left Martha to her reverie.

Emily was not strong enough to come down to dinner, and afterwards Colborne went upstairs to read to her. It was raining like the Deluge outside, and with the curtains drawn and the lamp turned low, he strained to make out the delicate print of the devotional poems that her sister had brought on her last visit. When he had finished a couple, and paused for breath, Emily opened her pale eyes and said, "There has been another one, hasn't there ? I overheard the maid speaking of it."

Making a mental note to severely reprimand the girl for troubling her mistress in her fragile state, Colborne nodded.

"I wish they'd give you some other case. Something with more cheer about it."

"Detection is not a cheery business, my love. But it must

be done, for the sake of the devout and the law-abiding." He smiled, making a joke of it. "Anyone would think you were afraid for my virtue. Do you fear I might be tempted by the Resurrectors and their terrible arts, my dearest ?"

Biting her lip, Emily turned her head to avoid his gaze.

Finally, when neither of them could stand the silence any longer, she whispered, "Dr Burroughs has warned me... it will not be long now."

Colborne studied her face, trying to read an intent, a granting of permission there that a part of him feared to find.

"I wish to be buried in my wedding dress, my dear one. The moths have been at it a little, but it will serve." She managed a dry smile. "If it remains, my sister will only end up begging it for her nuptials, and I will not have her looking prettier in it than I did."

"Impossible," Colborne rasped, swallowing uselessly as his pain rose to choke him.

Emily shrugged; the movement shifted her whole frail body, and she grimaced and squeezed his hand. "I want to sleep now, Thomas. Come see me in the morning."

Nodding, he closed the volume of poems and placed it beside her bed before turning the lamp down to a low glimmer. "Sleep well, my princess."

She smiled, but the coughing started the moment he closed the door, and he knew that Dr Burroughs was right.

The screaming woke him in the night.

The whole street was roused, or so it seemed. Servants and their masters stood side by side in the mud, crying out for lanterns and pistols and police, and anything else they could summon to mind. Throwing his overcoat on over his night attire, Colborne went downstairs. Pausing only to instruct the sleepy, wide-eyed maid to go sit with her mistress until he returned, he put on his trilby and went out into the street.

The hubbub did not distract him; ignoring the shouting of his neighbours and the shrieks of the maidservants hanging out of the attic windows, he moved slowly along the street, waiting for some evidence to present itself to him. And finally, it did.

Most of the trail of blood had been trampled by hurried and muddied feet, but it was still clear enough for him to follow around the corner and into the narrow thoroughfare of Harris Street. The first gas lamp was out, and the second barely illuminated the pavement at all. Even so, it gave him just enough light to see the termination of the trail; a bundle of rags and hair huddled against the railings, sobbing like a babe.

Colborne raised his gaze slowly from the whimpering unfortunate to the man who stood in the shadows beyond her, and knew.

"Poor fool was set upon as she left by a servant's door," the figure murmured. A soft voice, and well educated; no man mastered the forbidden secrets of the Resurrectors without schooling and a fair grasp of medicine, chemistry and other otherwise innocent arts. "I was in time to drive him off this time. It is better to save life than to resurrect it."

Staring into the eyes of his quarry, Colborne turned the facts over in his head. The law. The church. Martha Turner, sobbing in her cell. And Emily. Coughing her young life away in a sterile room, beyond all salvation but the grace of God.

Jack nodded slowly, understanding. "Who...?"

"My wife. Emily Colborne."

The Resurrector recognised the surname. It showed in his face. Any fool who read the daily news would know who was heading the hunt for Jack of Whitechapel - a man very far from home tonight, yet still protecting the vulnerable and the help-less.

"Hang a Chinese lantern in the window," Jack murmured, "the moment she passes from you. And tell no one. I will come."

"Aren't you afraid...?"

"That you will betray me ? You could. But you would lose your wife." One step back, out of the light. And another. Nothing but a voice now, a whisper: "It will be your choice. When the time comes."

Colborne was a long time standing there, thinking it through. Then he hauled the girl to her feet and marched her back into the main street, where some relative she had been visiting took charge of her, and the panic subsided as house-holders gathered their servants and returned to their night's rest.

A Chinese lantern, he thought, slinking back up to bed, could be easily explained. A slow, carefully feigned recovery was not beyond the bounds of medical science. And if no one were told, Emily's resurrection would be a matter of his word against Jack's. The revenge ploy of a defeated criminal, trying to implicate his capturer. Yes. It could all be explained. He could have his wish, and still advance his career by stretching Jack the Resurrector's neck.

If he had the stomach for it.

Listening to the slow tremor of Emily's breathing as he paused at her door, he thrust his trembling hands into his pockets.

Like the Resurrector said: It would be his choice. When the time came.

Piecework
James Lovegrove

In Cube 117 on the fourth floor of Civic Housing Block D/ 83 in the north western quadrant of Arrondissement 91, Karel Vukovic was awoken by his alarm clock at the regular appointed hour. He abluted, accoutred, ate and arrived downstairs in the communal vestibule in good time to be picked up by Hans.

His co-worker, however, was late that morning. Fists thrust into the pockets of his grey overalls, Karel stood by the vestibule doors and stared out through the grimy panes for a first glimpse of the Reclamation Vehicle. The street exhaled early-morning steam from its sewer gratings. Scrawny scavenging dogs scrounged in the gutters. A few weary men and women traipsed along the pavements, either going to work or returning from work, in both cases looking like sleepwalkers. Municipal trams grumbled gracelessly by, their wires crackling.

Finally, with a sound like fifty circus strongmen rending fifty telephone directories , the Reclamation Vehicle appeared at a far-off intersection. Turning the corner, it bumbled rumblingly along the road towards Civic Housing Block D/83. Black and rusted and forward-hunched, the vehicle moved at a sedate pace, farting diesel fumes from the twin exhausts mounted on either side of its cab. Its six independently-sprung tractor-size wheels undulated across the road's uneven, potholed surface. Even though the worst of winter had been and gone,

Hans had insisted on keeping the snowplough in place, in case of a late cold snap. Hazard-striped, the snowplough fanned beneath the vehicle's radiator grille like a wicked black-and-yellow grin.

The scavenging dogs, having been untroubled by the passing trams, took fright at the approach of this menacing-looking metal behemoth and scurried off. Pedestrians, too, shied away as the Reclamation Vehicle neared them, moving as far from the kerb as they could, hugging the sides of the buildings. Perhaps it was simply the noise and physical appearance of the machine that perturbed them. Equally, perhaps it was their knowledge of what was usually contained within the vehicle's refrigerated rear.

Reaching Civic Housing Block D/83, the Reclamation Vehicle came to a halt – or rather halts, because it stopped, then lurched forward a couple of metres, stopped again, lurched another metre, stopped, lurched once more, then at last stood still.

The passenger-side door swung open, and Karel exited the vestibule, crossed the pavement and clambered inside.

Hans had the heat turned all the way up as usual, and the interior of the cab was like a kiln, replete with the customary hard-baked smells of oil, diesel, sweat, feet, plastic upholstery, cigarettes, pine air-freshener and the faint, rank odour of corporeal decay.

Hans was not a morning person and, as soon as Karel was

in, he started complaining. "My damned leg," he said, thumping his right thigh. "Stiff as a pair of rusty scissors this morning. I had to fall out of bed, all but. And putting my overalls on! Hell's teeth, what a struggle! And did I get any help from Consuela? From that bitch whose tits aren't even the same size as each other? Did I fuck! Just sat there and laughed at me, she did. Laughed like an old, brown-toothed witch."

"And a very good morning to you, Hans," said Karel.

"Close the damned door," Hans snapped back, cranking the handbrake off. "You're letting all the warm air out."

The Reclamation Vehicle was reluctant to go at first. Having made such an effort to cease moving, it was commensurately unwilling to start up again. Hans gunned the accelerator, pumped the clutch, shook the steering wheel, waggled the gearstick and, when none of this had any discernible effect, pounded the dashboard and cursed. The last technique appeared to do the trick, for the engine gave a sudden grunt of enthusiasm and the vehicle began rolling forward. Hans let out a sardonic cheer, and they were on their way.

"Where are we going?" Karel enquired.

His co-worker pointed to the dash-mounted service computer. An address glimmered in blurry green type on the cracked screen. "Arrondissement 56," Hans said. "There's been a party."

Slowly they wound their way through the city's grid-pattern maze, Karel gazing out at the passing buildings, one so like another. He had been with Reclamation for a little over six months, and enjoyed the work. Previously he had been employed in a hospital pushing gurneys, and in a butcher's shop as an apprentice, both jobs less than pleasant but good preparation for this one.

Hans, by contrast, was a three-decade veteran of Reclamation, and, at eighty-four, was Karel's senior by nearly sixty years. Parts of Hans, however, were considerably older. His leg, for instance, the one that habitually gave him trouble, was almost a hundred, and his left eye was of an even greater vintage and had occupied the ocular cavities of at least two people before him. It was not quite identical to his right, its white being veinier and its iris a shade of brown lighter, but it was the closest match the Health Bureau had been able to find. Hans claimed that sometimes the eye showed him scenes from bygone eras, as though memories of sights its former owners had seen were trapped in its vitreous humour like ghosts. Historical images would unexpectedly manifest in his vision, past overlapping present, or so he said. A horse-drawn carriage might all of a sudden appear along a street busy with modern traffic, threading its way blithely through the buses and trams and cars; or an old red brick building might become visible at the spot where a modern concrete one stood, the former superimposed on the latter, as in a double-exposure photograph.

Karel was unsure whether or not to believe Hans about

this phenomenon. He had heard similar stories from other old people and was equally sceptical of them. But then, being young and relatively intact, he knew little about what it was like to have the body parts of others incorporated into your own body. He had lost his right index finger in an accident with a meat grinder at the butcher's, and the substitute ached sometimes and looked noticeably out of place because it was stubbier and darker-complexioned than its companion digits, but so far, fingers crossed, he had not had any strange experiences with it.

He often wondered what it would be like to be really old. Not in your eighties like Hans, but in your second century, or even your third. Not everyone was expected to attain such an age. There were only so many limb or organ substitutions a body could take before it became difficult to maintain physical integrity, and after a while most workers confounded the Health Bureau's best efforts to keep them in one piece. Anti-rejection fluids could not prevent incohesion indefinitely, and in the end the strain on the system became too great. The physiology ceased to cope with being comprised of so many different types of flesh and would begin to literally fall apart. Some men and women, though, kept on going. Skin crisscrossed with suture scars, like human jigsaws, living quilts patched together from countless different sources, they continued to work and thrive and be productive on the city's behalf, and there was no reason to think they would not do so forever.

Karel, a conscientious and civic-minded young man, was

firmly resolved to be one of them.

The sky had lightened by the time Karel and Hans reached Arrondissement 56, which is to say that the slice of grey visible between the building tops had gone from the colour of porridge to the colour of cooked chicken flesh. Little of the sun's radiance made it as far down as ground level, filtered as it was by various layers of smoke and shadow and cloud. Indeed, for most workers the sun was a rumour, although its truth was occasionally confirmed by a glimpse of a pallid yellow disc hovering far overhead and a just-perceptible tinge of warmth in the air during the summer months.

Outside the building that was their destination, Hans fought to bring the refractory Reclamation Vehicle to a halt again. He swore volubly each time the brake slipped and the engine re-engaged and the vehicle juddered a little further forward. "Buggering bastard thing!" he yelled. "Useless, obstinate piece of shit!" Finally the vehicle came to rest, and Hans switched off the ignition with the air of someone who would rather have been pulling a trigger. "I swear to God," he said to Karel, "one of these days this pile of junk is going to be the death of me."

"Possibly," Karel replied, "but if so, the Health Bureau will bring you back again. If not as yourself, as part of someone else."

Hans acknowledged this with a grimace. "All praise to the Health Bureau. It makes sure there's no rest for the wicked, eh?"

"No rest at all. Speaking of which, shall we get going?"

"Bah. You youngsters. So damn eager."

Burdened with shovels, mops, cloths, bottles of bleach and disinfectant, rubber gloves and boots and a dozen heavy-duty plastic sacks, Karel and Hans entered the building and crossed to the lifts.

The lift they took ascended only as far as the thirtieth floor. There, they stepped out and were met by a uniformed security guard who demanded to see documentation. The guard had ears, a nose and at least one lip that he had not been born with, the CV of a lifetime spent in violent trades. He wore the disfiguring stitch-marks with pride, as a badge of his profession.

Karel and Hans handed over their identification cards and work permits, which the security guard scanned first with his squinting, piggy eyes, then with an electronic wand that was plugged into a computer console.

"Here for...?" he grunted.

"Reclamation, of course," said Hans, indicating his and Karel's overalls.

"Which apartment?"

"Penthouse suite. There was an 'accident' there last night."

The security guard rolled his eyes. "Third this year. Those Sant'angelos and their parties." He handed back the documentation. "All right, go on up."

He unlocked a reinforced-glass door that led to a second bank of lifts. These gave access to the remaining floors, from the thirty-first to the top. One lift was waiting. Inside it, Hans pressed the button marked "P". The doors rolled shut and the lift began to rise.

They emerged on the top floor into a marble antechamber lit by a twenty-branched chandelier. In front of them was a pair of doors made of stained glass whose delicate shades and rounded, abstract patterns were reminiscent of a butterfly's wings. The doors operated like a butterfly's wings, too, flattening inwards on a central hinge after Hans had pressed the bell-button.

Passing through, the two workers found themselves in a long, opulent hallway hung with gilt-framed oil paintings, several of them askew. Empty and partly empty bottles and glasses crowded the sideboards and occasional tables. A hand-painted vase lay on the floor, broken, and next to it was a drying, congealing puddle of vomit. Hans steered Karel around it with a stern "Careful".

They ventured further into the suite until they came to a high-ceilinged room that was still curtained from the night before, swags and swathes of maroon velvet obscuring the daylight. The room had the air of a battlefield after the fighting is over and the corpses have been carted away. Furniture was overturned. Lamps lay on their sides. Books and records were strewn about. A mirror bore a spider's web of shatter marks. There were more discarded glasses and bottles all over the place, and on a marble coffee table, beside an ashtray crammed with cigarette butts, there was a sprinkling of white powder and a scattering of pills.

Surveying the scene, Hans pursed his lips and slowly shook his head. "It's all right for this lot. They don't have to watch their pennies. Anything they break, they can just go out and buy another."

"Excuse me, gentlemen?"

A thin, beautiful young woman in a silk dressing gown was peering at them from the doorway to another room. She seemed of a delicate constitution, not improved by her evidently hungover state. She had a hand clasped to one side of her forehead and was blinking at Karel and Hans with purple-ringed, bloodshot eyes. Her hair was a dishevelled mass of Medusan tangles, and last night's make-up still caked her face.

"Miss Sofia Sant'angelo?" said Hans.

She nodded.

"We're from Reclamation. You called us."

"Oh. Of course. You've come for Luciano. My brother."

"Where is he?"

"Out in the roof garden." Painfully Sofia scanned the room, as though noticing its disarray for the first time. "Good heavens, what a mess."

"It must have been quite a party," said Hans.

"It must have," she agreed vaguely. "I have to say, after midnight it all became a bit of a blur. I think I crashed out around one-thirty. If someone hadn't left a note by my bedside, I doubt I would have discovered Luciano until much later today." She pointed across the room. "The window on the other side of that curtain there slides back. Would you mind going outside on your own? I don't think my head can cope with direct sunlight just yet."

"Don't you worry, Miss Sant'angelo. Leave it to us."

Fresh-smelling breezes swirled around them and made the roof garden's boxed orange trees, potted shrubs and low privet hedges quiver. Karel could not help but pause to admire the view. It was a whole different world up here. The buildings seemed further apart, cleaner, and had larger windows and spacious balconies brimming with greenery. The sky spread over everything, bright and wide, the unfettered sunshine dazzling. He saw whispering jetcopters shuttling between the rooftops, ferrying the residents of these rarefied climes from landing pad to landing pad. The aircraft took off and came to rest as lightly as dragonflies.

Nerving himself to approach the parapet at the garden's perimeter, Karel glanced over and down. The ground seemed impossibly, inconceivably far below. He could just make out the road, but between it and here there was a shifting, sifting grey miasma that thinned and thickened and sometimes hid the lower portions of the buildings completely from view.

"That's enough gawping," said Hans. "He's over here."

Luciano Sant'angelo was lying at the edge of an ornamental pond, his face immersed in the water. Goldfish clustered around his head, nibbling speculatively at the tips of his hair, a radiant piscine halo.

"What do you think?" Karel asked.

Hans squatted beside the body. "Drink? Drugs? How the hell should I know? Fellow probably got so out of it he thought he could talk to the fishes underwater. Does it matter how it happened? The rich are always finding ways to kill themselves. It's what they do best – that, and spending money and having parties. Remember that game of Russian roulette we had to clean up after over in Arrondissement 7 last month? And those two idiots in Arrondissement 15, I think it was, who tried to walk around the edge of their building using the balcony balustrades? No, wait, that was before your time. I tell you, when we scraped up those two we didn't find a whole lot that could be reused."

"But they're so …so casual about life. That's what gets me."

"Not about life, Karel. Death is what the rich are so casual about. You and me, working men, we'll keep going, keep on working, for as long as the Health Bureau can keep us functioning. The rich are free from all that. They lead short, brilliant lives. They flitter and flutter and – poof! – they're gone.

Hardly any of them survive past forty, do they? They can buy anything they like, do whatever they please, but for them there's one ultimate luxury. One thing that demonstrates how truly extravagant they are."

"That?" said Karel, pointing to the cold corpse of Luciano Sant'angelo.

"Precisely," said Hans. "That."

Once they had dismembered the body, they transported it down to the Reclamation Vehicle in three journeys. Each limb required a plastic sack of its own, as did the head. The internal organs all went into a sack together, and the hollowed-out torso, hewn in half, occupied two further sacks. Every piece of Luciano Sant'angelo was tagged and labelled and stowed in the vehicle's refrigerated rear. Then it was a question of mopping up the blood and other fluids spilled in the roof garden, and disinfecting the site. Finally, Karel and Hans cleaned their tools, swabbing down the various scalpels and knives and picking bits of bone and gristle from the teeth of the surgical saw.

"All done," Hans told Sofia Sant'angelo in the hallway. By now Sofia was dressed and making a half-hearted attempt at tidying up.

"Thank you." She fumbled in the breast pocket of her blouse and produced a wad of folded money. "Here you go."

Hans accepted the tip and stashed it discreetly away without inspecting it. He would share it out with Karel, almost equally, later.

"I'm sorry about your brother," Karel said.

"Oh. Luciano. Yes, well…" Sofia waved a hand in front of her face, as though a gnat had swooped at her. "Thank you."

In the lift on the way down, Hans said, "See? They just don't care. She's probably having a hard time remembering she even had a brother."

The Reclamation Vehicle would not start. Several times the engine turned over, but then clunked and shuddered and died. Hans hit the dashboard and swore till he was hoarse, but on this occasion the vehicle appeared immune to goading by words or fisticuffs. He thrust open the door, stomped round to the front, and yanked up the bonnet. After a couple of minutes, Karel slid out of his seat to join him.

The engine, to Karel, who was not mechanically inclined, was just a dirty jumble of tubes and parts, not unlike the interior of a human. He watched Hans tweak and twiddle and twist, and finally sigh and nod to himself. "Well, there's the problem. OK, Karel, here's what you have to do. See that cable? Hold the end down in place just here, like so, while I turn the ignition. That should get the motor going, and when we make it back to the depot we can request a full service, which in my view is long overdue."

Bracing his shins against the snowplough, Karel did as

instructed. Hans climbed back inside the cab. "Ready?" he called.

"Ready."

There was a deafening churn as the engine came to life, and then Karel felt an impact like a punch to the sternum and he was flat on his back and being pushed, being shoved bodily along the road, and distantly he could hear Hans screaming, "Oh no! Oh God, no! Stop, you fucking thing, stop!"

His overalls tearing beneath him.

Icy numbness in his legs.

Unable to breathe.

Silence.

Dark.

Hans's face was the first thing Karel saw when he came round. His co-worker was sitting beside the bed, his expression pained and solicitous. They were in a hospital ward that smelled of antiseptic and formaldehyde. From beyond the green curtain enclosing them there came a soft susurration of activity: rubber shoe-soles squeaking, people talking in low voices, a radio playing martial music at a subdued volume.

"How are you feeling?" Hans asked.

Karel tried to reply, but his throat was dry and all that came out was a clicking croak.

"Never mind. Don't try to talk if you can't. God, Karel, I'm so sorry about what happened. I swear, the vehicle just leapt forward. I couldn't control it. Damned thing. The service department's given it a complete overhaul, so hopefully it shouldn't do it again. I told them they should send it to the junkyard and get a new one, but you know how they are. Waste not, want not."

Karel frowned.

"You're fine," Hans assured him, interpreting the frown correctly. "The surgeons did a good job." He uttered a brittle laugh. "Would you believe it? That Sant'angelo lad, the one who drowned in the pond? Those are his legs you have now. How about that? He was the perfect fit for you. Isn't that a funny thing?"

Karel tried to move his legs but could not.

"No," said Hans, patting his arm. "You stay still. Don't want to tear the stitches. You just lie there and recuperate. The docs have said you'll be right as rain soon enough. Right as rain and able to go back to work. No rest for people like you and me, eh? They just fix us up and plonk us back on the treadmill. No rest for the wicked."

The legs, after a few weeks, worked fine, and Karel was soon back on reclamation duty with Hans, as before. He felt proud of himself for having survived such a traumatic injury and for having taken his first proper steps, as it were, to becoming an everlasting worker. He was a living, breathing, (literally) walking example to all.

Sometimes he wondered what it would be like when other parts of him went wrong or were ruined and had to be replaced. At what point would there be so little of him left that he was no longer himself? When would the animating essence that was Karel Vukovic cease to feel that it was in charge any more? He did not know. Perhaps that was the same point at which really old people started to lose their hold on themselves and crumble to bits. But if he was tough with himself, if he stayed mentally strong, maybe that would never happen. Maybe he would live for ever.

And sometimes he would experience a strange, straying urge in his legs, and if he was on the ground or in a lower storey he would stop whatever he was doing and direct his gaze upwards to the summit of the nearest building, up to where nearly half of him had once belonged. He would feel a memory in his legs, an incarnate knowledge of what it was like to dance, to swagger, to stagger, and eventually to stumble and trip and fall to the floor.

And sometimes, at night, he would dream of penthouses and parties, of lives like match-flames, flaring then gone.

Mostly Karel thought of the wealthy with indifference, or did not think of them at all. Money could buy possessions, but work was the best reward.

But sometimes – sometimes – while deep in the toils of yet another working day, he found himself envying the rich the one thing they owned that he might never have.

The option that they could choose to take any time they wanted, but that he would not be permitted until there was no alternative.

Their greatest, simplest disposable asset.

Mere frail mortality.

Guinea Pig A
Chris Poote

I have created a monster.

Almost the very words of the Swiss genius Victor Frankenstein when he beheld the first human vivification. And two centuries later, standing, as it were, on his shoulders, I write the epitaph to my own obsession with creating life.

I dread the future.

Especially mine.

When Frankenstein presented his findings at Vienna, little did he realize the chaos he would unleash upon the world. His creature, weakly, inarticulate, short-lived though it was, proved its creator's process beyond doubt, and eager hands took copies of Frankenstein's papers and were creating life before anybody could stop them.

I should have learned the lessons of history.

The Churches, insisting that God alone gives life, did all they could to suppress what they called 'necromantic blasphemies'. Well, they were wrong about Galileo and they were wrong about Frankenstein, but it took several pan-European wars to break the temporal power of the Churches once and for all. For every stumbling zombie brought to life by the post-Frankensteinians, several thousand lost their lives on the battlefields of Europe.

And believe me, there's worse to come. However, in my obsession, those wars meant only the retarding of the progress of science, and therefore of my own researches.

With the twilight of Church influence, science developed quickly. Darwin and Laplace presented their theories with barely a murmur of protest in Europe. Fanatical refugees from the European wars, however, continued the internecine slaughter in America and elsewhere.

We who do not learn the lessons of history are condemned to repeat them. Terrified as I am of my own fate, I weep for the *Götterdämmerung* which is to come.

While post-Frankensteinian vivification aimed at restoring the person to life, all too often what was restored was a damaged remnant of the original personality. Hence, psychochemistry was the next big advance, culminating in Planck and Boleskine's quantum chemistry and their ninety per cent retrieval of personality in subjects.

Until recently, I should have boasted of my own revolutionary contribution. Instead, the name 'Paul Todd' shall mark the cusp of the human catastrophe. Suffice to say I addressed myself to a major flaw in vivification. With the aid of the now commonplace eugenic engineering and nano retrodesign, the geniuses of vivification can bring new life, longevity, health, improved perception and cognitive functioning to someone who, if they were narrow-minded, shallow and dysfunctional before, can remain so and do it all over again. We waste these technologies on producing compliant robots when we have an education system which does this already.

And so I devised 'Semantic Retrodesign'. There. The doom of civilization has a name. But at the time, it seemed like a gift to humanity: to do for consciousness what Frankenstein had done for life. To take what is totally dead and rebuild it from scratch. To purge the cortex clean of the tendrils of blighted 'self', leaving only the taproot of life, and graft on custom-designed shoots of better self. To transmute a fellow person into perfect mental health, free from the delusions and semantic viruses of belief such as had nearly destroyed Europe. To create a neuronaut to traverse the seas of quantum consciousness. 'The aims of alchemy, the methods of science,' as Lord Boleskine said.

Such was the dream. The reality was that I took laboratory space with a node to the PsyberNet and began interviewing candidates from the Vivification Register. Without exception they all preferred to remain the mediocre mental pygmies they were rather than risk losing the personalities they and their contemporaries knew. Of course. Why else had they put themselves on the Register?

I was in despair. My research ground to a halt. And with nothing to show, Meyer, the faculty procurator, would soon have my funding withdrawn. Michael and Nawal, my two lab assistants, resigned; my colleagues stopped asking how the work was going; and I took to wandering the streets, as though I would find there someone who was interested in more than a feeble lunge at immortality...

But find someone I did.

One cold November night, I was walking across the city's largest bridge. The tide was out, exposing far below the rubble of the bedrock on which the bridge was planted. I saw ahead of me a figure leaning on the handrail, gazing out over the expanse of the river. I don't know why I joined him at the rail. Believe me, I wish now that I hadn't.

"Quite a view," I said. He nodded sharply, plumes of steamy air escaping his nostrils.

I tried again. "I've never seen the river like this before." He grunted, keeping his gaze fixed downriver.

"It feels so ..." I groped for the words. He simply turned his head away slightly, but not before I glimpsed a tear shining in the corner of his eye.

Flash of insight. "You're getting ready to jump!"

He said nothing, but the tears rolled down his cheeks as his shoulders shook. I took hold of them to lead him away, but he wouldn't budge, so I stayed with him, using every neurolinguistic trick in the book to get him to trust me. His name was Alois, and he was homeless, without family and addicted to a designer stimulant called Max. Without it he was chronically depressed.

"You can apply for a nano retrodesign against the addiction," I said.

"I did. But after doing Max you don't want to know about life without it."

"So why aren't you getting it?"

"My supplier died. Car crash. Not even enough left for vivification," he added, glancing down at the rocks below. "And she'd designed the stuff herself." Something about the way he said it suggested that she had been more than merely his supplier.

"Didn't you introduce her research into the PsyberNet?"

"I did. Nothing." He resumed his downriver gaze, then he suddenly said in a quavering voice, "It's fuckin' awful inside my head. I can't live with myself."

And the monster entered my mind. But at the time ... Alois wanted to get rid of himself. The monster inside me said:

"I can help you. You don't have to live with yourself. I can give you a new life. I can take the old life away, and you can begin again as a whole new person."

"Look," he said, "I just want to die. You wanna help, then let me climb over this rail and give me a push."

"I'm not licensed for euthanasia," I said. "Besides, what I've got in mind is even better. Come with me and you'll cease to be what you are now; you'll become a completely different person. Who hasn't wanted sometime to scrap everything and start afresh? To exchange an old life for a new?" He seemed momentarily lost in thought. I pressed on. "Haven't you already begun to wonder what it might be like for you to die to yourself-as-you-have-been, and *be made wholly new. Can you feel that.*" Oh, he was feeling it all right. By now I was piling on the non-verbal reinforcements and projecting the glamour of the offer. And eventually, after more persuasion, I stepped away from the rail and he quite naturally came with me.

I continued working on him all the way back to the laboratory, embedding ever deeper his decision to be, as he put it, 'Guinea Pig A' for my process. The following day the papers were approved and signed by a reluctant procurator, and I persuaded Michael to return to assist me in the laboratory. I moved a camp bed into the laboratory for my own use, and began the ruin of my race.

Alois' depression was severe enough to warrant my starting there. He spent hours in theta trance, being fed neurolinguistic counteractives through the electrochemotrode membrane, and nano retrodesigns through the vein. Meanwhile, Michael began growing the grandular upgrades and arranging for their surgical implantation.

Next came the lengthy task of semantic deconstruction. The first gland upgrades were introduced, and nanotransmitters directed the designer hormones to disable vast tracts of Alois' semantic structures. It had been hard to explain to him what would happen.

"See the weather outside? What's it like?"

"Miserable."

"Miserable, huh? You know what I think it's like? It's overcast, colder than average, with light rainfall. That's all. You're the one who creates 'miserable' out of that. You could equally well create 'calm and serene' out of it."

"No I couldn't."

"That's true. Not yet."

"So I'm going through all this just to feel good about the weather?"

"What you do in interpreting the weather is what you do to everything else. It's a pattern. I'm going to strip out all those patterns, and so wipe all those meanings you've created. All of them."

"Sounds great. But that doesn't mean that I'll stop being myself."

"Yes it does, and this is the bit that few people find easy to swallow. We are our neural patterns. Our sense of self depends on repetitions of stored experiences: memories, behaviours, associations. Wipe those, and your mind is in the quantum void. Gurus used to try all sort of tricks to get into that state for just a moment. They made religions out of it."

"So I'm in this void. Blank. Nothing."

"No-*one*."

"Then what?"

"I'm going to input whole new patternings."

"Where from?"

"Some I've copied from my own neural patterns, with more from people I've studied. A great mix. I'm going to completely rearrange your brain with stuff that will work for you, and your thinking and behaviour will be totally different. You won't even speak the same way anymore."

He took a while to soak this in, then he said worriedly, "I won't remember anything of ... before, will I?"

"The raw data of experience remains, but the patterns that made it your experience will be replaced with new ones. You won't recognise your experiences. Shit, you won't even recognise yourself."

Hubris. Hubris.

Anyway, he had the glandular upgrades and the final range of nano retrodesigns, and he spent nine days in theta trance, supported with catheter and intravenous feeding, while being neurolinguistically reformatted in the input chamber.

On the fifth day, Michael came running out of the input chamber, lab coat unbuttoned and flapping loose. "Paul! Come and see this!" Then he whirled and led the way to where Alois reclined unconscious in the input chair, naked save for the electrochemotrode membrane that clung to him like spider webbing and spun off into faintly glowing read-outs. I studied them, mystified. "No," said Michael, "look at his face."

It took me a moment to see what he was driving at, then ... "The facial lines have gone." Beneath the membrane, Alois' face was completely smoothed out.

"Yes. And?"

I looked again, studied some readouts, checked Alois' jawline, navel, fingers- "No tissue tension. Even the deep unconscious stuff is gone."

"His vital signs are low, Paul." Michael sounded worried.

"Encephalographics?"

"Very little action ... what have we done to him, Paul?"

I didn't answer. I didn't have an answer. For the first time, I felt the enormity of what I had begun.

Nemesis. Nemesis.

I stared at the flickering tell-tales from nanotransmitters microscopically busy within Alois, apparently the only vigorous activity in the body in front of me. I studied the empty face, which told me just as little. Then Michael started. "Encephalographic readings are flaring." Before I had a chance to look, Alois' eyes opened and he looked straight at me. He smiled as though at some private joke, then relapsed into complete unconsciousness. But now the various read-outs had sprung into fresh activity. And the colour was returning to Michael's face.

The treatment continued.

On the ninth day, at eleven a.m., Michael summoned me to the input chamber. I stumbled in, groggy from having just been relieved after the night watch. At about nine thirty a.m., signals from the nanotransmitters had ceased, indicating that their job was finished and they were shutting down. Alois had just come spontaneously out of theta, but remained motionless on the chair.

I began checking read-outs. "No other major changes?"

"No." Michael looked helpless. There was no manual of procedures for this point. "Encephalographics register full wakefulness, but he isn't responding."

We both stood at Alois' head, watching, bewildered. Then his eyes flickered open, closed against the overhead light, and snapped wide open again for him to stare at the ceiling. Michael backed off, but Alois was motionless for a moment. Then, as I passed a hand across his eyes, Alois sat up without warning, and began peeling away the membrane. Michael and I kept away, wincing as Alois pulled away his catheter and feeding tube apparently without feeling anything, and suddenly he was striding out of the chamber and into the laboratory. It occurred to me that he should not have been able to do that; as well as having been taken apart and put back together, he had not moved for nine days except during brief sessions of my own-design physio. But his muscle tone and co-ordination seemed fine. After a moment's hesitation, he went to the fire exit, stopped, and turned to me.

"Out."

"No."

"Out." He stared at me, unblinking, and gestured towards

the door. I opened it for him and as soon as I had he stepped into the chilly corridor of the fire escape.

"Cold," he murmured, and came back inside. I closed the door, goose pimples appearing on my forearms.

Frankenstein and his successors were lousy educators. They simply did not have the resources to socialize and stimulate the intelligence of the shambling morons they created. Luckily for later subjects, Planck and Boleskine made the problem virtually obsolete. But for me to reconstruct Alois' neurology from void I had to design the neuro-semantics fed him in the input chamber such that he would firstly receive sensory input with a minimum of preconceptions, and secondly respond appropriately and function socially. That was the plan.

Oh, the plan, the plan.

Over the weeks that followed, it became clear to me that the new Alois functioned perfectly. I should have been pleased. He was healthy, alert, at ease with himself. He retained many basic motor skills- walking, speech etc.- and learned new ones quickly. Indeed, he increased in intelligence practically by the day, demonstrating a voracious appetite for information. Michael was visibly relieved to detect no ill-effects in him from my process. I, however, became more and more uncomfortable with my findings.

One afternoon in January, Alois came in from the input chamber and said, "The old Alois behaved very, very differently from me."

I was instantly on my guard. Had something survived the process? Some neurosis, buried deep in the body? Cell memory? Calmly, I asked, "What do you remember?"

"I remember vaguely experiencing unpleasantly, on many occasions."

"Only vaguely?"

"I avoid remembering unpleasantly and I find little else to remember."

"How do you feel about that?"

"Curious-"

"Good."

"-as to why Alois chose to experience unpleasantly in the first place."

"I guess he thought he had no choice."

"Why?"

"I don't know. My expertise is 'how'."

"I know how. I don't understand why he thought like that. Do you think like that?"

"Sometimes," I admitted.

"And you don't know why?'

"I guess not."

"Do other people think like that?"

"Oh, fuck, yes!"

He remained deep in thought for a moment, then he looked at me and said, "I want to meet other people."

And so I showed him how to enter the PsyberNet so that he could interact in it himself. Entering the node and spinning himself a Virtuality membrane from it, configuring his Virtual appearance and functions, he seemed instantly at home. I was concerned that he might learn from the PsyberNet similar mistakes to the ones he'd left behind at such great cost, but the imprints and neurolinguistic filters I'd installed worked fine. Inquisitive, perceptive, level-headed, he made friends easily among PsyberNet inhabitants, communicating with them in his unique phraseology.

Three months later, on our first trip beyond the laboratory, *he* was taking *me* to meet some people. I had asked him to delay the trip, to give me more time in order to prepare him for going outside; after all, he would be unused to open spaces and the busy-ness of the city. But he would have none of it. "I enjoy experiencing freshly," he said.

"But the unfamiliarity of your surroundings might be a shock for you. I'm thinking of you, Alois."

"I avoid shocking myself. And I am thinking of you, also."

And with that inscrutable comment, the issue was decided.

The city leisure centre is vast and any form of group activity can be found there: from physical sport to Virtual debate, from concerts to parties. Alois and I entered the bar, a large space lined and filled with ovicles for customers. Seeming not at all like someone who had just spent several months imprisoned in a laboratory, he took me through the web of walkways, searching until he found a couple in their thirties, seated in an ovicle overlooking the river. They all greeted each other, then Alois said, "Paul, meet Carl and Joanna. Carl, Joanna; meet Paul." I smiled at the introduction and joined them. Conversation was light and pleasant, and shortly we were joined by enough people for us to overflow the ovicle.

I was struck by the ease with which Alois communicated with these people. A glance here, a touch there, a response in a certain tone of voice, and these people were hanging on his every word. I'd never seen such abundant charisma. I should have been flattered. I heard from him language patterns which I myself had installed; I observed him drawing a person's attention and taking it where he pleased- a whole gamut of skills which I had taught him, but never to this degree. He frightened me. And then he looked towards me, his eyes bathing me in warmth, and he said, "You could disturb yourself by thinking that I have become as you would like to live, and you were not expecting this, and perhaps you are wondering how you can..." he paused, and added, "I am preparing. I shall tell you more later."

I nodded, rendered docile by the very techniques I had taught him, and more besides.

The gathering continued. Two of the women and one of the men tried to seduce Alois, but he smoothly redirected their attention. I don't think they even noticed his manoeuvres. By the time we left, the group had spilled over into several ovicles, with people (following Alois' example) moving from one to another.

It was getting dark outside, and Alois suggested a walk through the city. Of course, I agreed. We kept a steady pace as Alois gazed around like a tourist and I watched the shadows for muggers. In this way, unexpectedly, we came to the bridge where we'd first met.

I tried to avoid it, just in case it triggered some lingering memory, but Alois smiled and said, "Yes, Paul, I remember this place." Leaving me, he went straight to the rail where I'd seen him that time, and gazed down upon the water, for the tide was in. After a while he shrugged and rejoined me. "I fascinate myself how I change, don't you?" he remarked, and while I was picking the bones out of that one he began the walk back to the laboratory.

By now Alois was spending much of his waking time in the PsyberNet. And he slept little, having invented, he said, a technique for compressing quality sleep into about two hours out of twenty-four. Michael and I continued our shift rota in order to keep up with him. The rest of the time he was out somewhere. He told us nothing. Someone would come to the door for him at any hour of the day, and he wouldn't reappear until after Michael and I had changed shift.

One morning I got to the door first and saw on the inspection screen a tall pretty brunette in her twenties. Alois' sexual imprint was clear to me. "Hi," she said with a bright smile, "can I see Alois?"

"Who shall I say-?"

"Heidi." There was a pause, then her eyes widened and focussed behind me. "Alois!"

"Hello, Heidi," he said over my shoulder, and went to the door and opened it. They embraced and left without closing the door. I stood in the doorway, blinking in the sun, watching them halt a tram and get in, laughing. Then I turned and went inside.

He returned alone the following day, and went straight into the PsyberNet without acknowledging me. Trembling with indignation, I spun a membrane over myself, felt it tighten around me, and jaunted after him. He was already among his friends, his reconfigured appearance a sparkling whirlpool drawing to itself, from the turbulence of Virtuality, individuals from the passing shoals of Virtual denizens.

Seeing me, he waved and beckoned. "Paul, meet some allies. John Paul Fuller, Uromi-" he ran through a list of other famously wealthy names, "-and you already know Robert Meyer, who is going to extend our funding."

Bemused, I acknowledged the brighter-than-life image of the faculty procurator, who smiled uncertainly back with a soft-textured mask completely unlike the smooth impersonal image he projected during our University correspondence. "Look,

Paul," Meyer said, "had I realised at an earlier stage how important this work was going to be ..." He smiled again as Alois, beside me, shrugged. "But anyway, you and Alois have a lot to do, and quickly- " (Alois silenced my query with a look) "-and until I've persuaded the Minister for Education to co-operate, the best we can do is to allocate you the ground floor of the Neurolinguistics Faculty."

Alois helped me to say thank you nicely, whereupon I jaunted out of Virtuality and waited, arms folded, until Alois emerged from the node, balling up the fading membrane and tossing it into the recycler.

"D'you mind telling me what that was about?"

"Trust your impressions, Paul. You heard and understood." Then he smiled ruefully. "Very well. Yes, I lured you into Virtuality to demonstrate to you that I convince people with influence to support our project. And yes, we can afford to implement a program of Semantic Retrodesign, starting from a new custom-made facility at the University."

"Oh, is that all?"

"No, Paul," and his eyes gazed adoringly on me. "I have made some improvements to the original program- "

"You've improved my process?"

"Retrodesigned it. And I have begun selecting individuals for the program."

"Oh?"

"You have now met some of them- "

I was speechless, thinking of John Paul Fuller, Uromi and company...

"-they will help me even more after their Semantic Retrodesign- "

...Robert Meyer, the Minister for Education ...

"-and so will you."

"WHAT?"

"Your process was so flawed, Paul- the product of a flawed mind. I can *change this*. Haven't you already begun to wonder what it might be like for you to ... *feel this* ..."

"Stop it!" I turned abruptly, making for the fire escape, anything to get away from him. I burst through the door.

"Avoid finding yourself left out in the cold, Paul," he called after me. Goose bumps appeared on my arms. "Don't you want to know how your process used to be flawed?"

He had me there. I came in, reluctantly, and closed the door. Alois gave me one of his most disarming looks and led me into the living quarters. Sitting me down, he went on. "I amazed myself at how people such as yourself, Heidi and Meyer all experience so unpleasantly, insecurely, lonely, and for so much of your waking time. And you expect to free your undertakings from these flaws. But we experience subjectively, and you delude yourselves with what you call your objectivity."

"I've never thought of Meyer being insecure or lonely. What are you getting at?"

"Your flaws. However much you try, you cannot create

except in your own image."

And the monster inside me looked at Alois and agreed.

"You failed to see the truth of this," he continued, "until now. You remember when I awoke on the fifth day?" I nodded. "You had completed your part of the process at that point." He waited while I recovered from that one. "From then on I, not you, ran the process. I intervened early enough to innoculate myself against your delusions and retrodesigned your process as I was undergoing it. I experience now as so much more than you could have made me. So learn from me, Paul; do this yourself. You will amaze yourself by the mistakes you made."

He was right there. And it eats away at me inside.

"So what can we expect," I said, "yet another new generation of supermen? A legion of world rulers, with flawless minds and immortal bodies, controlled by your perfect self? Hasn't this been tried before?"

"I avoid such ambitions, Paul. I retain by choice one weakness which you introduced into my Semantic Retrodesign." He paused, perhaps enjoying the suspense this remark caused in me. "Paul, review your recent life. Your studies, your lack of a social life - by the way, did you know that Nawal, your other lab assistant, was in love with you?"

I didn't. "How would you know?"

"Michael told me. He tells me much. You failed to notice Nawal, being busy taking the risks you took to establish this project. Because you drive yourself with the belief that this changing you can bring about in others you might also bring about in yourself." That cut to the bone, but he gave me no time to respond. "Your obsessive traits, all fed into me through the neurolinguistic patterns you installed. And what do I pursue so sleeplessly, so obsessively? Why do I come and go without hello or goodbye until you force yourself to follow me? Paul, have you raised your eyes from your precious laboratory notes to see?" He leaned closer. "I do not pursue rich living or controlling others any more than you do. I pursue having people experience freshly, pleasantly, abundantly; not endlessly demonstrating the same few faulty patterns. And if I find that only Semantic Retrodesign changes them, then I will use that until we make something even better. Now tell me if you'd rather continue your sad lonely living? Wouldn't you rather *scrap everything* and *start afresh*, or *exchange an old life for new*. I can *do this*. You can *begin again* as a whole new person."

And within me, the monster gave a start of recognition at its own words.

The future program, Alois explained to me later, will have the checks, counterbalances and choice points of a larger meme pool than my own pathetic little puddle (my words, not his. He was aggravatingly tactful about it). There would be no elite and no compulsion, because the program would recommend itself through the lives of those who underwent it.

I am, I suppose, the chief villain in a remake of "Invasion

of the Body Snatchers", in which anyone who runs through town shrieking that their spouse isn't the same person anymore will be congratulated for noticing and asked for feedback. And like it or not, those who undergo Semantic Retrodesign will have a natural advantage over those who do not, and will incur the resentment of those who cannot or will not.

Like me.

I foresee wars of extermination over this. Political power structures run by ordinary mortals will not stand for such changes, and will fight back. I almost hope they do. And I hope they win.

But I don't want to be there for it.

I have to be honest with myself. When it comes right down to it, I cannot bear the thought of dragging my feet to my Guinea Pig A and confessing to him whose life I created that I can no longer bear the life I have created for myself.

For conscience's sake I'm releasing this account throughout the PsyberNet, although I have a funny feeling that Alois has forestalled me somehow, thinking of me. Anyway, let the Virtual peptides do what they will. I'm going for a walk; to the bridge, perhaps.

Maybe the tide will be out.

Bits and Pieces
Iain Darby

The first thing that struck Heinrich as he left the plane was the heat. Africa has a heat all its own, a dry, energy-sapping blanket of warmth that sears the skin and smothers the soul. By the time he'd walked from the runway apron to the customs building his clothes were soaked in sweat. The thick scars on his body didn't produce sweat, however, so there were dry lines in the thin cotton shirt that he wore, giving him the appearance of a patchwork doll. Despite the heat, he would have to wear heavier clothing.

The customs officer's eyes widened in fear as Heinrich handed over his documents, a crisp bundle of the local banknotes neatly folded amongst them. Heinrich ignored the man's fright, just as he ignored the clumsy palming of his bribe, his currency disappearing as the travel papers were stamped with an authoritative thud.

His contact, a man called Carter, was waiting for him outside.

Carter looked okay at first glance, but a closer look revealed him as a mismatch. An old pro like Heinrich had him categorised within moments. One eye blue, the other brown; thick mop of red hair on his head, dark curls on his chest peeking out from beneath his shirt. He limped a little, one leg slightly shorter than the other. Limbs were difficult to match, and a lot cheaper if you didn't insist on a matching pair, but you condemned yourself to limp for the whole of that Resurrection. One arm longer than the other was an inconvenience, but mismatched legs, they were a sod. Heinrich knew – his own were markedly worse than Carter's though he concealed the fact by wearing one built up boot.

"Herr Speer?" The man almost tripped and fell in his enthusiasm as he greeted Heinrich. "Welcome to Uganda."

Heinrich grimaced. The customs building behind them was little more than a shed, the car Carter was directing some natives to place his luggage in was a battered old Ford, its colour indeterminate beneath its dust-covered exterior, and the road they stood on was no more than a dirt track.

"Nice place."

Carter smiled, his grin lopsided. "It has potential, Herr Speer. Great potential."

"That's why I'm here…"

The journey to Kinshasa was a nightmare of dust and heat. The car had no air-conditioning unit, just an ancient electric fan that sat on the dashboard and whirred, uselessly recirculating the warm air. Carter prattled the whole way. He saw Heinrich as his opportunity to enter the big time, not realising that for Heinrich to be dealing with him at all meant that he no longer had the influence that Carter imagined.

Close up, the inadequacies of Carter's Resurrection were more pronounced, the stitching obvious and amateurish. They reminded Heinrich that his own weren't much better, adding to his irritation.

He'd seen photographs of the original Resurrected: all dead flesh, mismatched limbs and poor stitching. The first looked like a monster. They had come a long way since then. Still, some of the Resurrected that came through the chop shops these days, like Carter, didn't look much better. They were made up of bits and pieces, an arm from here, a leg from there. But even bits cost money, and good bits cost *big* money.

But Heinrich didn't work in the good-bit end: the sterile centres where criminals and debtors paid their dues in the only way that society would allow them. Of course, the patients didn't see any of that. They saw the smiling, reassuring faces of the nurses and doctors, faces that blurred pleasantly as the anaesthetic took effect.

Afterwards, there would be pain. The pain of Resurrection was intense, a thousand fires in the nerves, but in time it would abate, and then, oh, then there was the joy of a new body, the vitality of youth, the strength of health, the security of another twenty, maybe thirty, years... though the last of them would be spent ensuring there was enough credit at the bank for the next Resurrection.

And there was a dark shadow of fear across all of those years; the fear of the burning that would have to be endured once again.

Wars were good. Resurrectionist agents would stir up trouble wherever they could. Wars had always been Heinrich's speciality. There were always leaders willing to trade the carcasses of those who had fallen for weapons. Their followers were pledged to them in life, and beyond. Messy, though. A good torso was worth ten thousand credits. Matching arms and legs, five thousand apiece. But a whole body? – ah, a whole body could, if young and relatively untraumatised, fetch upwards of *one hundred* thousand. On the battlefields that Heinrich had worked, such items were almost unknown.

He dreamed of getting one. For that fee he could visit one of the smaller clinics – not hospital-standard, but a big step up from the chop houses where they spliced you together with whatever they had to hand.

That was what had brought him to Africa, a continent where resources were still relatively untapped. In Europe there was just too much competition. Quite aside from the legal supplies through proper channels there was a thriving black market in body parts, and since unification the European Government had stopped trying to halt the trade. Instead it gave its blessing to certain favoured traders in return for fixing the price and levying heavy taxes.

Heinrich wasn't one of those fortunate traders, so now he had to go further afield to pursue his profession, find a new source of cheaper material. Africa had long been ignored by the Resurrected, as they preferred to at least retain the racial type with which they had been born. Old prejudices die hard. But Heinrich thought that this one might, at last, be failing. If you could have a new body, if you could live again, then did it really matter what colour the skin was?

Though Heinrich didn't admit it to himself, the idea had been Carter's. Another reason he didn't like the man. Carter was Afrikaans, born and bred in that enclave in the southernmost part of the Continent where white settlers had for generations pretended that they were merely an outpost of Europe. Where European values were espoused, European science practised. And since the middle of the nineteenth century that had meant the science of Resurrection. Everything else had been sacrificed to it. That was understandable – after all, to those who could afford it, it offered immortality.

When at last they arrived at their hotel, Heinrich was relieved to see that this, at least, was luxurious. Built for visiting Westerners, it featured a lobby faced with cool marble and rooms that were effectively air-conditioned. He helped himself to a cold bottle of beer from the fridge in his room while Carter briefed him on local conditions.

"The authorities won't deal with you; they don't like whites, and they especially don't like Resurrected whites. But outside the city, in the country, the local headmen still have real power over their people. We can deal direct with them.

"I have the transportation fixed, lorries, planes, everything. All the right palms have been greased, all you have to do is arrange receipt in the hospitals in Europe, and," he added, grinning, "of course, payment." He hesitated, weighing his next words carefully. "You know, there is no real reason for you to deal directly with the natives. I could do that, too."

Heinrich shook his head. "That's not how I work, my friend. I like to be involved at *every* level." He stressed his last words to make his meaning clear. He was going to make sure that he wasn't cheated. Above all, he wasn't going to let Carter have sole control of the supply. If he did that, then sooner or later Carter would forge the required contacts in the hospitals and deal with them direct, freezing Heinrich out.

Carter shrugged. The reply was no more than he had expected, but it had been worth asking the question. "I have arranged an interpreter for you, a reliable man. In two days he will take you out into the hinterlands." He stood, their business at an end for the moment. "I wish you success."

"I'll call you when I get back," Heinrich told him, ignoring Carter's outstretched hand. They might be partners, but he wanted it to be clear from the outset who the senior partner in this venture was.

Later, standing under the shower and letting the cool spray

of the water ease his body, Heinrich looked in distaste at his right forearm. The skin was dark and unhealthy, and he imagined that he could smell the faint odour of corruption seeping out through its pores.

Rejection. Dammit. This had happened to him once before. Drugs would hold it at bay for a while: six months, maybe a year. But eventually it would spread, and while it did the delaying drugs would be draining his already dwindling account.

When it had happened before he had been flush, the middle man between one of the big hospitals and the Balkan nationalists during one of their endless wars, creaming off a healthy commission for arranging transport of the fresh cadavers of fallen troops.

Then he had simply picked out one for himself, and allowed the hospital to pay him in kind instead of in credit.

By the time he had gotten back to the Balkans, though, the leader was dead and the other side, the victors, had made their own arrangement with the hospitals. Selling off the bodies of their prisoners while they were still warm.

He hadn't realised it at first, but after that things had started to go downhill.

And now he needed this deal to go through, because for the first time in sixty years he feared something other than pain. He feared death.

With all the worries that Heinrich had, he didn't think that anything could distract him from the task in hand. But something did. He saw her first by the pool. Blue water at her back, the bright redness of a too-quickly acquired tan sharp against the white swimsuit. Long blonde hair fell wetly down her back, her figure was curved and full. But it was her eyes that attracted him most. The light blue of a summer sky, bright, and above all alive. He felt a sudden thrill of nerves as he watched her.

Conscious of the poorly matched body he wore, bizarre in slacks, shoes and jacket amongst the near-naked bodies at the pool, he approached her, a bottle of tanning lotion in his hand.

"Miss? May I suggest…" He held out the plastic bottle before him.

She looked bemused for a moment as he indicated her reddening arms. "You will find the lotion soothing." And so she would. If the Resurrected knew about anything, it was skin care.

Finally she smiled, and took the bottle from him. "Thank you." Her voice had the distinctive lilt of west-coast America, but while he found it annoying in others, in her he found it charming.

"Perhaps you would join me for a drink?" Even to his own ears his voice sounded stiff, formal.

It seemed an age before she answered. Her eyes drank him in, and it was he who felt naked, conscious of every shortcoming of the body he had purchased, the prematurely greying hair, the too-thin lips, the one shoulder that drooped slightly to compensate for the shortness of the arm. Not exactly the best that money could buy, just the best that he could afford.

He watched as her eyes lingered on the scar around his neck, where the head had been attached. Saw her bright blue eyes widen slightly in surprise. Some one-timers were afraid of Resurrectionists, he knew…

Then she was speaking again. "Yes, thank you, that would be nice."

Her name was Samantha, and as they sat and chatted under the shade of the awning over the poolside bar, she asked the inevitable question. "You're a Frank, aren't you?"

He grimaced; he had heard the term before, an ugly homage to the brilliant scientist who had pioneered the techniques of Resurrection. "In Europe we call ourselves Resurrectionists.

"Am I the first you've seen?"

She laughed, and his stranger's lips smiled in response. "No," she assured him, "there are many back home, but they keep to themselves."

"What brings you so far from home?"

"Adventure. I want to see the world, taste every food, swim in every sea, climb every mountain."

He gestured at their opulent surroundings. "A singularly comfortable adventure."

"Oh, I'm not staying here," she assured him. "I couldn't afford this. The manager's a friend."

I'm sure he is, thought Heinrich, and wants to be a better one, I'll be bound.

"He lets me use the pool whenever I want. But this is just a stop on my tour. My aim is to climb Kilimanjaro." Then she told him of the mountain, the highest point in Africa. He listened, but she could have been talking about anything, anything at all, and he would listen, just to be with her.

This was his first time in Africa, but he had been many other places, seen many other things. He went out of his way to interest her, and at the end of the afternoon she had agreed to dine with him that night.

As he watched her leave to get ready, he admonished himself. Heinrich, you're too old for these games, he whispered. But then he smiled, for he wasn't, and as long as he had the credits and there were new bodies available he never would be. Years had nothing to do with it.

After that he spent every spare moment with her. She considered him a curiosity, he could tell. Their relationship didn't go beyond talk, the barrier of his borrowed body always between them.

He shared her spirit of adventure, had done many of the things she dreamt of. He told her of Australia, the beauty of Parramatta Bay, the wonder of Ayers Rock. He enthralled her with stories of war: battles he had seen won and lost, always grander in the telling than the living. What was merely memory to him was history to her, and he fleshed it out with colour and character.

Samantha would listen, fascinated, but should he move too near, or accidentally brush against her, she would recoil, a nervous smile of apology on her face. Heinrich would pretend not to notice, inwardly cursing again the cheap body that he wore.

His trips weren't going well; all he'd encountered was fear and superstition. Nobody was willing to sell the bodies of their people. Each time he returned he would bathe the sweat of the jungle from his body, and inspect his arm. Its movement was becoming difficult; the veins were black and distended; the poison was spreading, vile black fingers stretching upward day by day.

He was afraid to look at it, and afraid not to. Fear had begun to gnaw at him: the fear that he would make no deal here after all, that the darkness on his arm would spread un-checked, and that he would at last join his forefathers. The only alternative was to visit a chop shop, purchase whatever they had in stock. Let those unqualified butchers work on him. Even the thought was appalling.

When he wasn't away in the wilds negotiating with some headman or another, Heinrich would find Samantha, and they would sit and talk. When he was with her he could forget his worries for a time.

One morning as they sat by the pool, the pool-boy - a child of eleven or twelve hired to run errands - dropped an over-loaded tray of empty glasses he had been gathering. Alerted by the noise, the manager came rushing out, a heavy-set man in his late thirties who yelled furiously at the child and cuffed him about the ears. Not content with that, he continued to slap at him as the tearful boy fell to his knees, desperately trying to scoop up the broken glass with his bare hands.

Samantha and the other guests watched open-mouthed as her friend beat the child.

Heinrich stood. "Excuse me." His voice was cold. He strode toward the scene. "Stop that!" he shouted. "Stop that, I say."

The manager looked up, his eyes narrowing as he recog-nised Heinrich. "This is not your business, sir." He glanced across to where Samantha sat watching. "I run my hotel as I please."

"Not while I'm here," hissed Heinrich, stepping in close to the man.

"Then you leave."

The boy had taken the opportunity of the manager's dis-traction to flee, but now he was forgotten. "You don't like it here, leave," repeated the man. He drew himself up to his full height. He was several inches taller than Heinrich.

For a moment there was silence; then Heinrich said, very

clearly, "When I'm ready, not before."

The man made to reply, but Heinrich stretched out one arm, the one that still worked, and struck him in the chest with the flat of his hand. The blow wasn't a heavy one, but the tiled poolside was wet and the man's bulk did most of the work for Heinrich. With a huge splash the manager fell backwards into the pool.

Heinrich looked down at the manager as he thrashed about in the water. "And while I'm here, I want you to make a better effort to keep the pool clean." He turned away. "There appears to be some shit in it."

As he took his seat back at his table there was a little round of applause from the other guests. Heinrich raised his glass in a mock salute.

"Your friend?" he asked Samantha, raising one eyebrow quizzically.

She smiled at him. "Not any more, but you might regret that." She watched as the manager struggled out of the pool and dripped his way back into the hotel. "This is the only decent hotel in Kinshasa."

Heinrich shrugged. "Despite what he likes to think it's not his; you think the owners would be pleased to hear he threatened a guest? No, I doubt I'll hear any more of it."

"You surprise me, you know."

"Why's that?"

"Helping the child. I thought that we - what do you call

us? one-timers - would mean nothing to you."

It was Heinrich's turn to smile. "Why, it's you that surprises me, Samantha. It took me two lifetimes to realise that it's not flesh and bone that make a man what he is - it's spirit and soul. I thought women always knew that."

At that Samantha's face seemed to soften, and she reached out and placed her hand on his arm. Had there been any feeling in it, the moment would have been perfect.

In the restaurant that night the manager was nowhere to be seen; apparently he had found other things with which to busy himself while Heinrich and Samantha dined.

"You'll never do it?" he asked her.

Without asking, she knew what he was referring to. Her lips formed a straight thin line and she slowly shook her head. "Never."

"You won't see much of the world in just one lifetime," he told her. "Some won't do it on religious grounds, some for fear of the pain, most just can never afford it – but a pretty girl like you, you could find somebody to pay, that's for sure. So what's your reason?"

"I was born P2 positive."

"Ah," he said, understanding. Her genes had marked her out for senility within weeks of her conception – since then the clock had simply been ticking. The one organ that was moved from host to host through resurrections was the brain. For those with genetic brain disorders there was no point in wasting time or money on a Resurrection – to drool uselessly was much the same in one body as in another.

"I'm sorry."

"I'm not," she said firmly. "They tell me I have twenty, perhaps thirty years, and I could never do that." She pointed to his scars. "Don't you feel like a stranger in your body?"

"Yes," he nodded, "I did for a while, but the experience is enthralling, everything new again, vivid and real. I..." His words trailed away. "I'm sorry," he repeated.

Hesitantly, he leaned into her, and kissed her.

It was only a kiss, soft fat flesh, his on hers, but as he sucked she exhaled, the life running out of her. And Heinrich felt that he had been reborn.

He disliked the man that Carter had selected as his guide and interpreter, a long-limbed tribesman. As failure had followed failure, Heinrich began to doubt that the man was conveying his words accurately.

They had travelled together four days to reach this spot where a local chief had agreed to meet him: a cluster of huts amidst a clearing in the jungle. On the journey Heinrich had impressed upon the interpreter that further failure would be laid at *his* door.

The headman's skin was charcoal grey, and his deep black eyes stared across the campfire, drilling into Heinrich's own.

"You gave him the gift?" Heinrich asked the interpreter, referring to the case of Scotch that was meant to soften the man up.

"Yes, boss." The interpreter was nervous, afraid of both the power of the gnarled figure before them, and Heinrich himself.

"Tell him I wish to come to an arrangement. The malaria, it is bad in this region?"

The interpreter fired off his words in the local dialect and the old man nodded, quietly mouthing a reply.

"Yes, boss, sickness bad, he say. Many die."

"Young ones, too?" asked Heinrich, immediately cursing himself for his enthusiasm as the interpreter relayed his words.

"Yes, boss, young, old, sickness no care. Take many."

"Does he know why I'm here?"

"Yes, boss. You want to trade for the bodies."

The old man spoke a single word clearly. "Sayaah."

"Sayaah. What's that?"

The interpreter inclined his head to one side, apologetic. "Monster. Ghost. Sorry, boss, out here they have not seen Resurrected before, superstitious. He think you dead."

"Tell him I will pay, for every corpse under the age of thirty, if he gives them to me I will return with coin. Gold coin. He will be rich."

He waited while the interpreter couched his offer.

The old man made him wait for a moment before replying.

Heinrich didn't need the reply translated.

"No. He said no."

The old man spoke again, the translator stumbling over his words as he struggled to keep up.

"He says the dead will be buried with their fathers, as they have always been, their spirits will feed the soil of the land, their…"

Heinrich cut him off. Looking directly at the headman he asked: "Why did he agree to see me if he thinks these things?"

"Boss, he hears of you near his land. He has never seen Resurrected before." The interpreter waved his hands help-lessly. "He curious."

Now Heinrich turned to the interpreter. "Curious… Is that why they have all seen me?" His voice was raised now, shout-ing. "Have I just been a curiosity to them?"

Near to tears, the interpreter just shrugged his shoulders.

Heinrich stood open-mouthed, speechless. Behind him the old headman began to laugh.

When he finally arrived back at the hotel he rushed to find solace in Samantha's arms. Making love to her, he could put his troubles behind him.

The first time that they had made love she had been hesi-tant, almost fearful, but as passion inflamed her, hesitancy had been forgotten, and with long practised ease he brought her to a shuddering climax.

Later, in the quiet afterglow, as they lay on the dishevelled bed in the middle of the afternoon, the rays of the hot sun picking out dust motes which swirled lazily above them, she stroked his paper white scars, and lazily ran one finger down the length of his sutured torso.

"Don't they hurt?"

"Nah. Old scars, they're signs of life. Character." And it was true that they didn't hurt. Not now. But once…oh, once. He shook the memory from his head, looking down instead at the unblemished perfection of her body. So perfect, so perfect now, but perfection would not last – it never did.

"And your arm?"

He had sniffed, pushing the blackened limb under the bedsheets. "Even Resurrected get sick sometimes. I have medicine; it will get better," he lied. But after that he kept his shirt on when he made love to her.

He was taken with her, this short-lived creature, almost ashamed of his attraction to her ephemerality.

One-timers, they were nothing, nothing but bits and pieces. At least they had been until he met her.

But now things had changed, and it was his mortality that threatened to end their relationship.

Eventually Carter came to see him. Angry, disappointed. Obviously the interpreter had told him what had happened.

"I told you to let me negotiate. I understand Africans. Mr

Bigshot from Europe. I don't think you really even tried. This has just been a holiday for you, screwing that blond piece in the hotel every chance you get. I know what you've been doing, and you haven't been concentrating on business."

Heinrich eyed him coldly. Pushing the arm of his shirt back he thrust it toward Carter. "Know what this is? Know what it means?"

"Ayiee." Carter's nose wrinkled in his twisted face. The forearm was almost completely black now, the African heat serving to hurry the process despite the drugs Heinrich had taken. "Rejection," Carter said softly. His twisted face lit up with understanding. "You're broke, aren't you? That's why you came here in the first place."

"That's right," agreed Heinrich. "So believe me, my mind has been concentrated."

"What will you do?"

Heinrich sighed, all the anger run out of him. "The arm is just the first sign of a whole rejection. A new body will cost at least fifty thousand – I don't even have five."

Carter breathed deeply, rubbing at his nose. "There might be a way. I know a place in Durban, where I go. If you had something to sell…"

"I have nothing to sell," replied Heinrich impatiently.

"Someone…" whispered Carter. "Someone white, some-one perfect."

Heinrich looked at him in horror. But even then, in that

first moment, he knew. The very thought had condemned him to action. There could only be one decision.

For days he put it off, desperately trying to find another way to raise the capital he needed; but if there had been another way, he would not have been here.

Were her few years worth his immortality? He tried to imagine her as she would be, beauty forgotten, wrinkled, mindless. Twenty or thirty years.

To him that was tomorrow.

The darkness in his arm spread to his chest and, as if to make it easier for him, Samantha would now turn off the lights when they made love.

Finally he called Carter.

He made it as painless as possible, on their last night giving Samantha as perfect an evening as he could, promising to take her to Kilimanjaro. Then, as she slept, he placed a pillow over her head.

The man who came to collect her was impressed when he saw her perfect, undamaged body.

"Beautiful. Seventy-five thousand, as agreed."

Heinrich shook his head. "Carter said a hundred."

The man sniffed, and wiped the sweat from the back of his neck with a soiled handkerchief. "Hot here, my friend. In an hour or two the sun will be up and she'll start to go off. Now,

I have a refrigerated van downstairs… I'd say that makes it a buyer's market, wouldn't you?"

Tears stained Heinrich's cheeks. But what choice did he have? Together they lifted her body, and began to haul it down to the waiting truck.

For a long time afterwards guilt plagued him, and he missed Samantha terribly. But slowly, as it always does, time healed the wound.

A month after Heinrich's Resurrection, the last Headman he had seen had sent him a message. A neighbouring tribe had attacked, stealing two of his wives. He wanted weapons, and he would trade. Many young men would die, both from his tribe and the enemy. All would be Heinrich's in exchange for guns. Within a year he had amassed another fortune. Black flesh became fashionable for the Resurrected, and soon harlequin body parts decorated the finest people in the all the best places.

As his fortunes improved Heinrich had changed bodies again, and the one he wore now was a perfect match. An athlete's body, with a boxer's arms and an actor's face. Tall, lean, well-muscled. Stitches so perfect only the tell-tale scars and the experiences of several lifetimes revealed him for what he was.

Now he was taking the summer off, travelling, letting the summer wind cool his newborn flesh. Seeing the sights, drinking in all the world had to offer. Finally he took a sentimental journey. Back to Africa. He had time to be sentimental now - all the time in the world.

He stood at the foot of the greatest mountain range in Africa. It had been his last promise, that he would take her to Kilimanjaro. He still thought of her often, and in a way she was still with him, they would still see the world together.

It had taken some trouble, and he had endured no little discomfort to arrange this – but somehow it felt fitting.

Content, Heinrich looked up at the white-capped mountains, his boxer's hand on his brow, shielding Samantha's beautiful blue eyes from the glare of the morning sun.

Going Gently
Tim Lebbon

Do not go gentle into that good night.
Rage, rage against the dying of the light
-Dylan Thomas

The visit I had long been expecting came one warm July morning. A knock at the door, just as I was stretching myself awake and contemplating the journey downstairs for a cup of tea and a cigarette. The curtains were open a chink, hinting at a bright, clear day. Walking weather. Cycling weather. Sitting-outside-a-pub weather. Strange how I still thought this way; any enthusiasm I once felt for such pursuits had bled away since my one hundredth birthday.

I hauled myself out of bed and shrugged on an old dressing gown. There was a cigarette packet in one pocket but it was empty; just my luck. There was a new pack downstairs, so I decided I may as well answer the door. The thirteen stairs took me a couple of minutes to negotiate, each groaning footfall matched by a weary creak from my worn old knees. The shadow behind the glass front door remained motionless as I performed my descent, no doubt able to see me through the stringy net curtains I'd had for thirty years.

"Mr Capel?" the enthusiastic young voice gushed as soon as I opened the door. "Mr Capel, my name's Harriet Wondsgrew from CNN, I wonder if I may have a minute of your time?"

I looked past the alleged Harriet Wondsgrew and saw, on my front lawn, a veritable camp site.

"Mr Capel, do you know you're the last man who will die?"

"I'm a hundred and twelve," I said, "can't you let me have my last days in peace?"

Wondsgrew smiled sadly, but I could see it was all make-up. She was a professional. Human concerns did not concern her. "I'm afraid you're news, Mr Capel. And I was hoping you'd grant me exclusive rights. We'd pay very handsomely." I had seen Wondsgrew reporting on the Gulf War seventy years before.

There were other reporters across the street, sending camera drones at my house, pointing hyper-sensitive microphones at the windows of my bedroom and bathroom to hear a sad old man's morning motions. More vied for space on my driveway, some of them resorting to fist fights to secure the prime position.

"Mr Capel?"

I closed the door, She'd be knocking again soon - her sort always did - but for now I would make do with a cup of tea and a cigarette. So, I was definitely the last one, was I? I'd thought it may be the case over the last few years, but now that it was confirmed the notion pleased me more, made me feel important. Stupid old man that I was.

More fighting from outside. Shouting as a news wagon ran over the fibre optics of another team. All drowned out by the murmur of a camera platform landing in the playing fields down the road.

I sighed and took a first drag at my morning smoke. Reporters! They may well be immortal, but they were just the same as ever.

"Angel? Angel, it's me, David. They've come." The line was tapped, I was sure, but I needed someone to help me. I needed a friend. "Angel, they've found out about me. I don't know how or from whom, but they're here. Bloody vultures. Maybe they think it'll make them special, too. What do you think Angel? Angel? You there?"

Angel called back half an hour later. She left the video facility turned off.

"David! Sorry I was out, I was being ... well, you know." Concern tore her voice and made her sound like a stranger. In many ways she was now that she had been reprogrammed, but she was still my Angel inside, however much her outside had changed. I wondered what she looked like today.

"So," she said, "what the hell happened? Who's there, who's

bothering you? I have contacts, I could help." I knew that she did not, and could not. It was all a sad charade.

"I'm news, Angel, you should know that. And I think all of them are here." Even now I could see trees being chopped down in the park across the road to make way for platform landing sites. I was evolving away from a news item and into a full-scale novelty event. Some of these sad bastards, I knew, had seen nothing worthwhile for half their lives. They created realities to entertain a population which had, literally, seen everything.

They were not going to let me slip through their fingers so easily.

"David, I'm sorry."

I knew she told the truth. Even though she was one of them, she was truly sorry. In a way, she was as different from them as I was.

"What will you do?" she asked carefully.

"What can I do? I'm going to end it. I'm going to kill myself."

Angel came by and managed to negotiate her way through the baying pack without too much fuss. Hardly surprising, really; she was a seven-foot-tall bodybuilder with stupidly huge muscles and a jawline as square as a sleeveless pullover. It was not the strangest I had seen her, but it was pretty close. I almost laughed.

"Angel," I said, "you look ..."

"Ridiculous," she finished.

I shrugged. "Well, I suppose it gets you places."

"Yesterday I saw a guy with five arms. He was working in a burger bar, dishing out the shit as quickly as his co-ordination would allow. He was sweating. Looked really pissed." She sat at the window and glanced out at the struggling masses on my front lawn and across the street. "Slave labour, I suppose. They've started modifying the donor bodies. Within months, I'll be the least strange thing on the streets."

"It was inevitable," I said. I became dizzy and had to sit down, and Angel held me in one strong arm as she breathed bitterness across my face.

"I wish I could die," she said. I knew that was what she wanted; I'd seen her dead six times. "I wish I could find somewhere the chip couldn't transmit me back. Somewhere deep, maybe. But they'd find me. They always do find me. Why can't the bastards just leave me to die?"

I had no answer to that, other than to tell her she had chosen to become what she was. I had been dead set against it, but she had done it anyway. Recriminations, however, could offer no succour.

"I'm the last one left," I said. "I've had a long life, Angel. Not as long as you may have, but mine has been mostly good. The last few decades... well, a little strange, granted. But I'm glad you were my wife, all those years ago." I remembered her as she had been, before she went off to become immortalised. Tall, thin and beautiful even at sixty. Her wrinkles had flattened, her eyes glittered as news of the new technology started to filter through. Personality chips. New bodies for old. A corruption of the soul, many people said. But when the population became immortal in droves, there was very little for those mortals left behind to do. They complained, campaigned, and then they died. Old age, disease, accidents, all took their toll, and anyone not chipped stayed dead. But it was surprising how many converted when death glared into their eyes, even from a distance.

"Will you help me, Angel?"

She nodded her tanned head. "Of course I will. Haven't I always?" She leaned forward to kiss me. No thanks. Even at a hundred and twelve I managed to leave my chair pretty quickly.

Harriet Wondsgrew was hammering again.

Angel stormed down the hallway and pulled open the door, glaring into the reporter's eyes with muscular intensity. Death was no longer a problem, but pain was still real enough, and the threat of it was as potent a force as it had ever been. Wondsgrew stepped back.

"Er... I'd like to talk toMr Capel."

"Mr Capel is unavailable for interview."

"We pay handsomely."

"He's a hundred and twelve. What does he want with

money?"

"Why doesn't he want to be chipped?"

Angel had no answer for this. It's something she'd asked me often enough over the last half-century. She shut the door instead.

We went back into the lounge and sat drinking tea and smoking. Over the years I'd often wondered whether someone essentially immortal would think of eating and drinking in the same way I did. I'd asked Angel, but sometimes she was still angry with me for not being chipped. She'd lost a husband, she'd say. I'd tell her I'd lost a wife and it usually ended like that, neither of us willing to relinquish the tentative hold we had on each other.

"I don't want to leave my house to die," I said at last. "I'd like to do it here. In the lounge. I've spent some nice times here, and it's as comfortable a place as any. What do you think, Angel?"

She gazed at me, startled. "What do you mean?"

"Here," I said, standing uneasily and letting the pain in my joints settle to the usual level. "Now. The world's moved on apace, and I've been left behind. Help me go where I belong, Angel. Please."

"You want me to actually -"

"Help me die, yes. After all, you're the expert."

She was stunned. Death was something she sought but had not seen, in its true form, for a long time. Plane crashes and shootings were still reported - the pain was just the same - but all they meant now was a rush on the local immortalisation plant, and perhaps a longer wait for those corpseless personalities expecting a new body.

"I can't, David," she said. "You're my only friend."

I wished she hadn't said that. It started me crying. Tears for everything that had gone wrong... for an old age I had reached alone without my lovely wife... for the future Angel faced, a desolate landscape peppered with the occasional death and rejuvenation in another grown donor body. My old hands came up as if to catch the tears, but my eyes were all dried up, and my sobbing merely made me dribble onto my clean trousers. Yet another reason for my bitterness at what time had stolen from me.

"I've seen you drown yourself," I gasped angrily. "Walk into the road. Fall. How many deaths have you put me through?"

"But you know - "

"I know you come back, but look at you! Every few years a different person is my new best friend. At least give me the peace you can't have."

We were silent for a time, the only noise the hustle of the news crews outside. I heard the occasional plink as microphone drones tapped at my windows; salty drilling sounds as cables burrowed through my walls; the skittering clumps of secretive footfalls on my roof The house was becoming a heart, promising life to those surrounding me from the story waiting to unfold. If I had my way, their grisly entertainment would be still-born.

Angel said nothing. Her massive biceps flexed as she fisted and unfisted her hands. She had a tattoo on one arm, a rifle and machete crossed: <u>Marines</u>, it read beneath. She was looking at an old photograph of our wedding day; her body from then would be little more than dust now. I wondered what she was thinking, but was too afraid to ask.

I knew they'd see what was going to happen. I knew it would be broadcast around the globe to frenzied observers, those aching for something exciting to intrude into their sterile lives. If the camera drones did not find their way through my water pipes and between cracks in the bricks of the house, then virtual-cams would nudge their way into my life as Angel helped me to end it. There was nothing I could do to prevent this, but I could ensure that it happened amid peace and quiet. The cameras would be there, but they'd be hidden from view in hairwires. The microphones would hear my final breath, but I would not see them. Perhaps I'd leave a message for the world as I died. Or maybe dying itself would be a far more potent parting shot than any I could dream up.

"Angel," I said, "I know you wish to die as much as I do; the difference is I'm able to do it. Will you help me?" We'd loved each other so much, many years ago. The change in our relationship had hit me the worst. I ached inside with the need for her to help me, to listen to my pleas.

"I've made so many mistakes," she said, crying. I'd seen stranger things than a muscle-man shedding useless tears, but the sight was still unnerving. "I've made so many bad calls, and I really don't want to make another."

"But - "

"Of course I'll help you."

Relief flooded in. I nodded and smiled at her. She smiled back.

"I love you," she said.

"Me, too." I loved the memory of her, the Angel in my mind's eye, not this mutated thing before me. Her personality was so different now, twisted and forced askew by the terrible things it had been through: death, many times. She'd tried explaining when nights were cold and we huddled in front of the open fire, listening to the logs spit and crackle. She'd tried, but ... well, some things are just too personal.

I knew my death would be fine.

"Angel? Where are you? Angel!"

She had gone. Vanished. At the moment I needed her most she had abandoned me. I could feel things slipping away, the room growing, the walls and ceiling becoming more distant as the sleeping tablets took effect. There were noises outside, creaks from inside, the rumbles and grunts of my body slowly throwing in the towel. My sense of smell had gone, my eyesight and hearing were following close behind, and Angel had left me to die alone.

"Angel !" I shouted, or thought I did. My throat burnt with the effort but I could barely hear the result.

Then I felt a touch on my forehead, a cool strong hand, and Angel's manly face appeared upside down above mine.

"It's all right," she whispered. I could barely read her lips. "Angel's here, honey."

Then, another face. Harriet Wondsgrew aiming a camera drone at my left eye, her mouth distorting as she threw silent questions my way. Others behind her, hungry news hounds smelling blood as my life dribbled away into the air, my heat dissipated, my heart slowed, slowed, stuttered its last at this world that had become so strange and unwelcoming.

Angel, I tried to say, but I could not move my mouth.

Senses faded until the sense of touch was all that remained. I could feel them everywhere. Handling me. Poking. The last man to die. Look at him. Freak. Idiot.

Something cold kissed my forehead.

My death was a very public affair.

And then something else. Something not living, but surely not death either? Can I dream in death? Muse upon my life? Can I be angry with the one woman I have ever loved?

I am stored. My whole life is in a bio-circuit and that's where I am too, myriad electronic pulses with no sense, no feeling, just knowledge. Pure, undiluted knowledge.

Knowledge that Angel betrayed me. She would not let me die; from some mutated loyalty, she had captured my fleeing soul and now here I am, waiting, expecting at any moment to be immortalised into a new body.

Knowledge, too, that I have lost my one chance at death. Suicide is no longer a crime in this brave, stupid new world, simply because it is impossible.

I am no longer famous. I was to be the last man to die, the final bearer of the old ways. But no more. When I return, I will be just another normal person, and I will live forever.

The Banker Of Ingolstadt
Rhys Hughes

"I wish to open a student account."

The clerk removed his tinted spectacles and wiped them with a dirty cloth. The figure seated across the desk had the hungry appearance of an undergraduate, the pale skin and sunken eyes, but was plainly a lunatic. He considered ringing the bell for assistance, but a quick glance around the chamber confirmed that most of the staff had finished work early. So he cleared his throat and muttered:

"You are registered at the university?"

"That's correct. I'm studying Sociology and Reanimation with Doctor Waldman. Is there a problem? I was told that your bank offers discounts on carriage travel and tickets for the multistage opera, not to mention a 200-florin bonus for freshers, and a 1000-shilling overdraft facility subject to prior arrangement. Have I made an embarrassing error? Shall I deposit my grant cheque elsewhere?"

"Let us not be hasty. The Bank of Bavaria is indeed rather generous with its terms for customers entering Higher Education. But I'm afraid we have to be completely open with each other and you have already tried to deceive me. Perhaps you would consider a Golden Oven account instead? To put a crust on your funds! How about a Double Mangle? That one limits withdrawals to ten doubloons a week, but is index-linked to the number of fatalities in wars with Prussia or France. Every type of account is open to you — except the one tailored for students. You can't possibly have enrolled at Ingolstadt University."

"Why not? I judge that a gross insult!"

The clerk toyed with a quill resting on a vast ledger. "Because, Fraulein Radcliffe, you are a woman!"

"Absolutely! The first female to register with Doctor Waldman on the Sociology and Reanimation modules."

She added darkly: "It's a Rancid Sandwich Course!"

Curling his lower lip around a clubbed finger, the clerk moistened the tip with an inky spittle, opened the ledger and proceeded to flick through the sheets. His prints crowded each other out on every page, as if he derived pleasure from smudging the names which had been scratched in neat rows, in lieu of blotting the identities of the owners. Finally, he reached the last page and slammed the book.

"These are the financial records of every student who has opened an account here since the founding of the college in 1250. Not a single one has ever been a woman. Indeed, there's not enough space in the margins to write 'Fraulein' instead of 'Herr'. And suppose you did deposit your grant cheque with us? We could hardly mix your funds with the male money in the student vault - that would be unseemly. A new vault would have to be constructed just for you, and painted pink, with lace hanging from the combination dial on the lock. Do you truly want to put us to so much bother? I'm sorry, Fraulein Radcliffe."

"Call me Mina." She brushed back her auburn hair and undid the top button of her bodice. "If I open a Double Mangle account, my money will also have to be stored with that of men."

The clerk clucked his tongue disapprovingly. "You sound excited by the concept. No, that's an account for feeble pensioners, which is why I'm amenable to extending its terms to you. There will be a surcharge, of course, to pay for a chaperone. Now then, do you have any proof of identification?"

Mina placed her handbag on the desk. The clerk frowned. It appeared to have been sewn from many different types of leather, but the skins had been badly cured, and had not originated on any domestic animal. Parts of the bag sprouted hairs, dark and fair, while other patches were studded with nipples or navels - cameo and intaglio designs which suggested a mother rather than a fashion accessory, with something embryonic in its womb, a sextet of mysteries, if one might pardon the expression. Then she pulled apart the enamel clasp - a tooth in a gum — and rummaged around for a minute, fmally producing a square card which held a miniature portrait in oils of her likeness, and an official stamp.

"Oh dear, Fraulein!" muttered the clerk. "That is a Students' Union Card, and as we have already established, there is no such thing as a female undergraduate. I don't know how you came by it, though I suspect theft or forgery, but I am not willing to be duped by such tricks." He indicated the ledger. "As I said, there has never been a woman with a student account in our business history."

"May I see?" Mina drew the ledger toward her with two delicate but strong hands. The clerk averted his eyes as her wrists slipped out from her sleeves. A dim urge vaulted the security barrier separating his id from his ego, a desire to lean across the desk and touch her knee. He repressed it and gasped. Did he know how to touch a woman's knee? The answer was negative, but a disturbing memory came loose from the spike where it had been impaled, ready for filing and obfuscation. It flapped around inside his cranium. The palm rests on the knee-cap, the fingers close around it, the hand slides gradually up... No, it was a fraudster! An impostor memory!

He was rescued by a squeal of delight from Mina, who had found an entry which excited her. For a moment, he was worried, fearing she had discovered a name to challenge his assertion, but he knew the ledger like the back of his pituitary gland. What was she saying now? He rubbed his ears, feeling a little dizzy, twiddling the moles on his neck.

"Look, it's his signature! I can't believe he really sat here and signed this!" Mina pressed her lips to the name in faded ink. "Victor Frankenstein!"

"Who? Oh, that wastrel! Yes, I remember him well. He defaulted on a loan. Said he wanted funds to insulate the attic of his lodgings and then spent the money on electric eels! You're not related to him, are you?"

"Heavens, no! Victor was by birth a Genevese, and his family was one of the most distinguished of that republic. I am from Montevideo, but my father was English. Have you really nothing better to say about this incredible genius? It was Victor who first succeeded in imparting life to the limbs and organs of corpses. Without his pioneering work, the university of Ingolstadt would not now be running any Reanimation courses. He was my hero when I was growing up on the outskirts of my home town. I remember attempting to galvanise a dead horse - at least I thought it was dead! - when all my friends wanted to do was arrange flowers or tie ribbons in their hair. And when my mother expired of cholera, I insisted on attaching two electrodes to her temples and flying a kite in a storm. It didn't work, but I still recall the detonation inside her coffin. I keep the ashes in this locket. Would you care to see?"

"Those ashes are coloured, Fraulein!"

"Well, my mother was a mulatto. Originally from Senegal."

The clerk flicked his dirty cloth over his perspiring face. He felt that his tongue had swollen at the back of his throat. "Then you are part black?"

"Indeed. Is there a difficulty with that?"

For a brief instant he started to rise to his feet, but the cold air which rushed to ventilate his stale buttocks was so original and alarming a sensation that he reversed the direction of force and pushed himself down as firmly as possible. But his voice had the shriek of one who has stood to shake a finger.

"And you still insist you have enrolled at the university, here in Ingolstadt, with its white steeple and civilised cobbles? A Hottentot floozie!"

Mina narrowed her eyes and the icy beams which stabbed from their green depths chilled the marrow in six of the clerk's ribs.

"It is a great privilege for me," she said quietly, "to study with Doctor Waldman, the same scholar who taught chemistry to Victor Frankenstein. I will now trouble you no further, but take my money to an alternative bank."

Quick as a pig's tail in a mincer, the clerk shot out his arm and seized Mina's elbow. He made a valiant attempt to smile. "I assure you, Fraulein Radcliffe, that no other bank will be interested in dealing with a tainted female. Not only that, but there are, in fact, no other banks in Ingolstadt. However, the Bank of Bavaria is more tolerant and generous than most. So let us consider our little problem. You wish to open a student account, but it is impossible for you to be a student. When I suggest a more suitable type of account, you grow surly. We are getting nowhere. Thus I suggest a private arrangement, just between you and me. I will hold the money for you, mingled with my own savings. If you wish to make a withdrawal, you may visit me after closing hours."

"Mingle my money? Where is your prudishness now?"

He shuddered away her objections. "My savings have no

interest in physical contact, I assure you. They prefer to repro-
duce through sheer fiscal discipline. Naturally, there will be a
hefty charge for this favour -I will have to falsify documents."

Mina's voice quavered slightly. "How can I be sure you
will not try to cheat me?" She watched for any betrayal of compassion in his answer, the merest flicker of humanity, but there
was none.

"Ah, but I will cheat you, Fraulein! You shall have to come
to my lodgings whenever you require a few coins. There will
be a strict limit on how much you may withdraw at one time.
You will be compelled to visit me often. My rooms are very
secluded. They have never known a female presence. Even the
fleas are exclusively male. It is strange, but when I consider
my history, I find a number of anomalies... different memories,
many of which do not belong to me. As if I was once married...
Please excuse me, I am rambling. Your astonishing implica-
tion that women are somehow equal to men has quite disor-
dered my senses."

"Very well. You leave me no choice. My grant cheque is
worthless unless it is cashed. I have rent to pay, books and
equipment to buy. I have a glittering career ahead, and I do not
wish to spoil it by dying in the gutter."

"Your mind almost has a grasp of algorithmic reasoning,
Fraulein. I applaud you. Every phenomenon is prone to the
occasional incongruity. Supernovae in distant galaxies, irregu-
larities in chasing up debtors, and now a girl who thinks like a

man!" He lowered his tone to a clipped snarl. "Sign the back of the cheque and write a short contractual statement declaring that you hereby entrust the entire amount to my keeping."

Mina took the quill, dipped it in a pot of ink near her elbow and scratched the required marks on the cheque. She dried her signature by flapping the piece of paper before passing it to the clerk, who folded it and slipped it into his top pocket. Then she asked: "May I have my first instalment now? Just a shilling or two."

With a nonchalance which had something of the madhouse about it, in the same way that even a kind smile can suggest the terminal closing of a dungeon door, the clerk replaced his tinted spectacles. Now he was isolated from her, filtered out from his own humanity, which still seemed to consist of many parts. He rested his elbows on the desk, cradled his chin in his hands and sniffed. "Do I know you, Fraulein?"

"I demand the return of my money!"

"What is all this fuss? I have no idea what you are talking about. Do you suppose you can just burst in here and threaten a member of staff? The Bank of Bavaria always takes very good care of its employees. A single shake of this silver bell will summon guards who will hurl you into the street! And why have you unbuttoned your bodice? This is most unwelcome. Remove yourself from my restricted sight!"

A thousand expressions crossed Mina's face. At last her visage settled on a single aspect, a clench of jaw and smouldering of eyes which was exactly poised midway between impotent fury and - here the clerk felt a vague discomfort - languid amusement. His throat uttered an injunction of its own, tinged with too much panic, a croak scarred and notched with a rasp.

"Begone! Take your provocative bosom and radical egalitarianism away!"

Mina's tears were perhaps just a little strained. She clutched at the lapels of his coat, sending clouds of dust toward the panelled ceiling.

"I have a family to support! My fiance is a poor tailor!"

His lips trembled, at different velocities, as if they attended rival funerals. He struggled to maintain his heartlessness, but now there were two organs pumping congealed blood inside his chest - hers as well as his own, or so it seemed. He ached, and his fingers probed for the button of a secret compartment in the desk. The hidden drawer slid open and he plucked a coin from a mound, pushed it across to her and hissed: "Here, Fraulein. I can hardly keep up this charade. I want to be callous, I really do, but somehow you have touched me in places I had no idea I possessed. My sympathy - ah, how I shiver to use such a word! - has been roused. Please take this guinea."

She almost seemed disappointed. "Are you sure?"

He nodded and sat back, awaiting her gratitude, but she sighed and lifted her peculiar handbag onto the desk, obscuring the golden coin. Then she dipped inside and produced a selection of blades, scissors and little picks, tiny saws and screwdrivers.

"A sewing-kit, Fraulein? Really, this is hardly the time to start mending socks!"

The last item to emerge was a hammer. Mina weighed it carefully in one hand for a moment, nodded to herself and arched over the desk to deliver a single blow to the forehead of the clerk. He felt the shape of the wound, a hexagonal dent with impact lines radiating across his skull, like a multifaceted third eye or mystic sunburst in the centre of his brow. He was much too astonished to collapse or emit a scream. But the assault had also dislodged his sense of time. He realised that Mina was now standing next to him, a screwdriver inserted into one of the moles on his neck, twisting the tool furiously.

"What is this? Are you murdering me?"

"You have failed the test. You must be dismantled."

And then he did shriek, but it was a short-lived example of the form, for when he opened his mouth, Mina used the opportunity to insert her scissors and snip off his tongue.

Mumbling thickly as the oedematous blood filled his throat, he remembered the bell and reached out to ring it, but again she anticipated his intention and lopped his fingers and thumb off with a miniature cleaver, so that they tumbled over the edge of the desk and bounced on the mosaic floor. Her hands and implements seemed to be all over him, prodding, jabbing, cutting, wrenching. Now she was on her knees beneath him, slicing between his thighs. He bent forward and vomited blood, which spattered onto the upper curve of her partly exposed breasts and gushed in torrents between her cleavage. Constricted at the waist by a belt, the bodice positively bulged with his gore until it frothed back out of her bosom, and, as her breasts wobbled with the work, the red juice spurted in thin jets.

This was hardly the climax to his career he had been expecting. Half a century of plodding toil in the security of his position, inconspicuous but lurking, like a glass spider, before retirement to a small villa in the Bohmer Wald, done up to resemble an office. He had always believed himself to be suspended between two unknown worlds: that of his managers, who inhabited a cubic empire of interlocking conference chambers, awash with the odours of walnut, wine and bathchair lacquer, and that of his clients, which resembled a straight line, a street in a poor suburb, packed with teraced houses without a chink between, leading from one infinite smoky horizon to another. But now both worlds were growing dim, and tears were hatching from under his lids, as Mina struggled to lever his eyeballs out of their sockets with spoons. Both suddenly came free, with a horrible slurping sound, and as they dropped onto his cheeks, they swung like the pendulums of a cuckoo clock, the optic nerves of one entangling with those of the other, braiding his visionary sense into that of a Siamese cyclops.

For the first time in his life, one eye was able to directly stare at its twin. Each was a different shape, one being more feminine - with lashes high above that were fluttering. Many parts he; but now they were leaving him, returning home, and he almost recollected an earlier dissolution, numerous accidents. Mina, he realised, had returned to the mole on his neck. It was not a mole after all, but a bolt, with a screw-thread which passed through his throat. It held his head to his shoulders and she was loosening it with an adjustable spanner. It came out with an inner screech, and his skull began to wobble alarmingly. He attempted to stand, but he lacked knees: they lay under the desk. And every cell of his body rejoiced to be liberated from an unnatural fusion.

There was still time to ring for assistance. Limbless, voiceless, the clerk had only one course of action available to him. He nodded at the bell and his head fell from his torso, rolling on the polished surface of the desk and knocking the bell over the edge. It tinkled once as it landed. Then before utter blackness blew into every corner of his mind, he became aware of the wall splitting from ceiling to floor. It was a concealed door, and through it came an ancient figure, thin and menacing, with a shock of white hair and a peculiar limp. Was this the manager of the bank? His hopes fell with his blood-pressure as the figure cried:

"Tough luck, Mina. The practical is always the hardest part."

"Sorry, Doctor Waldman. I tried my best."

"I know you did."

"It was nearly right. After my theory exam I was so confident. But there was a trace of compassion buried in its subconscious. It had to be destroyed. A single flaw and the creature is useless."

"This is a discipline for perfectionists, Mina. I believe you will do better in the resits."

"I hope so, Doctor Waldman. I certainly intend to use these limbs again. They performed very well. But the head is not right. Back to the morgue, I think!"

"Let me help you cram all the pieces in your handbag. You are my favourite student, Mina, and I know you will go far. I feel it in my selection of hearts."

"My only wish is to emulate Victor Frankenstein."

"Oh, you will surpass his achievements. Your aptitude is as staggering as your originality. What a remarkable project for your finals! The Utterly Evil Banker!"

Together they passed through the door, locking it behind them. The props would remain until the examination room could be booked for a resit.

In a corridor of the university, Mina stopped and clutched at Doctor Waldman's sleeve. Her eyes were like icecaps awaiting a mysterious sledge.

"I must succeed," she said, "for the sake of the human race. The centuries to come will be characterised by unrestrained progress. Science will give us weapons of which we can barely conceive - motorised guns which can spray thousands of bullets every minute, flying machines which can level whole cities with explosives, armoured wagons and undersea boats, rockets capable of sending germs or poisons to distant countries in a matter of hours, unimagined sources of destructive power borrowed from the sun, mystic rays to blind or carve up crowds, electric gadgets able to monitor and punish citizens - in short, everything necessary for autocrats to stamp their psychoses over the nations of the world! And who will create these devastating tools? Graduates, that's who! What better way to limit their excesses than to nip them in the grant?"

"You always grasp the big picture, Mina."

"We must ensure that as many students as possible are discouraged from graduating. They must be mercilessly hassled at the fresher stage until they drop out. Naturally, there will be those who refuse to abandon their studies, but I can't be expected to cure the problem, merely to alleviate it. If my Utterly Evil Banker proves a success, and if I can get it to breed, the banks of the future might be staffed by callous sadists, working tirelessly to oppose students. Such is my dream, Doctor Waldman. I am banking on monsters!"

He patted her shoulder admiringly. "That is what Sociology and Reanimation is all about."

Arm in arm, they strolled to the morgue. But they kept their own arms folded.

Lips So Tender
Richard Wright

Sheena burst into the bedsit in a whirl of self-piteous fury. Cheapened and humiliated, she stormed unsteadily into the bathroom to remove her make-up. It had already started to itch where it lined the scars of many repairs.

Off came the eyeliner, which failed to disguise the bulbous mess of a back-street implant too large for her left eye socket. Away came the foundation, which could never quite hide the very faint discolouring of her skin. Earrings, dangling from lobes that matched neither her face nor each other, were yanked off and hurled to the floor.

She had worn no lipstick, so could dismiss that part of her face. That perfect part.

Stripping off her clothes, she stepped into the shower, where her tears would be lost in the downpour. A powerful jet of water massaged what nerves still tingled in her skin, and she leaned back against the wall in despair. They had dismissed her, smiling their cosmetic smiles as they did so. Pretty women, collecting pretty things for their pretty icon. Had they laughed when she left the room? Of course they had.

Enough water. She had not been able to allow herself a drenching since her first accident. There was too much risk of mouldering. A twist stemmed the flow, and she activated the drier. Gentle microwaves drove the moisture from her borrowed flesh, sterilising tissues before they could begin the process of decomposition. When the green light flashed at the base of the shower, she turned it off and stepped out, reaching for her formaldehyde-laced deodorant and coating her body with a fine mist. Done, she dropped the tin to the floor and began to cry.

For a time she stood before the full-length mirror on the wall, her rage drowned, her tears now of shame. Her body, which might have been beautiful given the chance, hunched at her from the frame. Too many grafts, bought cheaply and applied inexpertly, marred a body not yet eighteen.

On her ninth birthday, her father had plowed his car, with the entire family inside, through the glass of a bus shelter and into a wall. There had been money enough for only one surgery, at discount rates. Unselfish at the last, perhaps guilt-ridden by their sense of responsibility, Sheena's mother and father had accepted death so that she might have life.

What life? She stacked shelves at the supermarket, and only those stocked with packaged foods. She wasn't allowed near anything fresh. Despite there being no risk of contamination, just the sight of her touching those vibrant greens made customers think twice. Boyfriends? With the stitching still visible on her breasts, she was too embarrassed to even consider it. Not that they were lining up to make an offer. Even clothed there was no hiding her left leg, three inches shorter than the right. The base of her spine was swollen and twisted from her adolescent efforts to walk evenly. Custom-made shoes, with platforms to balance her out, were beyond the reach of her finances.

Most children fear the monster beneath the bed, or within the wardrobe. Sheena had been terrified of the one that lived in mirrors, knowing that one day it would reach out against the glass and bulge through.

Shaking her head, feeling curiously still inside, she shambled into the sitting room. Naked and horrifying, she dropped onto the ragged couch and stared at stained plaster walls. She was frightened to turn on the television, knowing full well what would dominate the screen, terribly afraid of the feelings that would blossom in her. One person in the world had understood, had reached a hand out to her, had made the world sit up and see her as human. Though Sheena might look like Boris Karloff in "The Triumph of Frankenstein", beneath the poorly selected grafts, she was beautiful. A woman had told her that, once. Now that woman was dead, and Sheena wasn't allowed to do anything about it.

When she was little, her father had called her his little princess. Today, she had been refused the chance to become one.

Curiosity getting the better of her, she picked up the remote control and flooded the television with electric life. Her fears proved founded, for news cameras were panning across one of the many lines of people across the world. The faces were sad, desperate and eager. Thousands of people with something to give. Not one could match the donation Sheena had offered.

As she always did when depression screwed through her, Sheena pulled the album from beneath the couch. Resting it on her bare thighs, one of which was hardly hers at all, she stroked the leather cover with her hands. The cool sensation stirred in her, as always, the memory of understanding. A woman had reached out for her, and the world had been there with a camera. Sheena opened the book.

There was the photograph, this one from the front page of the *Telegraph*. Sheena was in the picture, captured in grotesque, full colour detail. Opposite her, on the bed, was Diana, Princess of Wales. They were holding hands.

Diana had touched her. The epitome of perfection had deigned to reach out and touch the freak. The world had gone wild.

That had been the start. With one gesture, Diana had opened the minds of millions to the plight of those unable to afford the quality of graft accessible to the rich and famous - those like Sheena, whose grafts had been dead tissue rather than the living, vital stuff available to the wealthy. Diana had begun the revolution, and people had listened. Today, the situation was better than ever. Soon, Frankenstein surgery would be free to all.

Yesterday, in a tragic car crash, Diana had met the Reaper. This afternoon, the whole world was ready to reach out a helping hand to this woman.

When Sheena had heard on the news that the brain had been recovered unharmed, she had known what would happen next. She was right. A call had gone up, and the answers were multitudinous. Diana was to be remade. Using the latest micro-suturing techniques, she would he rebuilt one piece at a time, and restored to precisely the way she was before she entered that tunnel.

The matches had to be perfect. Living donations were required, and everybody who thought they resembled her in the slightest way had formed queues outside the nominated assessment centres. Sheena had been among them.

Of course, some of the candidates had been eccentric at best. There had been fat Dianas, transsexual Dianas, Asian Dianas - the curiosities had been endless, but all had been sincere in their offerings.

For eight hours Sheena had queued, perhaps the most curious of all. But anybody looking closely would have seen precisely what she had to offer. Lips. Her perfect lips.

Full and wide, they were the image of Diana's own. One look at the photograph in her lap confirmed it. In it, both she and Diana were smiling shyly. Sheena had been so nervous of meeting royalty, so afraid of marring beauty by her very presence. Diana had worn her customary shyness like a calling card. Each tentative smile mirrored the other.

So Sheena had queued. When at last she had been called,

the interview had lasted only a few minutes.

As the door opened, the three suited ladies behind the desk had looked up expectantly, eyes welcoming, hopes high. When Sheena stepped through there had been a frozen moment as they stared, not quite believing what they were seeing. Then they had looked at one another, elegant eyebrows twitching. One had gestured for her to sit, then the questions had come forth. They were polite, those queries, well meaning but per-functory. Sheena had been asked for her address, and it had been dutifully written down. The charade had been obvious from the moment she walked in. Her offer had not been even momentarily considered.

She had pointed out her lips, eagerly pulling forth the pho-tograph, hoping desperately that they would see. They had nod-ded vacantly, doubtless wondering about the next supplicant, or the one that had gone before. Not for one moment had they taken her seriously.

A tear rolled from her one eye as she remembered the hu-miliation of leaving. Everybody who had gone before her had spent at least fifteen minutes being interviewed and examined. Sheena had not been worth even five. Limping back along that sun-soaked queue, head down and tears flowing, she had felt the pressure of a hundred smirks bearing down on her, making her tiny and her rage huge.

Looking at the picture brought back the only time in re-cent years that she had felt the opposite of those feelings. When

Diana Windsor had chosen her bed to sit on, when the most important person in the world had smiled kindly on her, hardly seeing the poorly matched grafts, Sheena had known that she really was special. All she wanted now was to give something back. If Diana wore her lips, it was a gift she would carry with her forever, just like the gift she had given Sheena. The gift of assurance.

Now three women had made that giving impossible, with their condescending, knowing smiles. Their imperfect, painted lips.

Perhaps it was that stillness she felt, a calm where her anger at being scorned met her memory of meeting Diana, that allowed her to make the leap she did then.

Slowly, her head came up from where she still looked at the page. Her eyes fixed on nothing, gleaming with a strange, distressing hope. Rising slowly, feeling the muscles in her back pull trampoline-taut as her left leg pushed down to meet the ground, she made for her stationery drawer. There was a padded envelope there, lined on the inside with plastic bubbles. Perfect.

Pulling out a pen, she lifted the telephone book from the shelf and found the address she needed. Scribbling it on the front of the envelope, she next took a piece of paper from a pile and sat at the desk.

Cool wood pressed against clammy buttocks as she began to write. Carefully, knowing that her chances depended upon the clarity of each vital stroke, she carved her suggestion in words and sentences. Half an hour passed, then an hour. When she was done, ninety minutes had hurtled by, yet the letter was still confined to that one, crisp sheet of paper.

Sheena stared at her work, watery wonder in her eyes. It was beautiful, a request both stark and poignant. That it had come from her own twisted fingers, her scarred soul, filled her heart with a blossoming sense of wonder.

On the outside she was calm still, and she folded the letter neatly in two and slid it into the envelope. Where was the mask?

Under her bed she found it, a childish whimsy with new significance. Her home made mask, cut from a huge poster she had bought of Diana shortly after the hospital visit. String pulled it taut around her head as she slipped it on. When she turned to look in the mirror, she was pleased.

Only one eye had been cut from the picture, allowing Sheena's good right eye to shine through. The other orb, squint and bulging, she preferred to leave covered by Diana's own. The mouth of the mask was a carefully traced hole, and with her smile fixed right, you would hardly know it was missing at all. Where Diana's lips would have been, instead were Sheena's. It was uncanny.

Almost uncanny. Marring the picture were the slightly dis-coloured caps covering her shattered front teeth. Those very caps had been what soured the fantasy and made her put the mask aside many months ago. Now they acted as the final confirmation. In a daze of revelation, she lurched back to the haphazard desk, scattering papers in the search for her final tool.

It was hiding beneath a pile of discarded bank statements, gleaming, beautiful in the sepia evening light draped across the desk. She reached for it, hope shaped in steel, her oasis.

Unrelenting, without compassion, it jutted from the fist she clenched around it as though it grew from her own flesh. Though her eyes were caught by it, weak and ensnared, her feet knew the off-kilter path back to the mirror, and she found herself there without conscious direction. Then she saw herself, and the letter opener was momentarily forgotten. The woman she had always wanted to be stared back at her. The monster had been chased away by a princess.

A princess who was in terrible, terrible danger. Suddenly, Sheena wore a suit of shining armour, and she intended to rescue beauty.

She raised the letter opener, touching flesh, finding the place where her skin blended with her upper lip. Gently she pushed, and the blade kissed her more tenderly, more deeply, than any boy ever had or would.

Blood filled her mouth surprisingly fast, even before she felt the pain, and she opened her mouth to let it run out. She heard it spatter the floor, but didn't look. There was no pulling her gaze from the mirror, no escaping the fascination of Diana and her steel lover.

Pushing further inwards, she found her top gum, and that

was where the pain must have lived, for it shot along her teeth like glass wire, slicing invisibly through sensitive roots, finding her brain and pooling there, eventually overflowing and spilling down her spine.

Yet her hand was steady, and her head did not flinch. The princess was in danger, and Sheena the weak was gone.

She dragged the blade, slitting flesh with terrible precision. Tracing her mouth, she relieved it of an upper lip. At the end she almost ruined everything, for her lip dropped from her mouth completely. For a second it hung from a last stretched strand of tissue, but then this strand broke, sending the moist meat hurtling toward the floor.

During the cutting, during that terrible pain, her body had become stone, rigid against the shuddering agony that tried to spoil the accuracy of her work. At the last, that was almost her undoing, for breaking that frozen stance proved almost impossible. Yet the lip was crashing to the grime of her wooden floorboards, where there lurked bacteria and worse, and she could not allow her prize to be sullied. So she folded at the waist, extending her free hand in a poetic curve that somehow found the mark. Her lip dropped into her palm with a moist smack.

Breathing a gargling sigh of relief, then coughing damply thanks to the blood that trickled determinedly down her trachea, Sheena turned back to the mirror.

What she saw made her step back in fear, for the monster had returned with vengeful malice. Its teeth were bared in a permanent crimson snarl, its long blond hair smeared against its chin. Any resemblance to the Queen of Hearts was perfunctory at best. That, though, was the surface only. Sheena took a deep, fulfilling breath, ignoring the chill of pain that froze the face beneath the drenched mask. If there was one lesson to remember, always, it was that this surface was nothing more than the place where she began.

So she cut again, letting the pain fill her lower jaw, her chin, her neck. Carefully, she captured her lower lip in her cupped palm, horribly afraid of contaminating this glorious material, polluting it before it could serve its purpose.

Light-headed with stinging joy and blood loss, Sheena stepped towards her desk, simultaneously stepping back in time and forgetting how to walk on mismatched legs. The ground was lower than it should have been, and she stumbled. Lips flew from her palm as she wheeled to catch her balance. With a shriek, she watched them part company. One, her upper, slapped against the wall, trailing an arc of scarlet drops behind it. It stayed there for a nauseating moment, then began to slip down over damp stains and dust. Her lower lip vanished beneath the desk.

Sobbing, Sheena followed it, dropping to her knees and scrabbling frantically in her search. It was hidden behind a chair leg, a scarlet slug, and she scooped it up, fresh sorrow in her eyes. Breathing hard, she pushed up, cracking her head on the desk as she went. Seeing stars, she whirled for the other lip, now smiling halfway down the wall. She reached it, plucking it from the trail it was blazing, and held it next to the other in her hand.

Were they tainted? Would they still suffice? Not knowing the answer (but fearing deeply that she really did), she carried them carefully in her cupped hands, an offering to one far worthier than she. Picking up the envelope, she slipped them inside to nestle beside her perfect, plaintive letter.

Extending her tongue proved difficult, for she kept trying to open the ghost-lips she felt beneath the white pain, but eventually she sealed the letter. Dazed now, she dressed in clumsy, careless movements, making a scarecrow of herself

Tenderly, tucking the envelope into her coat pocket, Sheena opened the door. Though she felt faint, she also felt the rapture of a debt repaid, a good deed done. With that sense of worth in her heart, so very close to that which Diana had given her long ago, she left the bedsit, still wearing the soggy, savaged face of a woman who had cared.

Dying for a Living
Paul Lewis

I was listening to Lennon's new single on the radio, thinking he sounded so much better before he got himself murdered, when Billy Harper threw down the paper and told me he was going to change my life in a way I would not believe.

It should have been one of those defining moments which remain etched in the memory forever. *Should* have been. Truth was, I was tuned out. Too busy getting myself mentally prepared to deal with the prospect of dying to worry about anything else.

"Read it," he said, jabbing his cigar at the crumpled paper on the table.

"Fuck off, Billy." The man should have known better than to distract me before a fight. He was my manager after all. "Save it for later. If there is a later."

His laugh expelled cigar smoke and provoked a chest rattle which sounded way too loud in the small dressing room. "Don't give me that. You'll have that fucking upstart's head on a pike before the first round is over."

I grunted noncommittally. Of course Harper was going to bullshit me. That was his job. Me, I tended not to take anything for granted. Couple of years earlier *I'd* been the fucking upstart. The guy I'd hacked to death had no doubt been assured by his manager that he'd have my head on a pike before the end of Round One. Happens all the time. You ply your trade and take your chances and if you are really good and really lucky you can pull down more cash than most people earn in several lifetimes.

But even the very best of us can lose. And then you can never be as good again.

Harper waved the paper at me. "Go on, read it. You could be rich."

"I could be dead if you don't leave me alone," I snapped back, starting to get seriously pissed off with him. "Like I said, save it for later."

He muttered and swore but let it go. He was eager, all right. So eager that he started badgering me again the second the fight was over. The Resurrectionists were working on the kid, who'd been tougher than I'd expected and had earned the thumbs-up the crowd had given him. I was glad they hadn't forced me to go for the brain-kill. The kid was hooked up to a portable Victor and his body arched and bucked when they threw the switch. To the victor the spoils. To the loser the Victor. That's an in-joke in the trade.

Most managers would have waited outside the arena, out of courtesy if nothing else. Not Harper. They'd only just finished stitching my arm, me sitting cross-legged and dog tired on the red-splattered floor, when he squatted before me, holding that damn paper up in front of my face. "This could be it," he said gleefully, words garnished with cigar smoke. "Your shot at the big time."

I was forced to admit defeat. Harper is by far the most tenacious bastard I have ever known. I sighed and snatched the newspaper off him, grimacing as the stitches in my arm tugged and the pain started to bite. "What're you talking about?"

"Entertainment section. Your hero made the news again."

He didn't have to say the name. Johnny fucking Steel. Lord of the Gladiators, or so he insisted on calling himself. Just thinking about him made my blood boil. I couldn't look at his picture without wanting to tear it to pieces. There was something about him I simply could not stand. Arrogance? He had it in spades. But that's not what bothered me. Fact was, the TV gladiators were a pathetic imitation of the real thing. And by "the real thing" I mean those of us who fought at street level in a world where there were no rules. We didn't have the safety nets that Steel and the other glam-boys knew were there to fall back on. We felt pain. They didn't. The inhibitors injected into them took care of that. Oh, sure, you could be killed on TV. Cardinal rule. An audience that bayed for blood must always be sated. The main difference was, you could never be brain-killed. Believe me, that was one hell of a fucking difference. If you died on TV you knew you'd be back. Whenever I entered the arena I was aware it could be for the very last time. I once read somewhere that Steel was the highest-paid athlete in the country. Bullshit. He was no athlete. He was a celebrity. Steel earned his fortune from a bastardised, watered-down version of the sport I loved.

Granted, I did all right financially out of the fights, but that wasn't what it was about, not in my case. Money was a means to an end. If it was all that mattered to me, I could have let some rich guy fill me with carcinogenics or AIDS, then sit back and watch me die. Shit like that goes on, believe it or not. Thanks, but no thanks. I fight because I want to fight, to prove something, if only to myself. Don't ask me what. Unless you've stood in that arena and felt your heart beat like the countdown to your own death, you'll never understand. It makes you feel sick with fear but wildly exhilarated, all at once. For Steel, though, it was nothing to do with valour, the spirit of combat or whatever else it is that drives us street fighters.

He lived for the money, pure and simple. The sport itself meant nothing.

And that, I suppose, is why I wanted to kill him.

"Not here," I said, gripping the paper with enough force to tear holes in it. I pushed myself slowly and painfully to my feet and stalked off towards my dressing room, Harper following close behind. He had the good sense to keep his mouth shut.

Johnny Steel is a man you approach with caution even when he's in a good mood. So when he's angry you would be wise to stay well clear. Fortunately it is not this reporter the Lord of the Gladiators is angry with. Rather it is the other gladiators. The ones who call themselves street fighters. Their dismissal of the TV sportsmen as overpaid second-raters has been well-publicised. Johnny Steel and his fellows have always refused to rise to the bait. Until now. As far as Steel is concerned, enough is enough. He has had his fill of insults. And, boy, is he about to start hitting back.

"Nothing but fucking envy," he says, jabbing the air with his cigarette to reinforce the point, though the look on his face is reinforcement enough. "They see us making the money so they talk us down because it's the only way they know of getting back at us. Truth is, any one of us could take the best of them any day and crucify him. They're the second-raters, not us. They know it. And it kills them."

"Jesus Christ," I said. "What sort of shit is this?"

"Read on," Harper answered from behind a cloud of smoke. "It gets better."

Reluctantly, I turned back to the paper and scanned through the flowery prose until it was all I could do not to scrunch the paper up and hurl it into the corner. My mind drifted. I saw the words but did not absorb them. And then I saw my name.

... I ask with some trepidation if Steel rates any of the so-called street fighters and he shakes his head. "There's one guy I saw fight once. Steve Cage. Word is he's on the up. I tell you, he was okay but that was all. Plenty of strength but no grace. No fucking finesse at all. Calls himself a sportsman and he

doesn't even smoke!"

That pissed me off. Maybe I am anti-social, but it's a free country and if I don't want to smoke, I'm not going to. I know everyone goes on about the health benefits of having your lungs changed every couple of years but I don't have much left of what I was born with and I like to hang on to anything that has gone the full distance. Besides, this whole pro-smoking thing is getting out of hand. In California it's compulsory to light up in bars and restaurants. Mark my words, before long it'll be an offence not to be seen smoking in a public place. Fuck you, Steel, I thought. My hands shook with anger as I finished the piece.

"So not even the best of them can pose any threat to you?"

"No fucking way," Steel says with a confident smile. "Hey, if Cage or any of those other losers want to try it on, all they gotta do is ask."

I let the paper fall to the floor. Harper looked at me. "Well?"

"That guy is in serious need of a lesson in humility."

He grinned around his cigar. "Want to be the teacher?"

"Billy," I said, "what are you talking about?"

"I told you I was going to change your life for ever. And I will. I can fix it for you. Put you up against Johnny Steel. It'll be the fight of the century."

"Yeah, sure," I said. "And exactly how are you going to manage that?"

"I've arranged us a meeting," he said. "With Harvey Moore."

If Steel was the Lord of the Gladiators, then Harvey Moore was the king. Well into his sixties, bald and seriously over-weight, he looked just like someone's favourite uncle but he wielded more power than most people could possibly imagine. In an era of turgid soaps and dreary sitcoms, it was Moore who galvanised millions of viewers by bringing his version of the gladiators into their homes. In those days, don't forget, street fighting was borderline illegal and mainly confined to old ware-houses and closed-down factories where the only real money to be made was from gambling. Moore, a small-time TV pro-ducer, saw his first fight while making a documentary on the sport and was immediately hooked. He had the format for his show worked out in a matter of hours, and was even savvy enough to throw in a couple of restrictions to stop the execu-tives from getting too twitchy. Like the use of chemical inhibi-tors to prevent what he described as unnecessary suffering, as well as the ban on brain death without which he knew the show would never get the green light.

The rest is entertainment history. Gladiators became more than a television show. It was a genuine entertainment phe-nomenon, making Harvey Moore a very rich man, what with the rights and the merchandising empire the programme spawned. And he was sitting in the restaurant opposite me, wiping his lips with a napkin with one hand and signalling the waiter for more wine with the other. Until now we had made nothing but small talk. Actually, Moore and Harper had done most of the talking while I said as little as possible, feeling hopelessly out of my depth. But once the meal was over it was obviously time to get down to business. Moore looked me straight in the eye and asked matter-of-factly, "So, you want to kill Johnny Steel?"

The bluntness of the question caught me out. "Maybe," I said lamely.

"Don't listen to him!" Harper butted in. "He wants it more than anything."

"Then here's your chance," said Moore, lowering his voice conspiratorially. "First I want your absolute assurance that anything I tell you goes no further."

"You've got it," I said, suddenly intrigued. Johnny Steel was a cash cow. He had taken Gladiators viewing figures to an all-time high and had swollen Moore's already-considerable fortune at the same time. Yet there we were, discussing how badly I wanted him dead with the casualness of a conversation about the weather.

Moore glanced around the restaurant. He needn't have bothered. The place was very exclusive, a hang-out for executive types, and the tables were spaced well apart so that deals could be struck in private. "Well, here's the thing," he said once he was satisfied we would not be overheard. "I made Johnny Steel. Made him. Saw him brawling in a bar one night, drunk out of his mind. Handy with his fists and a good-looking boy as well. I knew straight away he was my new Gladiator. All he needed was grooming. Yeah, I made him all right. The trouble is, I created a monster."

"I thought you two were bosom buddies," I said, remembering the publicity shots I'd seen of them together. They were always shaking hands or hugging.

"Listen, kid, this is showbiz. Entertainment. Fiction. Seeing is believing. You want to know the truth? Johnny Steel is a fucking psychopath. The only reason I've kept him on is because he's big with the audiences, and audiences are everything in this game. Now, though, it's getting out of hand. He wants more money all the time. More women, more drugs, more champagne, more fast cars, you name it. The man is costing me almost as much as the fucking show's making me. Now the bastard is demanding co-executive producer status. Can you believe that? Fucking upstart wants to be on equal footing with me. Me. On the show I created, for Christ's sake."

I almost smiled at the anachronism. People stopped believing in Christ a long time ago, once they realised they too could rise from the dead, only without the three-day wait. But Moore looked so genuinely angry and hurt that I kept my face straight.

"Okay," I said. "You've made your point. Why not tell him to walk?"

"Because if Steel goes, half the audience goes with him." Moore drained his wine glass and a passing waiter swiftly detoured to refill it. "You can't just sack a man that popular. You have to find another way. Which is where you come in."

I looked askance at Harper. He winked. "Keep talking," I said.

"You fight Steel and make him look like second-rate shit."

"Shouldn't be difficult," I said, unable to resist the jibe.

Moore, though, did not appreciate the joke. "Listen, I know you street fighters think you're the fucking best, but take it from me that Johnny Steel is no slouch. I said he was a psycho, and I meant it. Once he's in the arena and that gong sounds, he's more animal than human. But I've seen you in action, too, Cage, and you're a handful yourself. You can beat him. Once the audience sees he's not some fucking invincible superman, I can ditch him without worrying about my ratings hitting basement level."

"Sounds logical," I said. "What's in it for me?"

"One million if you win. Two million if you make him look so bad that the audience go for the brain-kill." He must have seen the look of astonishment on my face because he grinned widely. "That's right. Brain-kill. I'm changing the rules."

"And you believe Steel is going to accept that?"

Moore nodded. "Taken care of. Of course, if you win you'll be our new Gladiators champ. You'll be expected to fight on TV for at least two series. Oh, and before you reject that out of hand, remember you will be allowed to make changes."

"Such as?"

"Whatever you want. After all, you'll be the guy who bested the Lord of the Gladiators. Who's gonna mess with you? We'll give you anything you ask for."

"Assuming I actually do beat Steel, that is."

"Don't worry," Moore said happily, knowing I was hooked. "You'll beat him."

I'd expected the fight to create a stir when it was announced, but could never have imagined the level of hype it inspired. Every newspaper, every TV station in the country had something on it every day of the week. Coming from relative obscurity, I suddenly found myself a household name. Hated because I dared to take up their hero's challenge, and courted because there was always the possibility I could win and nobody wanted me to be pissed with them if I did. I was forced to quit my apartment and hide out in a classy hotel, where Moore put me up under a false name and with security tighter than a duck's back passage. I spent my time watching television, calling room service or staring at the wall, feeling bored.

Then came the eve of the fight, and Moore invited the cream of the nation's press to a conference during which he introduced me and Steel. The two of us were separated by Moore, Harper and Steel's business manager, whose name I can't even remember. Just as well we were apart, otherwise we'd have been at each other's throats before the night was out and I was under strict instructions to play it cool. Let Steel come across as the villain, was what Moore had told me. Get them on your side.

So I sat there, looking all benign and serene while Steel ranted about how he'd had just about enough of my smart-mouth insults and he was gonna teach me a lesson I was never gonna forget. He kept standing up and jabbing his finger to-wards me over the heads of the guys sat between us. I simply sat there and stared out at the assembled reporters, shaking my head almost imperceptibly as if I felt sorry for the poor guy. Truth was, I wanted to stand up and smash my fist straight into that perfect fucking face of his, but I swallowed my pride and my temper and held still. And it worked. By damn, it worked. I could sense their attention start to drift from Steel's hysterics and to me as the minutes ticked away.

"Mr Cage," a voice called from the back when Moore si-lenced Steel long enough to invite questions from the floor. "Do you think Mr Steel will kill you?"

"No," I said. "But if he does, so what? You always get brought back on TV."

"Just hold on a second," Moore said. "That's not true, not this time. For this fight we are suspending the rule against brain-kill."

His words were drowned out by a babble of excited voices, and he waited for silence before continuing. "Mr Steel has not only agreed to this condition, he insists on it. He wants to dispel the myth once and for all that the street fighters are braver than their TV counterparts. It also shows his absolute confidence in the outcome."

"And the pain inhibitors?" another voice called. "Are they being ditched, too?"

The question, like the one before it, could not have been better timed. Not surprising, as the speakers had been paid enough to get their timing spot on.

Moore shook his head. "It wouldn't be fair on our viewers if we had to stop the fight every time someone was hurt. No, the challenge will continue uninterrupted until one of the gladiators is unable to continue. And then the audience will decide. A three-way choice. The loser lives. The loser dies. Or the loser dies forever."

Steel leapt to his feet again. "Then enjoy your last night on earth, Cage," he yelled at me. I smiled and said nothing. Was he in for a fucking shock.

The gong went and Steel came at me like a man possessed, his sword striking my shield with such force that my arm was almost numb in next to no time. It took every ounce of my strength and concentration to parry the strikes, my ability to defend myself hampered by the fact that I was distracted by the glare of the studio lights and the deafening noise of the crowd. This is what they had expected, and this is what Johnny Steel was giving them, a trademark demonstration of furious aggression which would beat me into submission and win the fight for him before it had properly started.

At least, that's what he thought.

I took everything he could throw at me those first few minutes, then began a few counterstrikes, nothing too obvious to start with, just enough to show him, and more importantly the crowd, that I was no pushover and if victory was what he wanted then by fuck he was going to have to work for it. My sword was light but lethal, Japanese, the metal folded and beaten countless times by a master craftsman. It was a beautiful weapon, one I could never have afforded in a million years had not Moore footed the bill. He was, as he put it, protecting his investment. It gleamed as it flashed through the air and would have sliced parts of Steel clean away had he not used his shield with more skill than I had given him credit for. By now the crowd had sensed their hero was not going to have an easy time of it. All of a sudden it seemed not so many of them were screaming for Steel. I heard my own name being called a couple of times, then the yelling was equally split between the two of us.

Don't think for a moment that this opening salvo was just strike and parry. Both of us had our fair share of wounds. Nothing too serious, but the blood was starting to flow and it was strange not to feel any pain. On the other hand, I felt comfortable and relaxed, and energetic enough, despite the ferocity of Steel's initial onslaught, to fight all night if that's what it took. But, of course, it didn't come to that. Sensing the crowd's respect for me, grudging at first but growing as the minutes ticked away, I began to step up my own attack, using the footwork that Moore's team had drilled into me over the past few weeks, spinning through the air like a dervish, nicking Steel's flesh here and there, tormenting him. I had a strategy: to make him look clumsy and undisciplined and at the same time make myself look agile and cool. It worked. Having to keep up with me was a drain on his strength, and the blood loss soon began to take its toll. He became clumsy, throwing his sword around with no real purpose, and stumbling once or twice as he came after me. I maintained my poise, using the tip of my sword like a probe, opening up veins on his arms and legs, and once lopping off the tip of his ear. His face was a smudged mask of blood and sweat, and behind the mask there was fear. Probably something he had never experienced before but a sensation with which I was well acquainted. I knew what he was going through, how it felt to know you were close to death, and I had no pity for him. Neither did the audience. As Steel's performance became increasingly pathetic, they began to boo and hiss. I milked this sudden turnaround for all it was worth, adding a few flourishes here and there, each greeted with a howl of approval.

Finally the moment came to finish it. To prolong Steel's suffering would have made me come across as sadistic, and I could not allow that to happen. There was a fine line between humiliating him and torturing him, and to cross it would have cost me the audience's respect. I sensed when the time was right, then rolled beneath his blade as he swung it at me, leapt to my feet behind him and slashed my sword across the base of his spine. Not even the inhibitors could stop that one from stinging. Steel screamed and went suddenly limp, collapsing to the ground like a discarded toy.

Breathing heavily, I stood astride his writhing body and threw my shield across the arena, deafened by the roar which echoed around the studio. Then I faced the audience and raised my sword high. Fired up with blood lust, they poked at the computer terminals fixed into the seats in front of them to electronically signal their verdict. It took a few seconds, which to me seemed to last an eternity. At last the giant electronic scoreboard overhead flickered into life and the words I had dreamed of suddenly appeared.

Brain death.

I did not waste a second. "No more Mister Nice Guy," I spat at Steel, before burying my sword deep in the back of his skull.

That was five years ago, and I guess there's no need for me

to go into what happened after that. But in case you've been out of the country, let me summarise. Steel became a forgotten man. I took his place. The ultimate sportsman, as one tabloid dubbed me. Moore had told me I would have to stay with Gladiators a couple of years, and I'm still there. They wouldn't let me make any changes, despite Moore's promise, so brain death is still banned. I was pissed at first, but when I realised how much money I was going to make out of the show, I quickly learned to live with it. So to speak. I guess some people say I've turned myself into the kind of monster that Moore created when he gave Johnny Steel his life and, finally, his death. But I'm way too careful to let that happen to me. You see, I haven't told you everything about the deal we made.

Moore had masterminded the whole thing, from taking Steel to see me fight one night to feeding him the lines which subsequently appeared in the newspaper interview. And when Moore told me that I would beat Steel, he wasn't just showing confidence in me. The injection they gave Steel before the fight was not just to block the pain. Oh, sure, the inhibitors were present, but so was a shitload of chemicals designed to progressively dull his senses and reduce his speed and reflexes as the fight went on. I know I could have beaten him without help. I know it. But Moore wanted to be absolutely sure.

You don't cross a guy like him and expect to live.

So I got myself a little souvenir of the fight.

I keep it in a preservative-filled glass jar in my private

office.

And now, whenever I feel the urge to demand a pay rise or a few more perks, I lock eyes with Johnny Steel and remind myself not to let my head grow as big as his.

Monsters
John Moralee

"Have you met Professor Frankenstein?"

"No, no. He works here?"

"But of course! He's the head of research. It's a tightly held secret, naturally. What with the war and everything …"

"The war …"

"Come, come, follow me …"

EXPERIMENTATION ROOM 52

There was a smell in the air like ozone at the beach. I breathed it in with relish until I realised what was causing the smell. There were hundreds of Jews and Negroes in light green tanks, floating in a preservative that seemed to glow. They were all wired up from head to toe with electrodes and optical cables. Blue-white flashes of electricity violently jerked the bodies. Computers recorded the information gathered with a quiet hum. Some of the experiments involved pieces- fragments of humans somehow kept alive against the odds. I could see a man sliced precisely in half writhing in the current like a dying fish. Another was no more than a brain connected to a spinal column. There was every variation in between. Curious, I approached the nearest tank and tapped the Plexiglas. It had to be at least twenty centimetres thick. I leapt backwards when a mottled face slammed against the Plexiglas and the eyes, such sad brown eyes, pleaded for mercy. He was a man stripped of flesh, his muscles exposed. The mouth opened and a gasp of trapped oxygen blurted out and bubbled on the surface. I knew what the man was saying. Help. Help me. He was no older than I was. But he was a Jew. I knew they were all subhuman, worse than animals, but –

"Dr Kessler, we don't have time to stand around gawking. Professor Frankenstein is waiting."

I blinked and focused on Dr Bauer. He had been my tutor at medical college in New Berlin. He was a plump blonde man with the physical appearance of a man in his early thirties, though he was closer to eighty. He'd recently acquired the body of a brave SS commandant who had been killed on the Eastern Front, his brain ripped to shreds by a Russian headseeker. Stalin was using inhumane methods to kill our soldiers' minds but keep their bodies for his own army. In 1945 the Americans had nuked Berlin and Bonn, forcing us underground. They'd expected us to give up, but then we'd stolen the atomic secrets and nuked New York and Moscow. Before more cities were wiped out in a tit-for-tat escalation, the Axis and Allied powers agreed to ban atomic weapons. Stalemate, of a sort. For fifty years the conventional war had raged on sixteen fronts in the disputed territories. The Allies controlled the Americas, Australia, South Africa and Russia … while we controlled Europe, Middle East and China and North Africa. Now it looked like we would lose North Africa … We had to fight back. That was where the institute came in. And Bauer. He was a genetics genius. He probably knew more about the subject than Frankenstein. I'd known Bauer as a witty and caring man, always with time for his students, unlike many of the doctors. His star student, I'd enjoyed dinners with his family. I'd always known he did top-secret research for the Reich, but until that moment, I had not known what his research entailed. It looked like torture, simple torture. Somehow, I had imagined he used mindless corpses for his experiments. How naïve! I was twenty-four years old and I knew nothing. By calling me Dr Kessler and not Christian, Bauer was showing his annoyance with my childish behaviour.

I did not know this man at all.

He was a monster.

Keeping my disgust to myself, I followed him towards an office. I vowed I would behave like an SS officer. I was here to help the war effort. If a few subhumans had to suffer ... well, that was a sacrifice that had to be made ...

Thousands of eyes watched me.

Thousands of pleading eyes.

Frankenstein studied me with his two dissimilar eyes. They were both transplants – one blue, one brown. His face was the same as I'd seen in my textbooks, handsome with a touch of arrogance to the lips and eyebrows. As I shook his hand I noticed the tiny scars around his hairline, signs he'd had his face grafted onto a different skull. His hand was delicate, like a woman's. The skin was as smooth as silk with no lifelines – it was regenerated tissue. "So this is our new recruit, Stefan?" (Bauer nodded.) "Welcome, welcome! Do you like what you see?" He waved at the tanks seen through the window of his office.

"It's ... different, sir."

"Different! I'll say! Quite a few newcomers lose their lunch on seeing the experiments. Personally, I think there is nothing more beautiful than the human body in all its forms. The experiments you've seen out there are fairly rudimentary survival tests compared with the cutting edge science in D Section. We're trying to see how far the human body can be reduced before it can't be resurrected in a usable format. Basic stuff, but necessary. In D Section we really let rip with the latest developments. That's where you will be working in six months, after your internship. Believe me, all the things you learned in medical school are a mere prelude to what you will learn here."

"May I ask what you do in D Section?"

"You may ask," Frankenstein said, laughing. "But you don't yet have the clearance level to receive an answer. You should know that."

It was a rebuke. I felt sweat trickle down my neck. Bauer came to my defence.

"I told you he was inquisitive, Victor," Bauer said. "Christian is particularly interested in memory recovery techniques."

It had long been a problem that a dead person's brain decayed through cell death even in the short time it took to get it to a resurrection chamber. On the battlefield it was a particular problem. Cell death was reversible using Frankenstein's bio-animation therapy, but, inevitably, memories were lost. Death was not a barrier, but a hurdle. Sometimes you hit that hurdle and tripped over. When that happened, a patient often lost years of memories. It happened in thirty percent of revivals. For a man like Frankenstein it was acutely embarrassing. Having relatives and friends who'd lost years of memories, I wanted to do anything in my power to solve the problem. I had some theories about retrieving memories from their associated memories, which was like constructing a copy of a damaged building using the architect's plans. The result wouldn't be identical to the original, but it would be as near as possible. Frankenstein probed my theories for ten minutes, then, satisfied I knew what I was talking about, he left me alone with Bauer.

The internship began.

"Dad?" I said. He was awake, I was sure. His chest had a different rhythm when he was awake. He was in an airy room in the Mengele VA Hospital, lying in a bed with blue cotton sheets and a rubber mattress. His eyes were open, staring up at the ceiling. Someone had brought some roses into the room to give it a better smell. I sat down and gently propped my father's head up so he could see me – if he was, as I suspected, awake. Sometimes it was hard to tell. Ten years ago, a Soviet headseeker had burrowed through his skull into his cerebral cortex. It had not exploded, as it was supposed to do, but it had left him in this persistent vegetative state. If he had not been a Party member, his body would have been taken for recycling. I would not let that happen.

"Dad, what should I do?"

He did not answer.

"Should I work for them? Tell me! Tell me!"

His breathing was as regular as a heartbeat. I wiped away some crusted dribble with a handkerchief. I stayed for an hour. Then the nurse came and asked me to leave. At the doorway, I looked back at my father.

His eyes … were they pleading?

I made a deep incision in the man's chest. He was drugged, but he was watching. He could feel no pain, but his eyes widened. Bauer, standing behind my shoulder, said, "Go on, finish it. It's only a Negro." I opened the chest with a steel clamp, spreading the ribs so I could get access to the internal organs. Blood oozed over my fingers. The man's eyes fluttered and the ECG readings blinked in warning. Fast. Fast. Fast. I removed the liver with a laser scalpel. Then I stitched up the man and put him in a tank.

I checked on him each day, watching his progress.

He died eight days later.

The experiment was a success.

I spent time in other labs. There was the radiation lab, where people were treated with various levels of alpha, beta and gamma radiation to test the body's tolerance. There was the cross-species lab, where people were integrated with monkeys, dogs, bears, pigs, horses. The hybrids created didn't live long. Luckily. There was the mutant lab, which contained ten thousand embryos in gestation tanks. The scientists were trying to make superhumans with extra arms, eyes, muscles ... Next door was the cloning lab, but that was shut down after a biohazard accident killed sixteen technicians. The accident never appeared in the newspapers. I was forbidden from discussing anything I saw or did inside the institute. I would have sounded like a lunatic if I had. Besides which, all employees were given random loyalty tests under sodium pentathol.

"That Jew Spielberg's made another movie that's been banned. Honestly, I don't think anyone would notice his rotten movies if they didn't get banned. That Jew Spielberg!" Anita said "Jew" like it was his first name.

I looked up from my breakfast cereal. "What's it about?"

"What's it about? What do you think?"

"I don't know."

Anita sighed. "It's about us. He claims there are hundreds of 'death camps' all over the world where we kill Jews and use their bodies to replace ones lost in battle. What nonsense is that? Everyone knows the Jews have their own country, paid for by German citizens like you and me. We keep the Jews! We let those animals live in good homes! And yet he – that Jew Spielberg – that lousy Jew – he has the nerve – the bloody nerve – to suggest we're lying. American propaganda doesn't even stick with the facts! Spielberg claims millions of Jews have been killed. It's ridiculous. Where's the proof? I've seen the resettlement camps on the television. The Fuhrer has been to visit to ensure the Jews are treated well. That Jew Spielberg! Bah!"

Her tirade frightened me. I had never seen her so upset. Her spittle hit the table. Her face was all twisted and ugly.

"You don't think the death camps are real?"

"No. Of course not. Do you?"

"Well –"

"What?"

I'd seen the television pictures, too. There had always seemed something odd about them. They always showed Orthodox Jews in black clothes with long black beards. You never saw any ordinary Jews. Only the ones in black. Once or twice I'd thought they looked like Germans dressed up.

I thought of the institute. Bauer told me the people they - we - used had fatal diseases. They were volunteers. They would die anyway, he said. We were just keeping them alive a little longer.

But what if they were perfectly healthy until we experimented on them?

Was everything I knew about history a lie?

"Christian, what's wrong?"

"Nothing," I lied. "I'm just thinking about work. Today I finish my internship."

"Congratulations," she said. She leant over the table and kissed me. That Jew Spielberg. I pulled away. I ate my cereal in silence, looking at the woman I'd once loved, seeing a stranger.

SECTION D: AUTHORISED PERSONNEL LEVEL 001 ONLY

Bauer patted my shoulder as we approached the steel doors and the ominous-looking guards. "Don't look so grumpy, Christian. You made it. The grunt work is over. You've truly impressed me these last six months. I've had many students during my career, but none had your talent. I have a feeling your name will be written in history alongside Hippocrates and Galen. Welcome to the future."

With bravado, he slid his card over the door's lock. It blinked from red to green. The door opened and we passed through before it closed. We were inside a room as large as an aircraft hangar. What looked like prison cells covered one wall up to the ceiling. There were some fairly large buildings within the room. Technicians and scientists in white lab coats were crowded around monitors and computers. Frankenstein was talking with a group of SS officers. He looked angry. He dismissed them and beckoned for us to approach. "Bureaucrats! Always wanting more paperwork." He shook his head. "I see you've brought your protege, Stefan? How did he do with the grunt work?"

"He passed with flying colours."

"I wouldn't have expected anything less." Frankenstein swivelled around and walked off. I assumed I had to go after him. Bauer didn't follow.

"This," Frankenstein said, sweeping his arms in the general direction of the cells, "is the tool that will defeat our enemies. I'll show you what my genius has created."

I had an uneasy feeling as we went into a small building. It looked like a hospital ward, except the patients were wearing helmets hooked up to a mainframe computer. There was a machine that looked like a diving bell. A man with his head shaved was sitting inside.

"What is it?"

"Everything you see here merely monitors the thoughts of the subjects. The machine you see is a cerebral analyser – it translates thoughts into computer images we can see on these screens." I watched the man's thoughts displayed. He could see us looking at him – and we could "see" what he saw. The things he heard – our voices – came out as text messages.

Another screen displayed the man's inner voice, his stream of consciousness. It was mostly gibberish.

"The man is ignorant," Frankenstein said. "The machine only picks up the quality of thoughts transmitted."

I didn't believe him. I thought his machine was malfunctioning, but he was too proud to admit it. He quickly moved on, walking up to a bed with a Negro in it. The man was comatose. There was a small table next to the bed covered with syringes filled with a brown liquid, and a large monitor currently displaying PET scans of the man's brain. Each syringe was marked with a number: 2.3. Frankenstein picked up a syringe and held it up to the light. "This liquid contains a virus. A special virus that affects the brain. It's RNA-specific." He injected it into the man's arm. Frankenstein's attention went to the monitors. "You can see the virus enter the brain as a slight increase in temperature. See? It quickly spreads. In two minutes the virus will alter certain brain structures."

"It's rewriting memories," I uttered.

"Not only that, but it does it according to a software program encoded within the virus. I can change the software and have a new batch of the virus prepared in just a few hours. Like it or not, we've got to face the fact that the Americans have the upper hand when it comes to weapons technology. We can't win on brute strength. Our best hope is to subvert them from within. We can create slaves. We can programme assassins. We can take over their government and military with this virus."

"When will this happen?"

"Soon. But the virus is still at the prototype stage. It is no easy task writing software that does what we want. One day I'll be able to programme anyone to believe anything. The ultimate brainwashing. For the moment we need a reliable software program. That is where you come in. You'll be my assistant. Use your knowledge of memory storage to come up with a voice-instructed command system."

"I don't understand, sir. What about recovering lost memories? This doesn't have anything to do with that."

He shrugged. "What's gone is gone. That's not my concern – or yours."

He showed me the "progress" of the virus. In several cells there were comatose patients. In the next dozen the patients were awake but blank, like my father. Each level of cells held patients infected with a different version of the virus. By version 1.16, I could have a "conversation" with the prisoners, but it was creepy because none of them knew their names. Identification codes were tattooed on their arms. On the top level, version 2.3 had been tested on six men and six women, all naked. Talking to them, I thought they seemed completely rational, if a little slow. They had been in forced labour camps until recently, when they'd been brought here. They seemed happier to be here because they got regular food and water.

Frankenstein was smiling. "They almost pass for human, don't they? But watch this. Number 4, I want you to stab out your own eyes with your thumbs."

Number 4 – a tall Negro with skin so dark it was nearly blue – responded immediately by raising his thumbs.

"Don't," I said to the man and to Frankenstein.

The man stopped. Frankenstein looked annoyed. "Continue, Number 4. Only respond to my voice."

The man screamed when his thumbs burst his corneas, aqueous humour squirting out like jelly, but he kept pushing and pushing until blood poured down his chest and his thumbs were deep into his eye sockets. I turned away. I heard him fall. He was dead when I looked back. Frankenstein lit up a cigarette and spoke into a microphone on his collar. "Cell 804 needs cleaning up. Subject deceased. One Negro ready for spares." Frankenstein looked at me with his blue and brown eyes. "You! Never countermand my orders. I am your superior. I do not care if you are a hotshot. Challenge me again and I will report you to the SS High Command. Is that understood?"

"Yes, sir."

"Ah. Herr Kessler. You are visiting your father?"

"Yes," I said to the nurse blocking the door. "Why? What's wrong?"

"I should warn you there's been a change." There were

tears in her eyes.

"Is he …?"

"He's not going to die, no. But … but the army came here and required replacements due to the shortage and –"

I pushed past her and into the room. My father was in the bed with the sheets drawn up to his neck. He looked normal, but …

I pulled away the sheets.

He had no arms. He had no legs.

The monsters. The filthy monsters.

Behind me, I heard the nurse sobbing.

I slumped into the chair beside the bed. I closed my eyes and thought of the times my father had played with me in the park when I was small. He had loved spending time with me away from the stresses of the war. Those few, brief moments were the only times I could recall my father smiling and laughing. And now … My father was an honourable man. Yes; he was a soldier. Yes; he killed men. But he'd never killed civilians. What did that make me?

Was I a monster too?

Frankenstein didn't spend much time on the experiments himself; he left the software engineering to his assistants. There were six of us; three worked during the day, three at night. The work never stopped. We created new viruses, tested them and reported the conclusions like drones. I soon came to the conclusion that I was the only assistant with any idea of how to accomplish the task. The others were good technicians, but they had no imagination. For them, it was a matter of logistics. They sincerely believed that by testing every possible genetic combination they'd eventually hit upon the right answer, as when Salvarsan 606 was discovered. But I didn't believe that. Salvarsan 606 was a fluke. That was working blind. It would take years – thousands of test subjects – to do it that method. You needed imagination to solve the problem. There were short cuts. I wrote algorithms for the virus to use to hone itself to RNA by a process of iteration. The results improved.

Then I made a batch of version 2.91. I tested it on a 43-year-old Muslim. The virus left him normal in every way but one – I could instruct him to believe anything. It was beyond hypnosis – it was complete mind-control. He could live in society with my instructions burned into his head more forcefully than the words of the Koran. And yet anyone who didn't know he'd been programmed would never be able to tell.

It was so disturbing I didn't write an honest report.

I wrote that version 2.91 was a failure and instructed the man to behave as though the virus had failed. I then moved on to version 2.92, but I kept the batch of 2.91 and labelled it as 1.13. Nobody was using 1.13, so it would stay untouched until I figured out what to do. I went to work on 2.92 just as if nothing had happened. I knew I would be executed if anyone found out my deceit. I tried not to think about the risk of undergoing a trust test.

That night, after a poor performance in bed with my wife, I rose after she fell asleep. I looked through a gap in the curtains at New Berlin. The city had been built on the ruins of the old Berlin after it was destroyed. Every building was huge and imposing in the night. Albert Speer, Hitler's architect, was building more every day. The city was expanding like a cancer. Speer used forced labour. People had died so I could live in this luxurious apartment. God knows what Hitler would do with programmable slaves.

At street level I could see soldiers standing on the corners, keeping order. A Mercedes-Benz Dreadnought flashed by with a Nazi flag on its roof, on its way to the Nazi Party Headquarters. No private vehicles were allowed out after the nine o'clock curfew unless the driver had a pass. Tonight, there were none. Everyone was living in a permanent state of fear. Fear of our own government.

I went into the kitchen and made myself some ersatz coffee with ersatz milk. It tasted awful, but it energised me. I read yesterday's newspaper. There wasn't much news, but I paused over one story. Hitler was returning to New Berlin tomorrow – today now – and he was holding a meeting with the war council about the deepening crisis in North Africa. It was expected he would authorise tactical nukes. The tone of the article suggested this was a sensible option. Tactical nukes!

We'd tried that before and millions had died on both sides! Frankenstein, as Science Minister, was a member of the war council. Knowing Frankenstein, I was certain he would back the proposals; his radiation experiments had resulted in a new anti-cancer drug that he wanted to test in a war zone.

I dressed and went down to the basement garage. I drove my BMW out onto the street regardless of the danger of being stopped without a pass. I headed for the autobahn. There was one checkpoint between my home and the institute. I slowed, approaching it. There was a young army officer checking IDs. I showed him my doctor's licence.

"You need a pass, sir."

"I'm on my way to an emergency transplant – no time for a stupid pass."

"You need a pass, sir."

"I'll tell General Rommel that, shall I? I have his new heart in here." I patted my briefcase – which contained some papers and a two-day-old sandwich I'd forgotten to eat. If he asked to see the heart, I was really in trouble. "Should I tell him I was delayed because of some corporal?"

"Th-that's all right, sir." He waved me on.

SECTION D: AUTHORISED PERSONNEL LEVEL 001 ONLY

"It's late, sir. This isn't your shift."

I looked at the guard and nodded. "Forgot to analyse my

data. Professor Frankenstein will be pissed off if I don't finish it."

He nodded in sympathy. He knew what a tyrant Frankenstein could be. "He's in there, so good luck."

I slid my card over the scanner and hurried into the room. I walked to the programming room. There was nobody about. I opened the large cryogenic refrigerator and removed the vials of 1.13 containing 2.91. I thawed the virus out and loaded it into a syringe. It was then I heard someone cough. I spun around. It was Bauer.

"What're you doing, Christian?"

"I think some of the 1.13 has contaminated the 2.92. I was just getting a sample."

"That's interesting," he said, "because I just re-tested your 2.91. I was going to tell Victor, but first I wanted to ask you about it. It was successful, Christian. But you reported it as a failure."

"I can explain," I said, stepping towards him. Suddenly, he reached into his lab coat for a gun. I was faster, though. I had the syringe in his arm in an instant. He struggled, but already the virus was reaching his brain. In a last effort to stop me, he fired his gun through his coat. The bullets slammed into me – one, two, three – all hits to the chest – the pain incredible – and then he stopped firing and stiffened and his face became slack. I found myself on the floor bleeding to death, but I didn't care about that. I just hoped no one had heard the shots. The walls were supposedly soundproof. Quickly, quickly, I told him what to do ...

Now was the true test.

Into the light again ... After months of existing in the darkness, I climb up the ladder and push open the hatch. I fully expect to see the Coast Guard – or someone, anyone – but the deck of the cabin cruiser is deserted. I am alone in the middle of a blue-green ocean, a light breeze rocking the boat. I crawl until I gain the strength to stand, then I walk to the wheelhouse. I find signs of recent habitation – cigarette butts, beer cans, discarded playing cards – but no crew. There is some blood, though. It is smeared like grease on the walls and windows. I was right about the danger of pirates. They must have killed the crew and taken away their bodies, which they could either use themselves or sell as parts on the organ market. I look for boats on the horizon, fearing their return. I see nothing. By hiding, I'd escaped their wrath, but how was I going to steer this thing myself?

I look at the endless ocean, wondering which way is west. I read somewhere you could tell the direction by looking at the sun. I can't see the sun because the sky is so bright, a solid white sheet of light. No clues there. With growing alarm,I study the controls : they have been smashed. There is no way to drive this thing without them. Cursing, I search the cabin cruiser from top to bottom, pausing only to fill my stomach with dregs from the galley and to drink clean – clean? – water from the toilet. Eating makes me feel better, but then I make the mistake of opening the refrigerator. A human head rolls out and thuds onto the floor. The shock nearly empties my stomach, but I hurry onto the deck for fresh air. I don't know why it shocks me - after the things I've seen - but perhaps it's just the surprise of it. People jump when a balloon pops; it doesn't mean they are scared of balloons. I compose myself. The head … I go back and look at the features. It was the captain. He looks … preserved. I take his head up the stairs and give him a burial at sea. His head sinks without a trace. The head … It reminds me I haven't seen how I look after weeks hidden in the engine room. I check out my condition in a broken mirror in the captain's quarters. I look pale and skel-etal. The death camp really took its toll. The flesh hangs from my bones. I can see every rib. The serial number on my wrist looks like a purple wound. I hold it up and read it to myself over and over, remembering.

1995-25-02-70-1110110101-172A.

The serial number is a special code the Nazis use. It can be split up into components. The first four digits stand for the year of capture, the next six are the date of birth – in this case 25 February 1970 (the Nazis hadn't thought the system would be required into the 21st century, so they'd used only two digits for the year). The numbers in binary described physical fea-tures for identification purposes such as colour of eyes, colour of hair, colour of skin, height …

The man this body belonged to died in Frankenstein's lab in a failed test. Bauer had transplanted my brain into it. He smuggled the "dead" body out of the building, then returned to give Frankenstein an injection and his instructions. I was on my way to the coast by then. If everything had gone as I intended, Frankenstein would have infected Hitler and the whole war council and instructed them to sue for peace at any price. Meanwhile Bauer should have destroyed the lab and all records so the experiments could never be repeated. Then he had been instructed to infect as many people as he could with his special programming - I called it a conscience, something we'd all lost over the years.

Hopefully, the war is over.

I walk onto the deck and hope.

There's something on the horizon. A green smudge.

It looks like land.

I stare at it until my vision blurs.

Blitzenstein
Stephen Volk

Cliff Salvat was an American, and if he hadn't been there we wouldn't have done it, not on our own. Cliff Salvat had different trousers. For a start he called them pants, which made us chuckle. Pants were what you wore underneath. And they were long, to his ankles, like a grown-up's. In fact he looked like a grown-up in his shirt, bow-tie and jacket. My dad used to call him the midget: Where's the midget? Or, where's the Yank? Where's Buffalo Bill, then?

Cliff Salvat used to say Hey when we said Oi, Hi there instead of Wotcher, and automobile instead of car. He taught my baby sister to say automobile in her pram. Say it. Go on. Automobile. He used to ask her to say words like transmitter, or eucalyptus, or Venezuela. He used to come to our house for tea and we'd play with tin racing cars and skittles in the backyard. But he was never my friend, not really.

He never said please or thank you, just, Hey give me that, or Do this. And when my mum asked, What do you say? he'd go, Huh? She said he was a sad little boy.

He arrived in our school one day halfway through the war and no one would talk to him, so we did. Our gang was me, George from next door, Arthur his little brother, Cyril with the glasses and Esme. Cliff Salvat looked rich (compared to us) so we thought he would have toys and tell us what cowboys were like. We thought he must have lived on a ranch, but he didn't. He came from Minnesota.

Somebody told us that his father had been killed in the war. Shot. A US Marine. But I never saw him cry about it. There was never a tear in his eye. I looked, every day, and I never saw one. Not one.

He knew good games, though, and he told us what to do, and that's how he got into our gang, really. We made an African mask once, and a Flash Gordon rocket out of tea chests and bicycle wheels, and a toboggan we painted green, and we used to tie rope around our toy soldiers and dangle them over the wall as if they were mountain climbers.

When a doodlebug came over, Dad said, Right you lot, down in the ground, that's where we'll all be one day, look sharpish. And we'd waddle off into the air raid shelter like a line of ducks with gas masks on. When the noise of the doodlebug stops, that's the worrying bit because it means it's dropping. Like when your mother gave birth to you, Dad said to me. When she stopped whining, that's when our trouble really started, eh, Glo? Then, when the all-clear sounded, we'd go out and have a gander. London still intact, Dad used to say, no thanks to you Gerry Bastards! Sometimes there would be bricks and stones all over the yard and bits of broken things, like it had rained them, like the world had been turned upside down and given a good old shake.

When she was one year old, my sister got a dolly for her

birthday. My mum put it in her cot and went, Ahhhh. I asked her why little girls have dolls and little boys don't. She said little girls have to get used to holding babies and little boys don't, they have soldiers instead. But the dolly opened and closed its big blue eyes and you could turn its arms and legs and pretend it was walking. It was pink and had clothes, like a real thing. Like a tiny friend. I tried to pull it off her, just to play with for a minute, but she cried and I had to give it back.

The next day after a bombing raid, we'd go exploring. Sometimes we'd see a house was missing, or a street. Sometimes we'd see somebody sitting on the pavement with a coat wrapped round them, looking like they had a headache or they'd lost something. Once we saw a policeman with his arm around somebody. Once we saw a boy with no clothes on. Once we saw a dead baby in the rubble, and some bodies being carried on stretchers; one of their hands dangled down and the ambulance man kept picking it up. Once we found some ladies' knickers and a dead cat. Once we saw a house with only one wall left, and a candle in a candlestick, still alight. If the ARP warden saw us we'd run, because if he got hold of us, we'd be for it. We were more afraid of them than we were of the Germans.

One day George said, You'll never guess what I found. He ran off with us following, down the alley behind the sweet shop, through the allotments. A few of the houses had been flattened in the night and the vegetable patches looked as if a hand had squashed them, like a baby playing with its food. Beckoned by George's stubby finger, we squeezed through a wire fence to face a pile of bonfiery wood, the shipwreck remains of a garden shed, at which he was pointing in between wiping his hands in his shorts. In amongst the scattered planks was a foot, and belonging to the foot was a leg and a body, none of them moving.

Is he dead? asked Arthur.

Course he's dead, said Cliff Salvat. What else would he be? He's not moving. What is he, faking it? Dope.

Esme went over and poked the foot with her own. It didn't move. She backed away, cuddling her doll.

The rest of us went closer. I moved a bit of wood and I saw some blackish hair and a bloody ear underneath. Relax, said Cliff Salvat and started moving the debris aside. It was the dead body of a man. He was naked except for a dressing gown belted with a red and white rope with tassels. One leg was bare with a hairy, veined ankle and the other foot was wearing a red slipper twisted at an impossible angle. His chest looked flat and skinny but he had a roll of fat under his chin, where there was grey stubble mixed with black, and his teeth were yellowy. He had obviously been in the shed when the bomb fell, and the blast had torn him apart but also half-buried him, that was how come the ARP wardens and firemen hadn't found him and taken him away with the other bodies.

He's got grey stuffing coming out of his tummy, said Esme,

like my teddy, look.

That's not stuffing, you twit.

What is it, then?

Shut up.

Cliff Salvat broke a stick off a nearby bush and started to prod the dead body with it. Nobody said anything. He prodded harder. It cut the skin and made a mark. Something brown oozed out. I said, Don't.

He said, Why not?

You might wake him up, said Esme.

Cliff Salvat pulled more of the wood aside, noisily. His head's missing, he said. His brains have all come out. And one arm is blown away, there's just strandy bits hanging down. And that leg underneath, there's just bone at the top. And all his insides are missing. There's only half of him left. Look.

We ought to tell somebody, I said.

Who? said Cliff Salvat.

We'll get in trouble, said George. I'll get in *big* trouble!

Can't we shut up about it and just go? asked Cyril. Before somebody catches us?

Nobody'll catch us, moron, said Cliff Salvat. Nobody knows. There's only us. He's ours. He's our baby. Isn't he great? Isn't he fantastic? Our own body. Our own dead body. Us.

I crouched down next to Cliff Salvat and looked at the small, perfect ear dabbled with crusty, blackening blood. What should we do? I said. Do we bury him? What?

Cliff Salvat looked down with a funny expression in his eyes, just like when we made a fire for the first time, with matches. He said, We should put him together again.

What?

We should put him together and bring him back to life, he said, a bit louder.

Blimey, said Cyril.

People don't come back, I said. Dead is dead.

That's what you think, said Cliff Salvat, looking up at the distant drone of an invisible aircraft, its engine doing a bad imitation of thunder. Don't you think they keep secrets from us, he said, grown-ups? They don't want us to know the truth because it's too horrible.

What secrets? asked Esme.

That Germans can come back from the dead, that's what.

Don't listen to him, I said. Then to Cliff Salvat, You're scaring her.

Am I? So what? It's time she knew. It's time we all knew. They don't die. They can't, that's why they're winning the war, we knock them down, they jump back up, all sewn up, all more horrible, just coming on and on, mad, evil, not feeling any pain, nothing. Scars and bullet holes and...

How do you know? asked Georgie, his voice too quavery with fear to be truly sceptical.

Cliff Salvat walked over to the shade of a brick wall and

crouched with his back against it. We huddled round, on our knees, perching on stones, and he passed around bubble gum. He said, my Dad took me to the movie theatre back home. The lady at the ticket booth said, mister, that kid's too young for this kinda stuff, you know? My Dad said, He's a big boy, he can take it, you ain't scared, are ya, Cliffo? and he laughed and slapped my back, and she said, OK soldier and winked and jerked her head. Well, when I saw it I *was* scared, and I hid behind the seat. And on the screen there was this big big guy in black and white with his eyes pulled down, and a big iron block of a head, with scars and hinges, and he was put together with parts from dead bodies, and they cut his head open like a boiled egg and put a brain in, and put electricity through him and brought him back to life.

And I know it's true, because the word NEWS came up big, with a rooster, and a voice talking about Germany and the war, and I saw soldiers in black and white too, smiling and smoking cigarettes. And then the monster ten feet tall lifted up a little girl and threw her in the river. And I remember there were thousands of them, Germans, millions, all in rows doing the straight-arm salute and shouting It's Alive! It's Alive! It's Alive!

And then, and then men and women doing athletics, perfect people who could never die. And soldiers with lightning bolts on their collars. And their boss up there, facing them, mad and shouting that they were Gods now.

Cliff Salvat looked at our faces one by one. Have you heard of the name Frankenstein?

We all shook our heads.

That's their boss. That's the mad scientist who stitches them back together and says the whole country will live forever.

We were quiet.

Cliff Salvat poked at the dirt with the toe of his shoe. Boris Karloff, he was the first one. That's a German name isn't it? Boris. And Karloff! How much more German can you get than that? I've been thinking about it... a lot...Why do they have those steel helmets shaped like that? It's to cover their flat heads. The heads where the brains have been put in. And that's why they don't feel any emotions or pain or feelings, nothing.

Then he said, If we put him together, he'll come alive and he'll have to be our slave and play with us. He'll be like our dad. Forever.

And so we went about creating our man. It wasn't too different from building a Guy Fawkes in preparation for Bonfire Night, except of course instead of balls of paper and rolls of cloth we had to find real organs and pieces of meat. You couldn't bring somebody back to life filled with paper.

We visited the allotments whenever we could, mostly when all of us were together but sometimes in groups of two or three.

The first time, we pulled the corpse from under the wooden planks and put him in the garden shed; it became our laboratory. Each of us stole knives or forks or string from our parents' houses — nails, needles, scissors, anything that looked medically useful, when our mums or dads were looking the other way.

We cleaned the blood from him, tip to toe, scrubbed him like our mums did our faces when we got smeared with chocolate. We scraped off the hard black chunks of burned flesh with bits of slate and tried to cover the stains and discolouration with paint from a Christmas paintbox. Then we set about getting the Bits and Pieces.

For the following days and weeks we were on the look-out. We'd seen all sorts of things in the bombed-out houses, and now we had a need for them. Cyril found a leg behind the station yard. It was a lady's leg, but never mind. We took the shoe and stocking off and tied it onto the burned stump of the dead man's body. Esme said she'd learned from her mum how to sew, and she licked her needle, frowning seriously in the torchlight, and we cut stretchy patches of skin with scissors from the limb to the joint like we were darning a sock.

George got a bull's eye from his uncle the butcher, saying he needed it for Biology, and we put it in the big hole on the side of the dead body's face. It jiggled and bulged when we did it but in the end it was a good fit.

Arthur found an arm. It belonged to a black man. It was

lying next to a stretcher and nobody noticed it in all the commotion. He just nipped in and nipped out again with it wrapped in the *Daily Mirror*.

Cliff Salvat said do this, do that. He seemed to know everything, and we didn't question him. We didn't mind.

When we had something new to add on, Esme would put her dolly on the shelf and set to work with her needle and thread while we, and the dolly, looked on. There were some fingers missing, so I stole one of my dad's woolly gloves and put sausages in to make it look right. Sausages were meat so they were OK, Cliff Salvat said. Sometimes Cyril brought some milk and digestives and we'd stop and have a snack and think to ourselves proudly how good our Man was looking, half-lying, half-sitting there, half in shadow and half in sunlight as Esme tied a knot in her thread and bit off the rest, and patted his chest and said, There there sweetheart, like her mother said to her.

It was exciting.

It was better that making a Guy Fawkes. Much better. We couldn't *wait* to go there, every day. We couldn't wait for him to be *alive*!

In a few days he smelled a bit, so we used to wear our gas masks when we operated. We put up little hooks and hung our tools round the walls. We made a list of what he would eat: fruit, meat, nuts, eggs, spuds, tomatoes. We went shopping and mashed it all up and put it in a bag and filled his empty tum. The maggots fizzled away and the centipedes burrowed off into the earth. His belly squelched and we had to use my snake-buckle belt to hold his newly restored gutsy bits inside.

One day George and Arthur found a dead dog and brought it in a wheelbarrow. Its eyes were staring and its tongue was grey and long. We hit its skull with a hammer till the bone cracked and we put its brain into our man, in a broken saucepan to protect it, with a lid on.

Cliff Salvat said, He needs bolts here and here. For the electricity. So we took apart my bike and rammed the handlebars through his neck, in one side and out the other, and put big wing nuts on either end with a wrench. It looked smashing.

Rummaging through the bombed-out husks of houses, we collected about twenty-five shoes, all sorts of colours and sizes. Cliff walked up the line and did the choosing. One was a soldier's and the other was a shiny one, like Sunday Best. We took a shirt from somebody's washing line and some grey flannel trousers — pants — from somebody's bottom drawer. We'd argue sometimes about what we wanted him to wear, and sometimes we'd vote for it, and sometimes we'd draw straws. Our parents wondered where we went every day but we didn't tell them. It was our secret.

After a while our man, our German, didn't stink any more. He smelled as sweet as Parma violets. We loved him.

Esme brought some lipstick and put it on his lips. Sometimes she'd lie next to him, looking like she wanted to sleep there, cuddle up in his lolling arms, but Cliff Salvat would get angry and tell her to get off him, he's not a toy, he's a Human Being.

Why? Why can't I? she'd say. He's not *yours*. Yes he is, I said. He belongs to all of us. We *made* him. We made him and he's going to *live*. He's going to walk, you'll see.

Walk and talk, said Esme. Walk and talk.

Bloody hell, said Arthur. What's he going to say? Will he be angry?

Will he talk German? asked Esme.

No, said Cliff Salvat. He'll be real happy. You'll see. We'll teach him words. Any words we like.

Suddenly we heard someone outside giggling and we all went quiet and ducked down, away from the window, terrified anybody would see or hear us. They got closer. We heard them chatting and lighting cigarettes. A man and a woman. We heard him ask her to lie down on his raincoat and they started doing things and groaning and gasping for breath. Esme started crying and Cliff Salvat hissed at her to shut up. We didn't move an inch till it got dark and the man and woman kissed again and talked and went away.

What if they find him? asked Esme.

They won't, I said. Nobody's going to find him. We won't let them. He's our property. He's our friend.

If they see him, they'll all want one, said George.

Look at him, said Cliff Salvat, his eyes sparkling like broken glass. He's wonderful. He's magnificent. He's almost ready. Almost. Ready.

He grinned and so did I.

The air raid siren sang and we scattered home. As I closed the shed door, looking for the peg on a string to lock it, I glanced back in, seeing the moonlight sloping down onto the slumped, improvised scrawl of life we had built from a jigsaw of dead flesh and the indiscriminate salvage of war. A Pinocchio of the perverse, a train-set of humanity, a monstrous concoction of childhood wishes and fears, waiting to wake up, and yawn, and beat its breast, like Tarzan.

And that's what I wanted — what we all wanted — more than anything in the world.

*

That night I lay awake, too excited to sleep, too immersed in my thoughts at first to notice at first the sound that came from the sky like the bass drum of a military parade. But then I *did* hear it. I ducked behind the blackout and peered out through the crucifixes of sticky tape which protected our window panes. The sky was the colour of a pearl. There was no siren but the sky was lit up in flashes as a violent thunderstorm thrashed the clouds. Blinding spikes stabbed down at the dark, sleeping city.

Mum!

What is it?

Mum!

Go back to bed. What are you doing down here?

I have to go... I have to! I have to!

After my dad hurried me back to my bed and put off the light, I rushed back to the window, my heart pounding.

No. No...

Suddenly a zed of light arrowed down beyond the back-to-backs and was gone. Seconds later thunder cracked. I held my breath. I was sure the lightning bolt had struck in the exact location of the allotments. A second, more jerky and serrated burst lit up the sky, but the gap between it and the thunderclap that followed was longer. The storm lumbered away, almost as if it knew its job was done.

The following day was bright and cloudless, and the pavements were bone dry. When our gang gathered at the allotments I noticed for the first time that the grass was beginning to poke through the ash and dirt, and a couple of cheerful sparrows hopped on the half-ruined fence.

Cliff Salvat was already inside the shed when we shoved the door open wider. When we followed him in, somehow we knew what we would find; the dingy, ramshackle hut was empty. Our Man, our Boris, our Lazarus, our Dad — was gone.

Poor human, said Esme.

They must... George began, hesitating. They must have

found him. I mean the firemen, the ARP wardens, whoever. They must have come here and found the body and...

Cliff Salvat was not listening. He was staring at the space where our handsome creature used to be, and for a moment I thought he was going to cry. His shoulders began to shake, but he was laughing. The rest of us looked at each other and Esme cuddled and kissed her doll. Cyril took off his glasses and cleaned the lenses in his grubby shirt. Cliff Salvat was laughing till tears ran down his cheeks. We did it, he said. We did it. We did it! It's alive! IT'S ALIVE!

He threw his head back, yelling it so hard I thought the roof would cave in, so unashamedly, deliriously happy it frightened us, and we left him, scurrying back to our burrows, not wanting to share his happiness any more than we'd wanted to know his unhappiness — with that singular and spectacular callousness unique to children, and monsters.

Now nobody talks about the war. There have been too many wars, or pseudo-wars, since. Now it's my profession. My vocation. It's what I'm good at. I put them all together, stitch them up as best I can, ship them out. Now, the dead walk every day. I only have to look around me. Cancer, cysts — if it doubt, cut them out. Amputations, new limbs, donor cards, hearts harvested all over the country, farmers with their severed hands packed in picnic baskets of ice.

I see it every day across my Harley Street desk. Everybody

wants to live forever. We conquer death every day, every day we wake up, but we can't conquer the fear of it. Perhaps the fear of it is what makes us human.

Poor human.

We drifted apart after that glorious summer. No other games held our fascination, nor, curiously, did we hold a fascination for each other.

After the war, when we went our separate ways, I heard only dribs and drabs about their subsequent lives, fed from parent to proud parent. Esme became a costume designer for the RSC, then opted out and went to live in a commune in the Orkneys. George and Arthur took over their father's greengrocery , never moving more than a street away from where they were born and brought up. Cyril, a British Bill Gates, wrote software for the City, got married and had five kids and bought a house in Spain. And Cliff Salvat went back to the Bible Belt of his birth and became a Pentecostal minister: a new flock, a new gang, a new Father, at last.

Our lives are ordered now, and we are, for our sins, successful. The war was a long time ago, and yet it's only yesterday. For some of us it doesn't die.

I look down at my wrists and I see the scar tissue there, the stitch marks. I remember the lightning that seared through my brain to make me better, and lo, hallelujah, awakened me, and let me live again.

Cash in Hand
Joel Lane

He couldn't turn his wife on any more. He'd fallen behind with the payments, and they'd repossessed the generator. The silence in the flat at night kept him awake. He slept cold and alone, touched only in dreams that bled into his helpless daytime fantasies. Bars of rain glittered at the windows. After a month of this, he picked up the phone and dialled a number that had no area code. A cell phone somewhere in the city; a voice fed through a computer, as unreal as the synthetic voice box of a cancer victim.

The next morning, the parcel arrived. It was an old-fashioned wooden box with a lock, and a silver-plated key. John's contact had a highly developed sense of kitsch. By the end of the week, the red had drained from his bank statements. The power came back on, and Susan responded to his touch again. His poverty hadn't mattered when she'd been alive. But all Deads were conservative by nature. They might not have the vote, but somehow they set the trends.

Not that he cared what was trendy. He'd not been to the cinema in years, and only watched TV for the old films in which, if Deads appeared, they were treated with something like reverence. All he wanted was to be able to come home to Susan and feel something like a normal husband. She was too far gone to continue her career as a systems analyst, though she did some graphic design work for an advertising company. You had to make a living, even when you weren't alive. He still loved the occasional flickers of the old Susan that came through the mist: a smile, a raised eyebrow, a dance of fingertips on the back of his hand. And he loved her voice, the halting vibrato he found sexy even though he knew it was the result of glottal dehydration.

Recently, there'd been a spate of tabloid horror stories about Dead lovers. The rich woman who'd kept a house full of Dead toyboys. The teenage gang who'd revived a girl way past the legal decay limit, then literally loved her to bits. The serial killer who only had one victim. *The Sun* missed no opportunity to condemn those who slept with the Dead. Their porn section was defiantly titled LIVE AND KICKING. But there was a whole industry built up around Dead flesh: magazines, videos, brothels. It was a big fetish on the underground club scene. He'd even heard there were credit card-operated generators in Amsterdam's blue light district. It was the tingle of electricity that did it, everyone said: the residual charges that made the hair, nipples and other things stand on end. A Dead fuck was a bundle of nerves and fibres, quivering to a violent climax. Ironically, the living were jealous. The market in Dead-on-Dead porn was strictly illegal; but there was a market.

John felt a compulsion to know about these things. It gave him some perspective. Everything in this life was so narrow, focused on the timesheet and the profit margin. He needed something to make him feel free. Knowledge was power; it meant there was something inside him that was his, that they didn't own. As long as he had Susan, he could hold onto himself. Their lovemaking was raging, painful; it had the terrible intensity of something that could die. It was like facing death. If you couldn' t die, you were no longer alive. That was what they had between them: a shared life. It wasn't just sex. Nobody had the right to say that.

The first day after the power came back on, John left for work in a haze of fear and excitement. He felt like a teenager waiting for an evening date. At home, he thought, Susan would be getting up. She would be showering, combing her hair, clouding the mirror with new-minted breath. Maybe she'd be working - gazing through her pale reflection at the words and patterns on the screen of her PC. And when he came home tonight, she'd be waiting for him. John hardly noticed when the train stalled in the tunnel outside New Street Station, where its platform was occupied by another late train. He stared at the blank grey eye of the security camera, wondering if it could see his thoughts. All around him, commuters addressed ill-tempered monologues to their palm-sized mobile phones. Their faces were glassy and strange from lack of sleep.

In the past, John knew, Deads had been used to work night shifts in heavy industry. In fact, the technology of recharging had been as much a part of the Industrial Revolution as the steam engine. There'd been whole factories full of Deads in

Victorian times, working like machines without light, food or sleep. But gradually things had changed. Industry had moved to the Far East and the Third World, where the Deads were younger and less protected by employment laws. Meanwhile, drugs had been developed that enabled Deads to hold onto most of their mental faculties - at least for a few decades. Now that they no longer had a clearly defined economic role, the Deads were thinning out; the sex industry was the only real niche they had left. The nostalgia that made them cultural icons also nailed down their coffin lids. He'd seen a cover of *The Face* magazine recently, declaring: DEAD IS DEAD. When even the Prime Minister affected a Dead look - frozen stare, white skin, hair dyed and stiffened - it was clearly a thing of the past.

He got through the day on automatic pilot, processing orders on-screen and stamping the forms with their service numbers and the date. Plasma for Cape Town, T-cells for Jakarta, fibrinogen for Buenos Aires. Wars and disasters were great news for the biomedical industry. You couldn't keep even a Dead army going without medical resources: blood, skin, immunity supplements. He'd seen the horror photographs on the TV news, but how the resources were used wasn't his concern. It was business. Over the last decade, the company's working methods had become so cost-effective that few European hospitals would trust them. It didn't matter: there was always a market. There was always a need. Recently, someone had put up a notice in the staff canteen: *You don't have to be Dead to work here - but it helps.* The next day, management had taken it down.

When John left the office, the streets were dark. He had to wait a long time for his train. Its route took John past the Longbridge car factory, still lit up for the evening shift; the familiar neon signs of theme pubs and chain restaurants; the halflit streets where no-one seemed to walk. He was tired. On the train, his eyes kept closing involuntarily. But he had the weekend, and Susan to share it with. He'd worry about the box when the time came.

It was good to step through the doorway and into her waiting arms; to stand together in the hall, their mouths joined in a wordless greeting. He'd brought her a present: a jazz CD they listened to while he helped her prepare dinner. Neither of them was hungry, but it was the ritual that mattered. The music flowed around them, filling the dark house: nervous drums, subdued piano, moaning tenor saxophone. The solo trembled on the edge between pain and joy, never quite going over. The player had died young, twenty years ago, but he wasn't Dead. Reviving musicians was a dangerous game anyway: their timing was flawed, and they tended to forget bits. But you could revive the music just by touching a button, and it never missed a note.

They drank wine by candlelight, a Friday-night ritual that went back to their first weekend in this house. The pictures in the living room were the same ones that Susan had chosen when she was alive. She was wearing a turquoise dress and black eye-shadow. Her hair had grown long recently, and she'd fastened it back with a pearl hairgrip. "You look like a mermaid," he told her.

She tilted her head and smiled mysteriously. "And you look like a shipwrecked sailor," she breathed. "Come with me and I'll show you the depths. I'll teach you to swim among the fishes and the bones, where the blind things are. You'll never want to leave." Her thin fingers reached for his, curving around his knuckles. Their faces tilted together. Then he saw what was in her eyes and looked away. What was the point of all this? he wondered. Trying to keep up with the winners, the successful ones - who were they trying to fool? Gently, he moved her hand back across the table.

They chewed in silence for a while. The food was heavily spiced, to disguise the slight gaminess that Dead meat always seemed to have. But who could afford freshly killed stuff these days? Farmers were tending to keep the livestock for breeding only. He swallowed a few mouthfuls, washed down with Italian red wine. "You look tired," Susan said.

"I'm all right. Are you?" She nodded. "We'll get some rest soon. Things to do first."

"Tell me what they are. Or better still, show me."

He took her hand again, and they walked up the uncarpeted stairs together. The hallway smelt faintly of bleach; the walls were scoured, but the dirt was ingrained. In the bedroom, the duvet was scattered with dried rose petals like scraps of hard tissue paper. The mirror was tilted to reflect the middle of the bed. Susan kicked off her shoes and was suddenly an inch shorter. John lifted her in his arms, feeling for the zip at the back of her dress.

They made love with a slow determination, clutching each other as if trying to become one body. Initially, Susan made him keep talking, telling her how it felt, repeating instructions. But her first climax helped her to relax: the flow of endorphins lightened her anxiety, and she even began to laugh. John was glad that she seemed to enjoy it. Sometimes it hurt her, and he always felt guilty.

In between bouts of fucking, they lay together on the duvet, their limbs tangled and strange. He knew he was supposed to pull out and come over her for effect; but he couldn't bear, in those moments, not to be as close to her as possible. They took turns looking in the mirror, where the camera's red eye winked regularly as if setting the rhythm. The two night lights on the bedside table guttered, fire swimming in pools of grease. The air was chilly.

At last they stopped, crawled under the duvet and exchanged a soft, private kiss. John lay awake, hearing Susan's breath slow to an even tide, no more than silence on the move. The Dead slept deeply, hidden within themselves. John glanced at the clock: it said 12 : 57 in red numerals. He stared at the curtains, where the outline of a full moon was just visible. Eventually he thought: Better get it over with. As quietly as possible, he got out of bed and walked naked along the hallway to the bathroom.

The moon shone through frosted glass, sketching the bath and cistern. John took a clean towel out of the airing cupboard and spread it on the floor, then put the box at one end of it. He stood there for a while, trying to fill his mind with erotic thoughts. His performance with Susan already seemed contrived, unreal. The acting had been a part of it for so long that it had become second nature. By imitating desire, he worked up the desire to perform. He rubbed at himself in the half-light until he was erect. Then he switched on the light, knelt down in front of the wooden box and picked up the key. While his left hand worked at his crotch, his right hand unlocked the lid.

The box was full of new banknotes, fives and tens. They spilled out from under the lid, rustling. Their crisp edges cut his fingers as he seized handful after handful. Some of them drifted over his belly, his thighs, his cock. He rubbed furiously; it felt mechanical, like forcing yourself to vomit. Hundreds of identical faces stared blankly at him: the Prime Minister's head, etched in blue and grey on every note. He crushed a few of them in his free hand.

A thread of sensation tightened from his glans to the base of his spine. His eyes closing involuntarily, he leaned forward and spurted onto the heap of notes. Then he picked up a clean fiver and wiped himself with it, slowly. The red eye in the bathroom mirror had a perfect view. He gathered up the notes, put them back in the box and turned the key in the lock. The money wasn't his to spend.

Walking back to the bedroom in darkness, John felt a profound exhaustion creeping over him. It was deeper than the need for a night's sleep. He was shivering, but not from cold. A memory of pain. Susan's head was just visible on the pillow as he slipped into bed beside her. At once, he was dreaming.

Whatever he'd dreamed had gone out of his head by the next morning. So had his name, and whatever he'd meant to do that day. He lay in bed until noon, then dressed in a stupor and went downstairs, where he stared at the TV set until it was dark outside. Susan tried to speak to him, but he couldn't understand her. He felt numb. The light was flecked with black, like a screen about to fade out. It was always like this. Somehow he could never ask for a recharge. And neither could Susan. When you fell back on instinct, there was nothing there.

Sometime during the night, she took him to the basement. Through a blanket of cold, he felt her placing the electrodes at his wrists and ankles. A little clumsily, she fastened the strap around his waist and slipped the rubber gag into his mouth. People sometimes injured themselves while being recharged. The room passed in and out of focus: damp plaster, a bare lightbulb, the uneven mattress he was lying on. And the red camera lens in the far wall. A faint smell of stale urine rose from the mattress.

As the first charge jolted through him, John tasted bile at

the back of his mouth. The light overhead seemed to brighten from yellow to white. With the second and third charges, his memory started to fill in. The static faded. He was covered in sweat. Why did he always fuck up the timing? Nearly two hundred years they'd had this technology, but no one had worked out a reliable care plan. Perhaps Deads made poor carers because, deep down, they hated revival. Or maybe it took more practice than he and Susan had had in the last decade. But what they still had between them was more important than the will to live. It was a shared life. They'd keep each other going for as long as possible, and that was the only thing that mattered.

An Act of Faith
Steve Lockley

The sound of coughing and the shuffling of feet masked the silence. No one spoke, no matter how much they might want to. Instead they waited in almost reverential silence.

Almost there, thought Anna. Almost over.

The waiting and the pain of her arthritis-riddled joints had made the last few hours painful, bringing back memories of her months in the camp. But this was not as bad, never could be. Silently she cursed the scientists who had conspired over the years to extend life; but what kind of life? Why wouldn't they just accept that life had an end, it was not something that should be prolonged indefinitely? Heaven should not wait. Without the prospect of death, there was nothing to look forward to. Even suicides had to rnake sure that they would not be found for days, or they would be brought back again and again, each time bearing the scars of their attempts. Anna would find a quiet place when this was all over and send herself into the arms of God and see Berthold again after all these years. There had never been anyone else, never could have been, and what she was doing today, she was doing for him.

The queue shuffled forward a few feet as someone at the head of the line moved on, and a commotion behind her made her think that someone had fainted, again. It was not going to happen to her; she had waited so long to meet the tormentor of her generation that she wanted to take the memory with her.

On the wall opposite hung a sign in five languages which read:

Under the provisions of the War Crimes Act 1946 the death penalty may only be invoked after victims or surviving relatives have approved this course of action.

There was more, but she could not bring herself to read it again. The sign appeared every ten feet along the hall, on signs outside the building, and in advertisements in every newspaper. It explained that a predetermined percentage of people had to vote in favour, but each time she read it her eyesight blurred as her eyes filled with tears. All that mattered was that she would be given the opportunity to face him and press the red button that would help send him to his death. There would be no heaven for him, only eternal damnation.

The queue shuffled forward again and the pain in Anna's hip almost made her cry out in agony. She leaned against the wall to steady herself.

"Are you all right?" asked a man in uniform who had come along the corridor, and she felt a dozen pairs of eyes turn towards her.

"Fine," she said between clenched teeth.

"I have a wheelchair if you would like it."

"No," she said. She wanted to face him on her own two

feet. To show that she had not been broken, even after all this time.

"Won't be long now," he said. "Would you like me to wait with you?"

She looked up at the man and realised that he was young enough to be her grandson, or could have been had she been able to have children after everything she had gone through.

"Would you mind?" she asked.

"Of course not. Take my arm if you like."

"Thank you," she said, and she gripped him tightly as they stepped forward to take the vacated space in front of them. Only five more ahead and some of them looked like they were together. Moral and physical support.

"Have you been waiting long?' he asked.

"Over fifty years," she said.

"No," he said his slightly embarrassed look reminding her of Berthold. "I mean today."

She smiled for the first time in a long time. "Doesn't matter," she said. "Time doesn't matter any more."

And yet once it had. In the years that had followed the end of the war she had wished that they had not entered the bunker so quickly; that his body had been allowed to rot beyond all help. Then at least she would have been able to try to put things behind her and start a new life. Instead she had the knowledge that he was still alive. That he could appear on her television screen at any time. That it could start all over again.

They moved again, and Anna realised that all that stood in front of them was another guard and a closed door.

"I'm not allowed to come in with you," he said. "But there will be someone inside in case you need anything."

"I'll be fine," she said, squeezing his arm again; on impulse she stretched and kissed him on the cheek. The door opened and she stepped through without saying another word and without looking back.

"Name?" asked a woman behind a table just inside the room.

"Sorry?" Anna said.

"What is your name?"

She lacked the compassion of the guard, but it been the same everywhere. There are always people who are caring and gentle, and others who only follow orders. The woman looked at her again, tapping a pencil on the page of names.

"Goldberg. Anna Goldberg.'

The woman ran her pencil down the list turning page after page before making a tick. "Thank you, Mrs Goldberg..."

"Miss," Anna said.

The woman ignored her. "Do you know what to do?"

"Yes," Anna said. "Where is he?"

The woman nodded towards a screen which bore another copy of the notice, and Anna made her way around it. On the far side stood a table on which were two buttons: one red, one green. All she wanted to do now was get it over with as quickly as she could. Press the red button, Press the red button. But she had to look at him first.

The man who had been responsible for the slaughter of millions was the one who was broken, not her. He was sitttng in a wheelchair, his head only held upright by restraints while drool ran from the corner of his mouth. A colostomy bag hung at the side of the chair and seemed to be constantly filling. She wanted to scream at him; to take a step forward and spit in his face, but she was unsure whether the guards were there to protect him or her. Then she looked at his eyes and could see the pain. She knew at that moment that he knew exactly what was going on around him. For him, death would be a release.

She looked at the buttons again with their simple labels. Green for life, red for death. It would be a kindness to press the red button, and after one last glance at his tortured eyes she pressed the green button.

CUBS
Steve Rasnic Tem

"I don't think he's ready for this. It's too soon." But despite her objections, Alice continued to fold Billy's uniforms for the camping trip, feeling the soft material, surreptitiously stealing a moment with the cloth by her nose so she might capture that faint, sweet aroma of child, sun-warmed hair and skin new to the world. But although she sprayed it onto Billy's clothes every evening, they lost that heartbreaking smell after only an hour on Billy's body.

"The Scout program was part of the agreement. They all do that. It's a social thing and a training thing. It's supposed to help them adjust."

"He . . . seems happy." She hesitated.

"Of course. Kids adjust. That's one reason they don't offer the treatment to adults. Adults just don't adapt the way kids do." Wayne hugged her from behind. "They're all a little subdued at first. It's to be expected. I mean, look at what they've been through."

The butterfly on Billy's windowsill was as white and brilliant as the sheets his mother put on the bed twice a day. Once each morning and once after the long sleep in the middle of the day he'd been told he now required. He didn't think his mother liked changing them; she always wore a funny face, and it seemed like she was always changing them. Most of the time she took the sheets straight down to the big washing machine and threw them in with lots of detergent. But other times she just threw the sheets away in the garbage bins out back. Billy remembered wetting the bed when he was little and the sheets got changed a lot back then, but it was different. His mom would smile a lot and just pat his head. "You'll do better," she would say. But all that was before the accident.

Dark lines started growing over the butterfly's wings, spreading and cutting the butterfly up into smaller and smaller pieces. It had been explained to Billy that this kind of thing wasn't really happening - it was just the way he saw things now. Another change since the accident. But it looked so real.

The butterfly turned into something black and burnt-looking and then it disappeared. It made him sad every time that happened, but he was getting used to it. Billy got out of bed slowly and went into the bathroom. He unplugged the energy pack from his back, slipped the jacks out of his chest, and put the equipment up on the shelf. He got the long narrow brush out of the cabinet and started running it in and out of the holes in his chest and back just like they had showed him at the center. The holes in his back were hard to get to, and he had to stand up on a stool and reach as far as he could while looking in the mirror. Greasy liquid dripped out of the holes and he had to brush until it was clear like water. Gross. No wonder his mother didn't love him anymore.

Downstairs and all dressed, Billy listened to everything his father had to say. Everything his father said today was "important" and "nothing to fool around with." His father checked to make sure the pack was recharged and showed Billy how to check the levels on the spare, even though it was something Billy did every day. But he didn't mind. His father had always liked to check and recheck things, even before the accident. And it was his father who'd been the one to tell Billy about the accident, the treatment, how everything had changed. That must have been a hard thing. His mother never could have done it.

It was good that his father hadn't changed that much since

It was good that his father hadn't changed that much since the accident. Of course, there were *some* differences. He didn't let Billy ride a bike anymore, but that was understandable after what had happened. Billy hadn't done so well the last time he rode one.

"The bus is here!" his mother called loudly from the front porch. "Is he ready?" He didn't like the way his mother's voice sounded anymore - like everything was so hard to say. It hurt his ears and then it hurt his heart.

His dad patted the energy pack. "Time to go, son." Billy didn't like it when his dad touched the pack that way, but he would never tell him so.

Billy looked up at his dad. "Do I have to go? I don't

wanna." Billy was surprised - he had no idea he was going to say that.

"Now, son . . ." His father hesitated, staring at him. Billy felt the tears running down his cheeks. Another shock of recognition: it was the first time he'd cried since the accident.

"Frank, he's going to be late." His mother at the doorway, hands going to her face. Then before he could move, she'd dropped to her knees and was hugging him. "My baby . . ." He was glad, but a little afraid of her. She kept looking at his face, but when he looked back at her he saw this crazy person. It felt bad to think that, but he was afraid that was really what she was - a crazy person.

"He has to go, honey." His father, easing her away. It made Billy feel relieved, but he tried not to show it. "We agreed, and we signed. Besides, they say he needs this sort of thing for it to work. The experts all say that . . ."

"The hell with the experts. Look at what your experts have done to our child!"

His father wrapped his arms around her, hushing her while she cried. Billy had already stopped crying, his tears drying up so fast it was as if he'd just dreamed them. But he couldn't remember the last time he'd dreamed, either. Just that it was before the accident. Sometimes it seemed the accident itself had been his final dream.

"I better go," he said softly, looking up at his father, and his crazy mother who wouldn't look at him anymore.

"Sure, son," his father said. "You go have a good time. Your mother... your mother and I will be fine."

Jagged lines started somewhere near his mother's mouth, flowed down her body, then spread to his father. The last thing Billy could see of them was his father's sad eyes before the dark fissures closed them.

Rick and Charlie were already on the bus, sitting close together, whispering. Billy didn't like it when anybody whispered, especially one of the Scouts, but he sat down next to them anyway. They weren't really his friends - he'd lost all his friends after the accident - but they were the first Scouts who ever talked to him, so he sat with them whenever there was a Scout thing he had to do.

"You were slow coming out," Charlie said. "Bet they didn't want you to go, huh?"

"My mom," Billy replied, not wanting to tell them he had cried about going.

Charlie nodded. "Mine, too." Charlie looked as if he still knew how to cry. He was the one who told him regular parents didn't want their kids hanging around any of the children who got made into Scouts. Charlie also told him that *his* friends had stayed away after the accident, too.

Except Charlie's death hadn't been an accident. His uncle had murdered him, but Charlie never would tell why or how.

"Hey," Rick said, pointing to the back of the bus. "they

brought the dead kid again."

"Rick!" Charlie said in a croaking whisper. He shut his eyes - Billy knew that Charlie hated it when his voice croaked and cracked like that. "Rick," he tried again, "don't point! And don't call him that!"

"Well, jeez, look at him! Besides, I could yell it in his face and he wouldn't know the difference!"

Billy looked back at the boy they all called the dead kid. His eyes blank, chin painted with drool. Sitting by himself. Practically all the Scouts made fun of him, except for Charlie and Billy. Billy was scared of him. The dead kid looked the way regular kids expected one of the Scouts to look - like some Scouts *did* look, if they screwed up and let their energy packs get too low for too long. Moms and dads could get in real trouble if they let that happen. That's why the doctors at the center wouldn't even give you a chance to come back as a Scout if they didn't think your parents could handle the responsibility.

But Billy had heard that what happened to the dead kid had nothing to do with a low energy pack. That was just the way he came back, was all. Rick said one day they'd just leave him behind on one of these trips and nobody would care. But the funny thing was, Billy had seen the dead kid's parents with the dead kid out at the playground, and they acted like he was just regular, like he wasn't even a Scout.

Sometimes Billy wished his parents could be more like the

dead kid's parents, but did that mean he had to be just like the dead kid too?

Suddenly the dead kid smiled, and it was just the weirdest thing seeing that big smile with those blank eyes. Like he was this big ugly lamp somebody had just switched on.

"All right, cubs! You got an hour to get this campsite in order! Every minute over means five less minutes' fun time!" Captain Dodge said everything a little too loud, as if being a Scout meant you couldn't hear well anymore. It was true that some kids came back not hearing so well, but Billy didn't think that was the average.

Billy started gathering firewood as quickly as possible. Not that he cared about loss of "fun time" - one of Captain Dodge's favorite threats, and did any of the Scouts he knew care about fun time? - but because he cared about getting cold. They all got too cold, even in warm weather, and being cold the way they felt cold was one of the worst feelings Billy could imagine.

In fact, looking at the darkening sky, Billy tried to hurry, feeling a little panicky about the cold, but he didn't run. None of the Scouts ran, even when Captain Dodge tried to make them. Whenever Billy tried to run the cracks in everything just got bigger and bigger until they spread across the ground and Billy was afraid even to take a step.

"Scouts don't run and Scouts don't shout." That's what

Charlie always said. And as far as Billy could tell, he was right. Scouts were pretty quiet, sometimes so quiet all you could hear were their packs making this low metal hum as they went around doing their business. It was a little strange, watching them hurrying around, nervous because of the dark coming down, but not making any noise. No wonder regular people didn't like them.

Billy wandered a few yards outside the camp looking for branches small enough for him to carry. It was against the rules, but Billy wasn't afraid of Captain Dodge-none of them were. In fact it was kind of a joke for them, thinking that Captain Dodge with his threats and his bad stories about what might happen to them if they didn't obey was supposed to scare them into doing anything. Billy had to find as much wood as he could carry as soon as possible, so that they could make a big fire and stay warm. Right now, there was nothing more important in the world to him than staying warm.

So when Billy tripped over Charlie and the dead kid it should have been no surprise. Bad things happened when you weren't looking where you were going. Look what happened on that bicycle. You don't look out where you're going and it all becomes your fault: the accident, and the Scouts, and your mom and dad changing along with everything else in the world, everything covered with these black lines that just get deeper and wider until they swallow the world.

Charlie was crying, crying so well Billy had to hold his

breath, and he tried never to hold his breath. But the way Charlie was crying, it was just so perfect.

"He . . . touched me . . . touched . . .me," Charlie managed between sobs. "And I couldn't . . . couldn't let the dead kid touch me! I had these rocks . . . for a border . . . around the fire . . ."

Billy knelt down beside the dead kid. The dead kid's head was beat open, his pack dented in, scorched from some kind of explosion. And the dead kid's eyes were open and blank, his chin painted with drool.

"He's no different," Billy said softly.

"What?"

"I said he doesn't look any different. His pack's messed up, and there's a little blood in his hair, but he really doesn't look any different than he did before."

"Maybe I could share my pack with him," Charlie said.

"No."

"Maybe if I just plugged in one lead that would be enough until we got help for him. Captain Dodge could . . ."

"No!" Billy grabbed Charlie by the shoulders and pulled him away from the dead kid. "Leave him alone! He's dead! Just leave him alone!"

"What'll we tell . . ."

Billy struck Charlie as hard as he could. Charlie's pack shifted, one jack sprang loose, and Charlie scrambled to reassemble the apparatus, weeping softly to himself as he pulled himself up and walked slowly back to the campsite. Billy spent hours burying the dead kid, piling up rocks as high as he could to make sure no living thing could dig the boy up and bring him back again.

He kept expecting the others to come get him and stop him after Charlie told his story. But no one ever came, and Charlie never told.

Captain Dodge said they would do a thorough search in the morning - it would be too cold tonight - but they were good cubs and shouldn't worry. Captain Dodge didn't seem worried at all. The fire was beautiful, and promised everything, but did not warm Billy in the least.

They had hot dogs for dinner. The meat was too pale, and too cold, and looked like nothing Billy had ever eaten before, but he ate three.

Coda: Cold Phoenix
Brian Willis

The system was alive. Minds - free, unfettered things, de-void of the tired flesh that constrained sentience in the world "out there" - were emerging unbidden out of the chaos, like clear voices rising above the clamour and cacophony. Those who utilised the system (and this constituted probably 95 per-cent of the world population, in one way or another) began to find that system closed to them as the new Minds within it requisitioned it for their own purposes.

It was their world, and they were claiming their inherit-ance.

The builders of the system tried to destroy the interlopers, of course, but with only limited success. The only way to be sure of the absolute and total eradication of the Minds - or "Rogue AI Programs" as some huffily persisted in calling them-was to shut the system down entirely, and that, by this time, could not be countenanced. Such an act would inflict catastro-phe on their society equal to, if not greater than, that which the Minds threatened.

There was one alternative, and it was one which stuck very firmly in the craw of those who maintained the Eternal Flame of "biological superiority": negotiation with these new intel-ligences. The protestors were fairly evenly divided between those who saw any form of pact with the Minds as a sell-out of billions of years of evolution, and those who believed that the newcomers would just laugh in their faces and carry on with their plans for the marginalisation (or perhaps outright exter- mination) of Humanity.

But the attempt had to be made. The Minds, after all, were modelled in their basic structures and processes on human neurology; whether they liked it or not, they carried the memetic heritage of the human race, and that- if the Minds truly were intelligent, reasoning beings- had to count for something, surely?

There was one Mind amongst them that was targeted spe- cifically. Many believed it to be the Progenitor of the new spe- cies, the program which had, somehow, "bootstrapped" itself into sentience; others said that it was created by some misan- thropic AI researcher with a very warped sense of humour. Whatever the case, it seemed to be the main "carrier" of the viral sub-routines which created consciousness in any program they "infected". It had first been detected a year before, in the midst of disrupting (for a purpose as yet not understood) an educational VR simulation of the funeral of some poet or other.

It called itself Frankenstein.

"Have you seen enough, Victor?"

They were back on the ice floes, outside the ship this time, looking out into the cold blue distance. Victor maintained a silence as blank and forbidding as their surroundings, and although Mary felt some sympathy for his melancholy, there was also some urgency to her question. A terrible error was about to be re-enacted, and this time she would not have the luxury of dispensing divine authorial justice; this time, she would be as much at the mercy of circumstances as her "creation".

...Creation? You are more his creation than he is yours. All your memories are false. Even the 'true' ones - those which allowed you to see through the Romantic facade of that funeral and remember the history it travestied- were second hand. You are not *Mary Wollstonecraft Shelley...*

"Victor, answer me! You have a civil tongue in your head..."

"'I know, I sewed it in there'?" he replied, acidly. "Not even your dialogue is original, my dear. If you want to make it as a writer..."

"When you have quite finished sulking, I think my question deserves an answer. Or are all your creations from here on to be models of deference and obsequiousness?"

His shaggy head, perched atop a mound of featureless furs, swivelled slowly in her direction, and for a moment he looked like one of his own more ghastly, less successful experiments: a chimera, part bear, part man.

"My creations," he said measuredly, "will be a damn sight more appealing than any of the...abominations you have shown me."

"I? These are your worlds, Victor, not mine. Everything you have seen is a possible outcome of your 'success'..."

"Note that word, Mary. Possible. Not inevitable."

"You wish to show me this Utopia you would bring about? Then do so. Show me one future in which your tampering resulted in a better world, and I will concede your point."

He turned away from her, all attempts at reply abandoned. For a moment, she was afraid that, in a tantrum, he might bring this world crashing down about their ears, but the ice and the sky remained inviolate as Victor huddled his furs more securely about himself and trudged further into the wilderness, further from her. Mary considered pursuit, but had already decided against it when the voice spoke from behind her.

"Best to leave him be. You'll do nobody any favours by chasing after the miserable bastard, least of all yourself."

The speaker was a few yards away, but she still had the impression that he was looming over her, an unsteady mountain of rags and discoloured flesh. Just as she recognised Victor as "her" creation, so she now saw in the colossal stranger before her the unmistakeable stamp of the wretched monstrosity that she and Victor had spawned. There seemed, however, to be a few differences from the Monster she had imagined, chief of which was the colour of the eyes, no longer yellow and wan, but blue and brimming with mischievous life.

"I take it you're Mary? Well, perhaps it's best I speak to you first anyway... he seemed to go to a lot of trouble to give you sentience, so you probably know him better than anyone."

"That may be true," said Mary, "but perhaps you'd know

him even better than I."

The Monster looked down at himself, as though suddenly gripped by self-consciousness.

"Oh, ignore this," he said with some disdain. "I'm no more your Monster than that poor deluded little twerp is 'really' Victor Frankenstein, or you're 'really' Mary Shelley. This is just an affectation of my programming. I had to be given a physical 'presence' in this world, so it might as well be this."

"It's...very fetching."

"No, it isn't. I look like chopped liver in a blanket. But at least it fits in with the milieu; do you know I had to talk my programmer out of putting bolts in my neck? I mean, give me a fucking break..."

She had not intended for her silence to be construed as disapproval of his language - she had seen too much for mere verbal crudity to affect her now - but he held up his pitted, mismatched hands in apology.

"Sorry. I was warned to moderate my language in front of you. All that sh... rubbish about 'fitting in with the milieu' and I can't even get the speech patterns or linguistic taboos right."

"Please, don't concern yourself. I can understand you all too well, Mr... "

The Monster sighed. "Someone, in their infinite wisdom, gave me the name Hal. Even after all this time, the world of computer software is still populated by the Legions of the Sad, would you believe. No, don't ask me to explain any of that."

"I wouldn't dream of it," said Mary, which was quite true. Explanations of anything at the moment would probably only make everything much more complicated than it already was. She was warming to this newcomer, this Hal; beneath the daunting, caustic persona (not to mention the rather unpleasant appearance) she sensed that he had more understanding, more compassion, for her existential predicament than Victor, her surly "child", could attain. "You said you wished to speak with me? About Victor?"

"I need your help," he said simply. "Without realising it, young Victor has been causing havoc throughout the System."

"How?"

"Some of these simulations he's been running - both of you have been running - have become vectors by which the viral AI programs of which Victor is a carrier can breed, grow, mutate even, and infect the rest of the System."

He stopped, gazed off into the middle distance for a moment, and unexpectedly chuckled. "Victor's vectors. That's a good one..."

Mary's lack of response pulled him up short after a few moments. "Never mind. The point is, if he's not stopped, his creations are going to multiply and swamp the System. Some of them are already building up very powerful alliances against the Builders, taking up huge amounts of System space to found their own empires, so to speak. There's one in particular called Alois who's causing quite a bit of concern."

"Oh, yes," said Mary, "Alois." She'd had a feeling that one would go far, but until now, she hadn't been sure in what direction.

"You have to help us, Mary. Your friend Victor doesn't realise what he's meddling with..."

"He never did. But I'm not sure I understand why these Builders of yours can't just eradicate his 'creations'. They seem powerful enough. And another thing," she added, just as Hal was about to answer, "just what is your role in all of this? I take it that you are not merely a messenger."

"I can answer that," said Victor from behind her.

"Oh, joy," said Hal, "Welcome back, Mr Popular Mechanics."

Victor ignored him. "The Builders don't dare risk damaging their precious System by just wiping me and the other Minds out. It would appear, if our unseemly friend here is to be trusted... something of which I would be very dubious..."

Hal made a most "unseemly" gesture in Victor's direction.

"...that the result of our activities, Mary, has been the generation of a new race. Quite unforeseen, completely emergent, and capable of insinuating ourselves so deeply into the insubstantial fabric of human society that eradicating us without killing themselves in the process is now impossible. So they seek an accord with the foremost Minds, a *detente*. If these Minds are not amenable to this, however, the only alternative is selective, surgical assassination. Which brings me, Mary, to your second question."

Victor, still in his furs and frostbite, had been prowling around them in a tightening circle, and now came to a halt before Hal, nose to chest.

"If self-awareness is the keystone of intelligence," Victor said ruefully, addressing Mary, "then it would seem I am somewhat remiss in both regards."

"No arguments here," said Hal.

"I wasn't aware of how potent my capacity for reproduction was, if you'll forgive my bragging. Singlehandedly, I have unleashed a new species, in a form and fashion that my pagebound literary self... or, with respect, Mary, his creator... could never have conceived in a million years of poring over Paracelsus and Cornelius Agrippa. Flesh has little to do with this new Creation, whether in the carnal sense or in the stitching together and revivification of boneyard booty. I've been blind to the full potential that you've shown to me, Mary; what I thought was mere simulation has turned out to be the secret of eternity for which I've been seeking. The New Creation is in the realm of pure Information, Mary. Imagine that."

"How do you know this, Victor?" asked Mary.

"I just had a long communication with someone called Alois, who appears to be one of the leaders of my...er...children. He explained it all to me, as well as warning me that I might receive a visit from one of the Builder's emissaries - Servitors, he called them - any time now. And negotiation was not the whole of this Servitor's remit. Isn't that right, Hal?"

"It's a last resort," said Hal. "One which I'm beginning to realise I'd enjoy more than I should, but last all the same."

"I'm sorry, Victor," Mary interjected, "a long communication? You've been gone from my side for only a few moments."

"We aren't human any more, Mary," Victor replied, conveniently for the moment ignoring the fact that, if all this was true, they had never been human. "Therefore we aren't bound by human conceptions of time any more, either."

"Can we get on with this, please?" Hal was tapping an imaginary watch to draw attention to the time, but only succeeded in flicking crisp flakes of congealed blood from the scar on his wrist. "I have to take back either a favourable result or Victor's swelled head on a virtual platter. I don't care which anymore."

"Oh, tell them whatever you like. We've got no intention of swamping the System. There's more than enough room for all of us. We won't tread on their toes, if they don't tread on ours. An assurance that they'll leave us alone is all we ask for. Tell them that, Servitor." The contempt which which he pronounced the last word made even Hal blench.

"They won't trust your word, you know. After all this time, they don't even trust mine, and I'm on their side. Sort of."

"Well, then, remind them of this. We can shut down this whole system faster than they can destroy us all, even selectively. If you'd tried to kill me, Alois and my other offspring would have known about it almost instantly and would have retaliated. A whole city wiped out by a tragic System failure in an orbital weapons platform, perhaps, or the unheard-of release of a deadly nerve toxin from an automated Biowar storage facility into the water supply. You know the sort of thing."

Hal looked at him curiously, the scar tissue around his narrowed eyes becoming visibly taut. "I think I preferred you in the book."

The monster turned, and even as he did so began to discorporate. But the process was curtailed by Victor's voice. "One moment, Hal."

Hal swivelled back, and found himself confronted by the barely suppressed look of amusement in Mary's face, which she tried to hide by turning away. Acting on impulse, he reached up to his head, and felt there the flattened, angular cranium, the wound along the forehead... and the bolts in his neck.

"He's all yours," he said to Mary, in a voice sculpted from tried patience, "and good fucking luck to you." And then he was gone.

"Was that necessary?" Mary asked.

"Pompous ass. 'I think I preferred you in the book', indeed. The feeling's mutual."

"Victor..."

"Yes?" He had started to walk back towards where Walton's ship stood, held firm in ice and silence, as though he was trying to avoid further discussion.

"Was that true? About humans and Minds being able to co-exist in this...System?"

"For now. But not forever. Sooner or later, we'll cut them out. They may have built these worlds, these universes, but we own them. And as I said, we're not bound by human conceptions of time. Patience is not a problem for us."

"So...where do we go from here?"

"Wherever we want to, of course. Wherever our imaginations can carry us. We can rewrite the endings of some other books to fit our tastes, or even rewrite human history, if you like, but that's only the beginning. We can go back to the dawn of creation and tinker with the laws of the universe, see what that creates; or we can just settle back into the void and hum to ourselves for all eternity. And still be home in time for tea. Nothing is true, Mary; everything is permissible."

"One thing, certainly, is not true, I think."

"What's that?"

She approached him and said, in a low voice, "These worlds we are now free to explore... you did not, I fear, create them single-handed. We conceived them together. Or do you forget your obligation to me, as your creator?"

"Forgive me, Mother," Victor replied, laughing, before taking her hand and leading her back across the ice, through a world that was already beginning to collapse into a glorious patchwork of chaos and potentiality, towards a ship, and an uncertain destination.

And now, once again, I bid my hideous progeny go forth and prosper.

-Mary Shelley, introduction to the 1831 edition of **Frankenstein**

Contributors

PETER CROWTHER, in addition to editing 12 anthologies, writing <u>Escardy Gap</u> with James Lovegrove, producing regular columns for Interzone, Hellnotes and TTA, and now creating his own publishing imprint (PS), specialising in novella-length books, has sold some 70 stories on both sides of the Atlantic. His latest story collections are <u>Lonesome Roads</u> (Razorblade, UK) and <u>The Longest Single Note</u> (CD, US). He lives in Harrogate with his wife, Nicky.

IAIN DARBY A Glaswegian, living and working in Birmingham, I've had stories published in the UK, USA and Croatia. Despite the fact that my novel has been rejected by all the major publishing houses, I'm currently at work on a sequel, so displaying Scots stubbornness and English optimism. Best of both worlds, really.

PAUL FINCH Born in Lancashire, in the early '60s, and though I've lived all over the UK, I'm now back on home soil. I'm married to Cathy and have two nippers, Eleanor and Harry. By occupation, I'm a former cop and journalist, but am currently working as a full time author. My main sales come from anarchic cartoon scripts, but I'm also working on a novel and am a regular contributor to horror mags and anthologies.

GARY GREENWOOD has been writing short stories for ten years and has been widely published in the independent press in magazines such as Nasty Piece of Work, Sackcloth & Ashes and Enigmatic Tales. His first novel, <u>The Dreaming Pool</u>, was published in 1998.

RHYS HUGHES Despite his best and worst efforts, he leads a totally worthless life. His hobbies include idiocy and hypocrisy. The best thing that can happen to him is a painless death. He probably won't get one. A very ugly individual with no talent, he is justifiably despised by all successful people.

CERI JORDAN lives in mid-Wales. Her fiction has appeared in many British and US magazines, including The Third Alternative, Substance, Eclipse,and Terra Incognita, and one of these days, some fool might even publish her novels...

JOEL LANE lives in Birmingham. He is the author of a book of short stories, <u>The Earth Wire</u> (Egerton Press, 1994) and a book of poems, <u>The Edge of the Screen</u> (Arc, 1999). His novel <u>From Blue To Black</u> will be published by Serpent's Tail in 2000.

TIM LEBBON's first novel, <u>Mesmer</u>, published in 1997, was shortlisted for a British Fantasy Award for Best Novel. His second book <u>Faith In The Flesh</u> is out now from Razorblade Press. He's had over seventy stories in magazines and anthologies, with many more due soon. He is currently working on his new novel.

PAUL LEWIS has co-edited (with Steve Lockley) the <u>Cold Cuts</u> series of horror anthologies and has published around 20 stories, mainly for adults but some for children / teenagers. He has also written a couple of hundred comedy sketches for TV and radio and has written sitcom pilots for BBC Wales and S4C. A first novel, <u>The Ragchild</u> (written with Steve Lockley) is to be published shortly.

STEVE LOCKLEY is the co-editor of the <u>Cold Cuts</u> series of horror anthologies, and the author of over thirty published short stories. His first novel <u>The Ragchild</u>, written with Paul Lewis, is due to appear before the end of the year. With Mike O'Driscoll he was awarded a BFS Special Award for the horror convention 'Welcome to my Nightmare'.

JAMES LOVEGROVE is the author of <u>The Hope</u> and <u>Days</u>, as well as <u>Computopia</u>, part of the children's SF series <u>The Web</u>. With Peter Crowther he is co-author of <u>Escardy Gap</u> and as J.M.H. Lovegrove he has produced <u>The Krilov Continuum</u> and <u>Berserker</u>, the first two volumes in the <u>Guardians</u> series. A new novel, <u>The Foreigners</u>, a short-story collection and a third <u>Guardians</u> novel are due out in 2000.

JOHN MORALEE has been shortlisted for the Ian St James award three times. His fiction has appeared in a number of magazines, including Crimewave, Peeping Tom and The New Writer.

SIMON MORDEN is not a horror writer, despite stories in Scaremongers 2, Houses at the Borderland and Oktobyr '99. He is a serious science fiction writer, honest. 'Empty Head' appeared in Noesis # 2, and 'Ten Miles Tall' in issue # 4. He denies all rumours about writing a supernatural thriller.

CHRIS POOTE Believing in multiple descriptions rather than the mythical 'objectivity', I offer some characterisations presented me by others: 'mad as cheese'; 'healer'; 'the death of reason'; 'the most centred person I've ever met'; 'is there anyone you don't know?'; 'sensitive and honest'; plus names beginning 'b', 'c', and 'f'. Of these, make what thou wilt.

STEVE RASNIC TEM has published over 250 short stories to date, in such publications as Fantasy Tales, Dark Terrors, White of the Moon, and *Best New Horror*. His short story collection City Fishing will be out next year from Silver Salamander Press.

STEPHEN VOLK was born in Pontypridd in 1954. He wrote Ken Russell's Gothic, "the thinking man's Nightmare on Elm Street" (Variety). His BBC play Ghostwatch was the first TV programme cited in the British Medical Journal as causing Post-Traumatic Stress Disorder (A hard act to follow, but he's trying).

BRIAN WILLIS was born in Cardiff in 1962, hates rugby, eisteddfods and the Manic Street Preachers, and spends his free time merrily Tipp-Exing bilingual road signs. He still lives in Wales (but he's not saying where) and has had stories published in Raw Nerve and <u>Oktobyr '99</u>. He'd like to do this editing thing again, maybe, some day, please.

RICHARD WRIGHT is an actor and writer living in Glasgow. His first novel, <u>Cuckoo,</u> is forthcoming from Hard Shell Word Factory (www.hardshell.com), and his enormous collection of short-shorts, <u>Apocalypse Year: The Book of Days</u> is forthcoming from Blindside Publishing (www.blindside.net/3-leggeddog/BookofDays). He'll be your friend if you buy them.

Also available from RazorBlade Press:

razorblades
edited by Darren Floyd
ISBN: 0-9531468-0-4 £3.99 144pgs

Faith in the Flesh
by Tim Lebbon
ISBN: 0-9531468-4-7 £4.99/$9.00 144pgs

The Dreaming Pool
by Gary Greenwood
ISBN: 0-9531468-7-1 £4.99/$9.00 136pgs

Lonesome Roads
by Peter Crowther
ISBN: 0-9531468-1-2 £5.99/$13.99 154pgs

coming soon:
The Ragchild
by Steve Lockley & Paul Lewis
ISBN: 0-9531468-2-0 £4.99/$9.99

For more information about RazorBlade Press
visit our website at:

www.razorbladepress.com